T0196310

THE LAST GOODNIGHTS

THE LAST GOODNIGHTS

assisting my parents with their suicides

{ A M E M O I R }

John West

COUNTERPOINT
BERKELEY

Library of Congress Cataloging-in-Publication Data

West, John (John Stuart)
The last goodnights : assisting my parents with their suicides / John West.
p. cm.
ISBN 978-1-58243-448-3
1. West, John (John Stuart) 2. Assisted suicide—Biography. 3. Parents—Death—Biography.
I. Title.

R726.W47 2009
179.7—dc22

2008035698

Paperback ISBN: 978-1-58243-557-2

Cover design by Gopa & Ted2, Inc.
Interior design by Megan Cooney
Printed in the United States of America

COUNTERPOINT
2560 Ninth Street
Suite 318
Berkeley, CA 94710
www.counterpointpress.com

"Death is as natural as life, and should be sweet and graceful."
—RALPH WALDO EMERSON

"Life is pleasant. Death is peaceful. It's the transition that's troublesome."
—ISAAC ASIMOV

CONTENTS

THE LAST GOODNIGHTS

foreword

I DON'T KNOW WHAT my booze bill was for that time, but I'm sure it was big. I had a good reason, though: I had to kill my parents. They asked me to. Actually, they asked me to help them with their suicides, and I did. And if that doesn't justify throwing back an extra glass or three of Jameson's on the rocks, then I don't know what does.

My father was Louis Jolyon "Jolly" West, MD, a world-renowned psychiatrist and former chairman of the department of psychiatry at the University of California, Los Angeles, age seventy-four. My mother was Kathryn "K" West, PhD, a respected clinical psychologist at the West Los Angeles (Brentwood) Veterans Administration Hospital, age seventy-five.

Jolly and K were wonderful people—brilliant, academic medical professionals, highly cultured, and well-rounded. Neither was at all religious, but both had deep insight into the human condition. They knew what was what. And they knew what they wanted.

So when they made their wishes clear to me, I wasn't about to argue. I respected my father and mother, and I loved them. And I believe, as they did, in freedom of choice, the right to personal privacy and self-determination—which includes reproductive

1

choice (as the law now recognizes, although it didn't used to), the right to refuse medical treatment (as the law now recognizes, although it didn't used to), and the right to choose death with dignity (as the law does *not* recognize—not yet—although a few states are getting close).

My father's desire to end his life did not shock me, especially since his newly discovered cancer—a particularly vicious type—was literally eating him up and would take him from playing tennis to lying dead in just five months. Should Jolly have been forced to endure a few more days or weeks of agony just to satisfy some people's notions that death should be "natural"?

And what about my mother? K had midstage Alzheimer's disease, plus osteoporosis and emphysema. Should she have been forced to deteriorate into a walking vegetable, soiling herself, wandering into traffic, hunched over like a crab, and coughing up blood, just because some people say that's how it's always been and always should be?

Jolly and K said no. And I agreed.

ONE

— ·— —

The Beginning

I HAD NO IDEA WHAT my father wanted to talk to me about that afternoon in early November 1998 when he asked me to step into his bedroom for a private chat. But I was used to Jolly's secretiveness, so I didn't find it odd that he would suggest it, particularly with a houseful of visiting relatives and no privacy anywhere but behind a locked door. I assumed he had some additional bad news about the status of his cancer, something he wanted to tell me first, since I would be his successor in the role of what Jolly liked to call "the man of the family." An outdated concept, perhaps, but one that, unfortunately, applied more to our family than I liked. After Jolly's death, I would be the one member of the family who could be called solid, competent, and reliable. My mother had once been an ultra-competent professional, but various illnesses had left her needy and dependent. I had two sisters, both older than I, but Jolly never felt they could properly handle complicated or stressful "real world" matters. Years of experience and many disappointments had informed his opinion.

I sat in the big leather chair by the bookshelves, prepared to wait. Whenever Jolly talked to me about something important, he approached it in a roundabout way.

But not this time. Straightaway he said, "John, I need your help."

This startled me—doubly so. He was being direct, which was rare enough. And he was asking for help. Jolly *never* asked for help. His smoothly contained persona, Mr. Totally In Control, had just popped open right in front of me. Not that any outsider would have noticed, because Jolly's demeanor was exactly the same as it was whenever he discussed anything important: His voice was measured and smooth; he sat squarely on the edge of his bed, leaning forward with his elbows on his knees and his hands clasped; he looked straight at me, seriously and intently, but his face showed little more than mild concern. His face rarely gave anything away. Only his words betrayed him now.

"I'm dying," he said. "That's no secret—everyone knows it. I don't have more than a few months, at most. But I do have something that is very important to me. I have options about how and when my death will occur."

He paused to let this sink in.

"At some point," he continued, "not too long from now, I will decide that enough is enough. By that time I will be full of all sorts of drugs, particularly the morphine that I'm already taking for pain. A little extra of that should do the trick, without anyone having to know and get upset."

He paused again and looked out the window.

I sat up in my chair. I suddenly felt hot and cold at the same time, as I realized what he meant. But as powerfully as his words registered, the idea behind them didn't seem strange at all. It made sense. He was about to die anyway, so why linger in pain? I knew I'd want to do the same thing if I were in his position.

I didn't know what to say, so I kept quiet and waited for him to continue. I don't know if I could have said anything even if I'd wanted to, because I was still somewhat stunned, not only by the intensity of what he'd told me, but also because I'd never expected him to share thoughts like these with me.

Still looking out the window, he continued, "My body is full of cancer. If I knock off a little ahead of schedule, nobody's going to know the difference, and I'll have saved myself a hell of a lot of pain."

Then he looked straight at me. "But I'll need you on board, to help me."

A question was implied, but we both knew what the answer would be. I nodded and said, "You got it."

I didn't register much of what he said right after that, because I was still having trouble processing the whole strange scene. Here we were, my father and I, sitting in his bedroom, calmly talking about him committing suicide. With me "on board," whatever that meant.

What it meant, I soon learned, was more than I had ever imagined. And then some.

SIX WEEKS EARLIER, Jolly had phoned me at my home in Seattle from his office at UCLA.

"I have some bad news, Johnny," he said.

I stopped stirring the soup I had on the stove. My first thought flashed on my mother: K had been declining, with a variety of ailments, for a few years now. Had she taken an unexpected turn for the worse? Or was Jolly just being overdramatic about something else, something relatively innocuous? He often did that.

"What is it?" I asked warily, hoping he wouldn't confirm my fear about K.

"Well," he said, taking a deep breath before continuing, "I had a pain in my hip that I thought was just my arthritis kicking up. I tried to ignore it, but when it got to the point where I needed a cane to get around, I thought I'd better get it looked at."

I was relieved that the bad news wasn't about K, but suddenly realized that it must be extraordinarily bad news about Jolly, because he never talked openly about his own health problems. Never.

"The radiologist took an X-ray of my hip but didn't like what he saw on the film, so he did a full-body bone scan."

My stomach sank as I instantly imagined the worst.

"When he put the scan film up on the box, it took me about ten seconds to register what I saw. There were metastases throughout my skeleton. Cancer everywhere. I realized I was looking at a death sentence."

He paused, but I couldn't speak. I was too surprised, completely unprepared for this. He'd been just fine, last I'd heard, and now he was about to die?

He continued, almost casually, "The radiologist said he thought I had about six months to live. I think that's optimistic. I'd say it's closer to four."

I stood there frozen, the phone jammed against my ear. I couldn't believe it. This wasn't possible. Jolly had always been extraordinarily healthy and strong. Hell, he still had more hair than I did. And even though he'd been overweight for many years, he'd never seemed unhealthy—just incredibly big, powerful, sturdy.

Part of what stunned me, surely, was the suddenness of it all, and hearing it over the phone, instead of in person. The soup I'd been cooking started to boil over on the stove, but I couldn't move. I waited for Jolly to say something else, but the phone was quiet.

I didn't know what to say, so I just blathered the first things that came to mind.

"Jeez, Dad, I'm really sorry. Are you in a lot of pain? What happens next?"

"Well," he said, then sighed heavily, "I'm not in much pain. Not yet. Typically, the next step would be to start a regimen of chemotherapy and radiation, but I'm not sure I want to subject myself to that. I'm going to get additional information over the next few days, and then start making decisions."

Dozens of thoughts jumped through my head, but I tried to focus on practical matters. I started to pace, the long phone cord whipping back and forth in my wake.

"What about Mom?" I asked. "How is she holding up?"

"She's okay at the moment, but she's putting on a brave face. I know she's worried as hell, and, of course, I'm worried about her, too. Her health isn't much better than mine. That's something else you and I will have to discuss when you're down here next."

"Of course, of course," I said, the implications of his words starting to ignite in my mind. K's fragile condition could deteriorate rapidly from the stress of Jolly's illness and eventual death.

Then another worry hit me: "What about Anne and Mary? Have you told them about your diagnosis yet?"

"Yes, I've talked with both your sisters."

"How are they taking it?"

"Well," he sighed again, "pretty much true to form—you know how they are. Annie is wound up beyond all reason." He chuckled sadly. "I had to spend almost an hour calming her down and reassuring her that I wasn't already in extremis. Mary was shocked and flustered at first, but put on a good show of acting calm, even though it's obvious she's frightened." He paused and then said pointedly, "You know that both your sisters are going to need your help with what's ahead."

"I know," I said. Both Anne and Mary had had deeply troubled relationships with Jolly and K over the years, and I'd fallen into the role of sometime caretaker. Relative calm seemed to prevail with my sisters at the moment, but Jolly obviously anticipated that would change. At the very least, I knew that Jolly's illness would be extremely difficult for them to cope with.

He continued, "Annie said she's coming to L.A. immediately—to 'help'—which your mother and I are not exactly looking forward to. It'll probably be the other way around, for the most part. And Mary said she'd try to come see me more often, but that damn husband of hers makes it difficult."

"Yeah," I said, "I know."

"What about you?" he asked. "Will your schedule allow you to come down here for a visit? I know you're busy lawyering and helping folks."

"Don't worry," I said, "I'll make arrangements. I'll clear some things off my calendar and come down there as soon as I can."

"No rush," he said. "I'm really not feeling too bad. And I'm not going anywhere. Not yet, anyway."

I could tell by his tone that he was trying to joke about his impending demise, so I chuckled appreciatively and said, "Right." He chuckled too, glad I'd gotten it.

Then I said, "Keep me posted, all right? And if there's anything I can do to help out down there, just let me know."

"Okay, Son," he said. "I'll keep you apprised."

"Okay, Dad. Talk to you soon."

"So long," he said, and hung up.

I STOOD THERE staring at the phone, still stunned, until the smell of scorched soup demanded my attention. As I cleaned up the stove, I replayed the phone call over and over in my mind. It didn't make any sense. He *sounded* healthy, and he was only seventy-three. Maybe his doctors had made a mistake and would catch it any day now. But even as I thought that, I knew it was a typical denial reaction. There hadn't been any mistake. The cancer was there. Jolly was dying.

I knew that Jolly had access to hundreds, maybe even thousands, of doctors at UCLA Hospital, where he worked, and that he'd get the absolute best medical care. My offer to help was an instinct, a reflex, what someone says. I didn't know what help I could actually be. But I found out six weeks later, when he called me into his bedroom for that private chat. Jolly's directness and request for help during that conversation had surprised me, but I understood what it meant: all business. He would be as detached, dispassionate, and professional in ending his own life as he had been during any other medical crisis in his fifty-year career. And he would expect me to follow suit. But although I knew (and he did, too) that I could remain calm and professional in a crisis, this was not a professional situation—this was my father, and his suicide, and my participation. I knew I'd have to steel myself like never before in order to handle the pressures that would surely come.

I was used to pressure. A career as a trial lawyer is not for the easily rattled. I could think on my feet, stay calm, and keep a straight face. But assisting Jolly with his suicide promised complexities I wouldn't be able to anticipate. It would be like getting plucked out of my office and tossed into the middle of a jury trial without knowing what the case was about. I'd still be expected to do my job—and maybe I could, to some degree. But this wasn't a court case; it was my father's life.

I knew I couldn't talk about this with anyone, not even my closest friends, because it might put me, and possibly them, in legal jeopardy. They could be forced to testify against me, or one of them might accidentally let it slip to somebody else who might call the cops or possibly . . . I don't know—I just didn't feel that I could run the risk of exposing such intimate and potentially incendiary information to anybody. Keeping professional secrets is stressful enough, but *this* . . . damn!

Another thing I found troubling was that I had no idea when this business would happen, or how long I would be involved in . . . whatever it turned out to be. Would I have to be in L.A. a lot? How could I schedule my absences from work? It isn't easy to leave a small law firm, or any small business, for more than a few days at a time, particularly when you're the person in charge. Even though I had a partner and support staff, there wasn't much work I could delegate. My specialty—representing victims of employment discrimination and sexual harassment—required an extra level of personal attention because of the intensely personal nature of the harm my clients had suffered. As an attorney I sometimes felt like St. George battling the dragon, particularly when I represented women who had been sexually assaulted in the workplace.

I always put too much of myself into my work. I felt it would be nearly impossible for me to do my job properly if I weren't in the office and able to deal with my clients directly and promptly. All I could think to do, to at least try to lessen the demands on my time and my mind, was stop taking new cases. Maybe that would give me the mental elbow room I knew I'd need to deal with whatever Jolly wanted from me.

JOLLY'S BIRTHDAY

A week after Jolly called and told me about his diagnosis, and five weeks before he asked for my help during that bedroom chat, I flew from Seattle to L.A. for his seventy-fourth birthday. We all knew this would be his last, so my sisters came too: Anne from New York City, and Mary from Northern California. Neither brought her husband.

I felt nervous about seeing Jolly, and not just because of the extreme changes looming over him and the rest of the family. Until he'd phoned me with his bad news, I hadn't planned on attending his birthday party—or any other event involving him—because our recent relationship had not been good. For a long time, Jolly's phi-landering had been an open secret in our family, but it had never intruded directly on our lives until two years before. Decades of polite, quiet disagreement about Jolly's behavior had finally become pointed conflict when he made the bewildering decision to start bringing into our home, and into the homes of old family friends, his newly admitted illegitimate child—an adolescent boy. I had told Jolly that this was highly inappropriate and painful to the family (and embarrassing to the old family friends), and that it was espe-cially hurtful, insulting, and disrespectful to K. I stood up for K because she was in no position to stand up to Jolly anymore, due to her failing health and increased dependence on him. K and I had always been close, and now that her health and strength were declining, I felt more and more protective of her.

I'd told Jolly that if he wanted to spend time with this boy, there were numerous other places they could go—places on the other side of town, where the boy's mother lived; places that wouldn't be so offensive to basic notions of decency, discretion, and tact. Los Angeles is not a small town; it has plenty of such places.

Jolly didn't like my telling him that his flaunting a gross indis-cretion was wrong, and he refused to stop it. He even tried to twist the situation on me by saying how sad he was that I "didn't like the kid," but I set things straight immediately: I told Jolly that it wasn't the boy I disliked—I didn't know him well enough to like or dislike him; I'd met him only a time or two, when he was a small child, and long before I'd learned his true lineage. Rather, it was *Jolly* I didn't like, for behaving in such an astonishingly bad way, especially to-ward K, his wife of more than fifty years. He'd had no reply to that.

I'd been angry at Jolly for several months afterward, but over time my anger had faded into sadness and disappointment as I mourned the loss of the man I'd once imagined my father to be, and began to know him—and try to accept him—for who he really was.

And now, after learning of his illness and thinking—a lot—about our relationship, I decided to put our recent conflict aside and act like a son, not a judge. Jolly and I hadn't resolved our old business, but life isn't governed by parliamentary procedure, and the new business—end-of-life issues—now took priority.

Besides, until these rough last two years, Jolly and I had had a fine relationship—friendly, warm, adult. Other than the standard turbulence during my teen years, we'd had a smooth trip. I always felt like I could talk to him about anything. (The fact that he was a doctor made some of what we talked about a lot easier, especially when I was struggling through puberty.) We had the kind of understanding that some fathers and sons have, where the son somehow intuits what his father expects, and does it naturally—and feels proud to have gotten it right. Behavioral scientists probably have a fancy name for it, but it's a common enough phenomenon: sons learning how to please their fathers. And as much as I always refused to admit it—thinking I had escaped such mundane motivations—I realize now that I'd always had a deep need to make my father notice me and be proud of me.

Of course, when I was a child I thought of Jolly as a deity, and his frequent absences from home only added to his mythology. He would be in Washington, D.C., battling with the National Institute of Mental Health. Or in Tokyo, pontificating at an international medical conference. Or just over at the hospital, working late.

Ah, yes, "working late." Jolly was a doctor—tall, handsome, successful, charming, magnetic, and powerful. Catnip to women. (Picture a young Orson Welles, whom Jolly resembled in his youth.) And so it began, and so it continued—even after he had aged and gained so much weight that, sadly, he'd come to resemble the older, ursine Orson.

Jolly attracted men, too, but in a different way. Men admired him and wanted to be his friend and colleague. This quality made him a formidable recruiter, and over the years he used his persuasive talents to attract many bright young doctors to his department.

Jolly had a true gift for making people feel special. When he wanted to, he could look you in the eye and talk to you and make you feel like you were the most important, fascinating person he'd ever met. Whenever I received this treatment from him, I felt as if Zeus himself had just smiled upon me. He was perhaps the consummate politician. In fact, many have compared him to Bill Clinton because of his powerful charm and intellect (as well as his marital lapses).

ONCE I ARRIVED at my parents' house and settled into the familiar living room, my earlier nervousness about seeing Jolly subsided. Somehow, everything seemed as normal as ever. Jolly held court from his usual end of the sofa and, surprisingly, showed no sign of his illness. I sat near him, in a chair in front of the fireplace. Mom sat in her usual spot—the opposite end of the sofa from Dad—and tried to keep a poker face, although I could see her fretting. Anne and Mary dealt busily with dinner preparations and last-minute gift wrapping and such, occasionally bouncing in for a quick comment, while I caught up with the folks.

It seemed like old times: The conversation was easy and smooth, the usual rhythms. At one point, Jolly said something a bit too humorous and cavalier about his dire condition, and K gently growled at him, "Jolly, don't exaggerate." He sighed and said, "Yes, dear." She rolled her eyes at his response, then said, "Now knock it off, or you'll scare the children!" And they both chuckled. Classic Jolly-and-K banter.

I finally asked Jolly about his plan for dealing with his rapidly advancing cancer. He replied with great sangfroid. "I'm a physician," he said. "I know when my number's up. It's just a question of how to go through the decline. The 'cure' in a case like this is worse than the goddamn disease. I'm not going to do anything drastic to fight it. What's the point? Maybe I'd live a few more weeks, but I wouldn't be able to do anything except lie in bed and suffer."

I was a bit surprised to hear him say this, because I knew he'd already started chemotherapy and radiation treatments, but I also knew that he often said and did contradictory things. Maybe he felt he needed to "keep up appearances" for his colleagues at the hospital by going through the standard treatment regimen. Or maybe he thought, as he did about so much in his life, that things would go differently for him—that by the sheer force of his considerable will, he could avoid the inevitable side effects of the chemo and radiation.

As Jolly continued, Mom did a good job of remaining stoic. Anne dashed all across the emotional landscape, alternately weeping and vowing grandly to stand by Jolly no matter what, and help him beat the cancer if it was the last thing she ever did. Mary put on a happy face for the most part, although it was obviously forced, and she seemed to shrink in on herself at times, retreating from the intensity of the conversation. I asked questions, remained calm, and tried to be supportive. So we all stayed true to our established family behavior patterns.

Dinnertime came and went, Jolly opened his presents with great gusto, and then the party came to an end because I needed to leave for the airport and catch the last flight back to Seattle. I had to be in court with a client the next morning, so I couldn't stay overnight in L.A. I was about to call a cab when Dad volunteered to drive me— another surprise. He usually hated chores like that. Perhaps he felt the need, as I did, for a few minutes of private conversation.

I kissed Mom and my sisters goodbye, and then Jolly and I got into his car and headed down the freeway to LAX. Jolly loved his Cadillac—the fanciest car he'd ever owned. When he'd bought the Caddy only a few years earlier, he'd joked about its being black, saying it would be the last car he'd ever own, and that we could drive him to his funeral in it. Now, as he steered it down the freeway, I realized that the joke would come true. I didn't say anything, though— surely he'd thought of it. I just shook my head at the sad irony.

As we drove along and made small talk, I could tell he had something on his mind—probably our unfinished old business— but I knew it would be hard for him to raise that painful subject. So, as we neared the airport, I waded in.

"Listen, Dad, there's something important I want to talk with you about, and I think it's important that I tell you in person, before I get on the plane."

"Okay," he said; he sounded neutral, but I sensed him bracing himself.

"You and I have been having this big disagreement for a couple of years, but I want you to know that I'm through with it. I've been thinking a lot about the whole situation since you told me your medical news, and, well, life-and-death matters—like what you're facing—are simply more important. So I want you to know that all that other stuff is moot. It's over and done with, as far as I'm concerned."

I heard him exhale slowly, and I thought I could see his shoulders relax. He didn't say anything for a few seconds, but I could tell he was concentrating, thinking how to respond. He glanced at me, then looked back at the road and said very quietly, "Thank you, Johnny. You don't know how much that relieves my mind."

Then we had to stop at a red light, the last light before we entered the LAX causeway for departing passengers. As we sat there waiting, I heard him sigh, and then the sigh turned into a sob, and I looked over and saw a tear roll down his cheek just before he reached up and wiped it away. It was the only time in my life I ever saw him cry.

Then the light turned green and we drove on in silence. I pointed out the terminal, and Jolly maneuvered the car over to the curb and stopped. We both got out and he came around to my side, his eyes still a little moist. He put his arms out and we hugged, and again he said, "Thank you."

I picked up my briefcase. "Well . . . I love you, Dad."

"I love you too," he said.

And then I had to go.

TWO

———

Honors and Horrors

UCLA HAD BEEN PLANNING to honor Jolly with a special tribute to his career the following April, but when word leaked out about his advanced cancer, things sped up. The tribute was held on December 1, in the main auditorium of the Neuropsychiatric Institute (known as the NPI).

As various doctors and professors droned on about Jolly's work at UCLA, I thought about how truly amazing his entire career had been: He had examined Jack Ruby after Ruby shot Lee Harvey Oswald; he had served as the chief psychiatrist for Patricia Hearst's defense when she was prosecuted for bank robbery (despite the fact that she was a hostage of the Symbionese Liberation Army at the time); he was the first white psychiatrist to testify on behalf of black South African prisoners who had been tortured by their white guards; and he was frequently asked by local, national, and international news media to comment on newsworthy (and usually unpleasant) cult activities, such as the 1978 mass murders/suicides at Jim Jones's People's Temple in Jonestown, Guyana, and the 1993 David Koresh–led, Branch Davidian tragedy in Waco, Texas.

Jolly's early professional celebrity had expanded beyond the medical world, into politics and entertainment. He'd been an activist for integration and civil rights since his college days, and was probably the only white person from Oklahoma to attend Dr. Martin Luther King's march on Washington, D.C. His accidental friendship with the actor Charlton Heston in New York in the late 1940s—well before either man had any professional fame—led to other friendships at the highest levels of Hollywood, especially after Jolly left the University of Oklahoma and took the top job in psychiatry at UCLA. His social realm came to include film stars, directors, producers, and studio executives; painters, sculptors, and classical musicians; professional athletes; wealthy industrialists; literary nobility such as Patrick O'Brian; and politicians such as senator Jacob Javits. He was a big man and he'd led a big life.

The high point of the tribute to Jolly's career came with the (expected) unveiling of his official portrait and the (completely unexpected) announcement that the auditorium had been renamed in his honor. Jolly beamed with delight, as did K and my sisters and I. And the crowd cheered with approval.

Jolly had had the foresight to pre-record his thank you remarks on videotape, in case he wasn't feeling strong enough to make them in person. That was prescient, because by the day of the event—less than three months after his diagnosis—he was so weakened by the cancer (and by the chemo and radiation treatments) that he couldn't give a long speech easily. He even needed a wheelchair to get from the parking lot to the auditorium, but as much as he hated being seen in a wheelchair, he wasn't about to miss this event and all the people singing his praises.

His videotaped farewell remarks made a powerful impact, in no small measure because everyone knew he was not simply retiring from UCLA—he was dying. It was startling, too, to see how healthy he appeared on the videotape, made only a month before, compared with how weak he looked in person, sitting in that wheelchair at the end of the front row. And when his taped remarks ended not only with "thank you," but also with "goodbye," most of us had lumps in our throats, and even a few of the tough old doctors got misty-eyed. Jolly always did know how to reach his audience.

SOON AFTER THE UCLA tribute, it finally dawned on me that maybe I should get realistic and investigate the legal issues surrounding assisted suicide. What did California law actually say about it? What was I really getting into?

It didn't take me long to find California Penal Code Section 401, which states:

> *Every person who deliberately aids, or advises, or encourages another to commit suicide, is guilty of a felony.*

Hmm. But what was the penalty? A little more research, and I learned that I was looking at the possibility of spending two to four years in prison. Great.

But I also knew that "the law on the books is different from the law in action"—a concept my law school professors had drummed into me and my classmates years ago. So now I needed to find out how such cases were actually handled. What were the procedures, the prosecution parameters, the factors causing differences in sentencing lengths—that sort of thing. I found very few reported cases in the law library, and none with factual situations similar to what I imagined would take place with Jolly. And I couldn't exactly call the L.A. County district attorney's office and ask.

The statute books say, "No assisting," but everyone knows it happens all the time. People get help from their doctors, nurses, knowledgeable family members, and friends—it's just not talked about. So how could I learn the ways of that world without exposing myself to undesired scrutiny?

I decided to get in touch with the Hemlock Society, a relatively well-known outfit that tries to educate people on the various practicalities of what it calls "self-deliverance." I'm sorry, but whenever I see or hear the word "deliverance," I just can't help but think of the movie *Deliverance* and I start remembering that goddamn banjo music, and Jon Voight looking scared, and Burt Reynolds with real hair, and poor, poor old Ned Beatty. So I just can't take the phrase "self-deliverance" seriously. It's only semantics, I know, and maybe I watch too many movies, but there must be a better way to put it.

How about "Self de-Termination"? It may be a bit too "on the nose," but at least it combines the two issues involved: personal autonomy (privacy, choice) and the end of life.

Despite their distracting catchphrase the Hemlock Society people look at this issue clearly and practically, which few others seem able to do, so on my next visit to L.A. I gave them a call. I figured I could get some general information from them without leaving too much of an evidentiary trail. Their telephone number might show up if my parents' phone records were ever checked, but not even Joe Friday would be able to tell who had placed the call. I needed to start thinking ahead and taking precautions like this now, because one small slip, and I could be doing two to four in Folsom.

When I finally found a little privacy (in Dad's bedroom, appropriately enough) and placed the call, I got an answering machine. An elderly lady's voice told me I could leave a message and someone would get back to me within a few days.

Swell. That's *really* secure. Let me see, what should I say? How about, "Hi there, my name is John West and I'm about to assist my father with his suicide, and I was just wondering what suggestions you people might have, and by the way, what's the address of the nearest police station where I can turn myself in for being such an idiot as to leave a message on your answering machine"?

So the Hemlock Society was a bust, and I didn't feel like I could ask any of my lawyer friends about assisted suicide now. I knew that any discussions I might have with a lawyer *after* the fact would be absolutely confidential and protected by the attorney-client privilege, but I wasn't sure that the privilege would protect discussions *before* the fact, so I decided to keep it all to myself. I would just have to handle things on my own, use my brains, and not get caught.

Why was I going through all this? Certainly I had the right temperament for it, the experience of handling high-octane stress and keeping secrets. And I believed it was the right thing to do. I respected Jolly's choice, and I felt I could give him whatever he needed. And I'm sure my old habit of wanting to please him was in there somewhere, too. But beyond all that, I think I must have been responding to something larger—perhaps what some Jungians describe as "the call to growth." I'd been asked to do the most important, most challenging thing I'd ever done. It went way beyond "doing good works," as some lawyers, doctors, teachers, and others choose to do with their skills. This was both an intensely personal and an intensely political act. I was certainly worried about, even scared of, the potential legal consequences, but at the same time I felt I had to answer The Call.

A FEW DAYS LATER, a little more than a week after the UCLA tribute, Jolly fell as he was getting into the shower. The cause of his fall was something called a pathological fracture of his upper right femur. Translation: His hip spontaneously broke, snapped like a twig, because the cancer had eaten it away so deeply that the bone could no longer support his weight. Boom! On the floor. Naked. In agonizing pain.

The paramedics took him to UCLA Hospital, just down the street. The collective medical wisdom was that his only chance of ever walking again was to have hip replacement surgery. So that's what he had. In fact, he had double hip replacement surgery, because X-rays revealed that another pathological fracture was imminent in the femur just below his other hip joint. The cancer was so advanced in his yet-unbroken left femur that almost the entire upper bone was compromised. It, too, could have snapped at any time.

I thought it strange that Jolly agreed to the surgeries, given his advanced cancer (and his plan to end his life "early"), but later I realized he had good reasons. The most important of them? Autonomy. Without the surgeries, he'd never get out of bed again. But with them, if he recuperated quickly enough, and if the chemo and radiation slowed down the cancer (some major "ifs"), then he might be able to walk again. And the sooner they did the operations, the sooner he'd recover, although his general health was declining rapidly. Surgery was his last chance to avoid at least one of the indignities of the dependency that he despised.

Another reason was as simple and sentimental as the season: Christmas was near. Jolly truly loved Christmas—the tree and the lights and the cards and the music and the food (especially Mom's oyster dressing) and giving lots of presents. He wanted to be able to participate—not just lie in bed and watch.

Another possible reason: his image. If he didn't agree to the recommended surgeries, it might look as if he were "quitting," and he certainly didn't want to be remembered as a quitter.

Yet another possible reason dawned on me: strategy. Maybe Jolly didn't have a sufficient stash of drugs at home to do the trick, and needed to undergo the surgeries to get what he needed to make "The Plan" work. And if the surgeries were in fact successful and he could walk again, then once he had the drugs he needed and felt ready for Self de-Termination, he could simply walk into his bathroom, get a glass of water, take the drugs, stroll back to bed, climb in, go to sleep, and that would be that—all on his own.

Which takes us back to the first reason: autonomy.

CHRISTMAS 1998

Not very merry.

Jolly had hoped to come home by Christmas, but his doctors strongly advised him to stay in the hospital a while longer and get more physical therapy for his new bionic hip joints; he was recuperating very slowly. Grudgingly, he agreed.

Christmas Eve was particularly somber. Mom gathered Anne and Mary, their husbands, and me together in the living room and, quite formally and carefully, stated her desire to not go on living after Jolly died. She said she'd stay around for a while, but not long, and then she would choose to end her life.

This was difficult for Mom to talk about, but not for emotional reasons. Her professional training and decades of work as a psychologist had enabled her to put emotion in its place. What she found difficult was organizing her thoughts and speaking the words, because she had midstage Alzheimer's disease and the additional complication of advancing aphasia—a neurological speech impairment, often associated with Alzheimer's, that made it challenging at times for her to articulate her thoughts smoothly.

It's not easy to hear your mother tell you—on Christmas Eve, no less—that she plans to end her life soon. But it wasn't a complete surprise. Years earlier, both Jolly and K had made the family well aware of their desire to not become medical basket cases at the end of their lives.

Nevertheless, Anne became upset by K's announcement and started complaining about not wanting Mom to abandon her so soon after Dad died. As Anne grew increasingly strident, I could see Mom withdrawing, retreating into herself. In the past, Mom had been able to weather Anne's frequent emotional tornados, but the Alzheimer's had robbed her of most of her strength and her ability to wrestle Anne back to reality and calm her down.

I was about to jump in and remind Anne that this was not about *her*, but about Mom, when Mom beat me to it! What I'd interpreted as K's withdrawal had really been a gathering up of her energy, a focusing. She snapped at Anne with crystal clarity: "Stop it! Just stop it! If you aren't going to listen to what I have to say and be supportive of my wishes and join in the family group, then you will not have a place here." This shocked Anne into silence, which allowed Mary to step in and make a few well-chosen remarks about everybody pulling together, and somehow we got the subject changed. Soon thereafter, the family meeting broke up and we all went our separate ways to bed.

But instead of going to sleep, I stayed awake, thinking: Could Anne's emotional instability and unpredictable behavior cause problems in implementing The Plan with Jolly? Could she become an obstacle? And what about K's announcement? Could that somehow lead to additional scrutiny of Jolly's death?

With plenty of questions but no ready answers, all I could do was toss and turn and eventually worry myself to sleep. Happy Holidays? Not so much.

ON CHRISTMAS MORNING, everyone at the house glumly ate breakfast and joylessly opened a present or two. Then we loaded up the car and took presents to Jolly at the hospital. He seemed in pretty good spirits, all things considered. Given the location and the circumstances, it was hard to be festive, but we tried our best—singing Christmas carols, untying ribbons, and opening boxes for about an hour—and then Jolly said he needed a nap, so we straightened up the room and left.

Back at the house, we went through the motions of Christmas dinner, but of course it didn't feel right. We knew it was our last Christmas with the family intact, even though Dad wasn't physically present at the table. And we knew he would never again sit at the head of that table and preside over a holiday meal.

THE NEXT EVENING I went to see Jolly alone, and we talked candidly about The Plan. He said he wanted to do it the night he got home from the hospital. He thought he'd have plenty of morphine available, given what his doctors would likely prescribe for him to take home, but he was concerned that they might give him only the liquid form, in intravenous drip bags, which might not be sufficient. He said he'd ask his pain-management doctors for a strong opiate, like Seconal, as a sleep medication, but he wasn't sure they'd give him enough—for his special purpose, anyway.

He asked me to take an inventory of all the drugs he had on hand at the house (in his bathroom, where he seemed to have more pill bottles than a drugstore), and report back.

The next day, when we were alone at the hospital again, I told him what I had found that seemed most useful: about twenty methadone pills, about fifty heptabarbital, one hundred phenobarbital, and a few other things. Several of the bottles looked pretty ancient, and I mentioned my concern about the pills' potency. I had heard that some of these drugs didn't "keep" too long. Jolly didn't respond to this, but asked if I had seen a smallish green bottle with no label. I said I hadn't but would look again (even though I knew I'd checked every bottle in his bathroom). He thought for a minute, then said he wasn't sure he had enough drugs at home to do the job.

He said he had already been contemplating various options that wouldn't require so many drugs to accomplish. One of them was to stage an accidental drowning in his bathtub, as if he had fallen asleep and been so full of pain medication that when he'd gone underwater he hadn't had a strong enough gag reflex to wake up. I told him I thought the bathtub scenario would automatically raise suspicions because he never took baths, just showers. Besides, as I gently reminded him, he probably wouldn't fit in his standard-size bathtub—he was just too big. He weighed about 250 pounds, even after radiation, chemotherapy, surgery, and several weeks in the hospital. Three months before, when he had gotten his diagnosis, he'd weighed about 325.

Another option, he said, was to achieve the same result by "taking a dip" in the swimming pool. He told me to crank up the pool heater in case he decided he wanted to go that way. Again I had to say it wouldn't look right, because he hardly ever went swimming— besides, he couldn't walk without assistance, so his presence in the pool would raise the question of who had helped him get there.

His other idea was Mexico. He'd send me down to Tijuana to pick up a few items, in case he couldn't get them from his doctors. For half a second that seemed possible, because certain narcotics are available without a prescription in Mexico, but then it hit me: I'd be transporting these narcotics across the U.S./Mexico border. *No thanks!* I didn't think I could help Jolly very much if I were rotting in prison for attempted drug smuggling, and I called this to his attention. He chuckled ruefully at the obvious flaw he'd missed, and I chuckled too, but I was faking it; actually, I was getting angry.

Jolly was infamous for having big ideas but relying on others to do the scut work. This dynamic applied to both his professional and his home life, where Mom had handled all the practical details until her Alzheimer's interfered. But if Jolly wanted an autonomous death, he had to do things for himself. And he hadn't done much of anything besides consider a few unrealistic options. His insufficient drug stash was a real problem. Luckily, he later succeeded in persuading his pain-management doctors to prescribe some of his take-home morphine in pill form and a decent supply of Seconal tablets. I knew he couldn't talk openly with any of his doctors about his end-of-life choice, but maybe he made enough vague references that they realized what he had in mind, and did what they could for him without overstepping their ethical boundaries.

Jolly had asked me to bring him his stationery, both personal and professional, because he had a few letters to write and another plan he wanted my help with. (*Another* plan? Now what?) He said he'd been thinking about the possible consequences for me if my role in assisting his suicide were suspected, and he thought a "goodbye letter" from him might help throw the hounds off my trail. He also wanted to write a private letter of farewell to K so that after he died his "natural" death (and after any investigation was over), she could learn the truth of the matter and perhaps feel a little better. He probably also felt he owed her an explanation, because if she hadn't had Alzheimer's, Jolly would have turned to her, not me, for help with this sorry business.

We talked about where to put these goodbye letters, and Jolly suggested I tape them to the underside of the drawer in his nightstand. But that seemed a bit too melodramatic to me, too much like a bad spy movie. We finally settled on putting them underneath the liner paper inside that drawer. Not very original, but if there was an investigation, the letters would be found easily and might protect me. And if they weren't found right away, then I could steer Joe Friday to their hiding place without much trouble.

I sat on the couch by the window of Jolly's hospital room and snacked from his dinner tray (they always brought him the deluxe meals, although he never ate much more than the Jell-O), while he composed the letters in his head and then wrote them down on the stationery. As I snacked, I contemplated the fact that we were only a few days away from the actual event. It didn't feel real, somehow, perhaps because Jolly seemed so calm. He'd always had a great talent for making things appear easy—an essential quality of his above-it-all persona—and it wasn't failing him now, even though he was full of cancer and had just had two artificial hips stuck into him.

Perhaps it was natural that I remained calm, too. I've always been relatively coolheaded, and I'd already experienced the untimely deaths of several close relatives and family friends. In addition, I'd had serious professional training. But underneath all that was the fact that I was unquestionably my father's son, and following Jolly's lead was second nature to me. Sometimes I even felt myself slipping back into ancient patterns of behavior around him—joking a little too much (for attention), deferring a little too quickly (for approval)—things I hadn't done in years.

But even when I had these "relapses," I remained aware of the gravity of my situation. I was facing serious medical issues and legal consequences—playing with real fire—and I didn't want to get burned. I already felt singed: Jolly's bathtub/pool/Mexico planning problems, Anne's increasingly erratic behavior, several clients in Seattle having additional troubles . . .

I mentally steadied myself to cope with the intensity of what loomed. I felt like I was about to enter a tied football game with a minute to go, or parachute out of a plane for the first time—into a combat zone.

Jolly wrapped up his letters and said he needed to call it a night. I put the letters in a manila envelope and drove back to the house, where I installed them in their appointed spot.

Afterward, I poured myself a small glass of Jameson's and went outside onto the patio to think. The darkness and quiet and cool night air helped me relax and gather my thoughts. As I sipped my drink, I found myself recalling a poem Jolly had worked on over the years, which ended: "Too soon dead. Too late wise. Make my bed. Close my eyes."

MONDAY, DECEMBER 28

It would have been reasonable to expect a smooth and orderly transition in getting Jolly from his hospital room to his bedroom at home, especially since we were dealing with the world-famous UCLA Hospital and its care of an important UCLA professor and hospital department chairman emeritus, a bigwig of the first order. He would get the best possible deal, right?

Not even close.

The UCLA social worker assigned to coordinate the move seemed to care a great deal, as did the woman from the hospice service, and they both assured me that everything would go smoothly, but absolutely nothing did. Instead we had rank chaos—exactly what a dying cancer patient and his family don't need. During the few days before Jolly's expected return home, as we tried to convert his bedroom into a medical ward, the UCLA people didn't seem to know what the hospice people were doing, and vice versa, and neither group knew which medical-equipment company was delivering what or when or where. Even the rented hospital bed frame and its special mattress came from two different places at two different times. What a mess.

So I became a quick-study expert on the intricacies of the medical-supply industry and other bureau*crap*ic (another new term I've coined) matters related to getting a sick person home from the hospital. But I had to wonder how other people cope—people who can't get time off work during the day, or who don't have a head for details, or who don't have long and close ties with the hospital in question.

Stay healthy, people. I'm not kidding.

Friday, January 1, 1999

Happy New Year?

Not exactly. Except that Wisconsin was playing UCLA in the Rose Bowl, and whichever school won, Jolly would be happy. He'd been raised in Madison, Wisconsin, and had attended the university there before joining the Army in 1942, and he'd spent the last thirty years on the UCLA faculty, so the two schools he felt closest to were in the big game. Final score: Wisconsin 38, UCLA 31. His hometown team won. How appropriate. He was going home tomorrow. In more ways than one.

I went to the hospital in the late afternoon to see if there were any new developments that Jolly wanted me to handle. There weren't, so we just shared a last bit of father-son football viewing—not something we'd ever done much of, except around the holidays, grateful for the break from all the family talk, and for the chance to rest our mandibles before the most important holiday activity: eating.

At halftime Dad decided he needed a nap, so I left. It felt good to get outdoors again, to breathe real air, not the recirculated, sterile stuff served up inside the hospital. It was like the difference between drinking distilled water from a plastic jug and fresh water straight from a mountain stream: The distilled stuff may be "cleaner" but it tastes like hell by comparison. Maybe that's what Hell really is: a place where everything is bland, neutral, and tasteless.

SATURDAY, JANUARY 2

Jolly's D-day. I got a reveille phone call from him at 8:30 AM, and I'd been out late with friends the night before, so I wasn't at my sharpest, but what he told me jolted me into focus. We had a major snafu with his prescription for Seconal, the main drug he needed for his early exit: UCLA's pharmacy didn't carry it. Unbelievable! How could a major university hospital not carry such a common drug—especially if its own doctors were prescribing it? And if they didn't have it, who the hell would?

I stumbled into the kitchen, got some coffee inside me, grabbed a phone book, and started calling pharmacy after pharmacy until—finally—I found one that had a supply of Seconal in stock: good old Horton & Converse. But wait—Jolly's prescription read: "30 pills, 50 mg. each," and the pharmacist on the phone said the standard size was 100 milligrams, which was what they had in stock. I relayed this information immediately to Jolly, and he got hold of one of his docs, who rewrote the Seconal scrip for 100-milligram pills.

What a way to start the day.

I had another cup of coffee, showered and shaved, and drove to the hospital to start the process of getting Jolly home. A couple of his doctors dropped in, looked him over one more time, and then issued the discharge orders and take-home prescriptions. Their patient seemed more cheerful than he had the day before, probably because he was finally leaving the hospital. And that meant, as he'd told me privately just a few days before, that he could finally do what he wanted to do: end the agony as soon as he got home.

This was it. Tonight was the night.

I HAD THE UNENVIABLE task of getting the long list of Jolly's prescriptions (other than Seconal) filled in the hospital's dreary basement pharmacy, where during the interminable wait I had a wild idea: What if the prescriptions that a patient needed to take home were simply ordered by the doctor, filled by the hospital's pharmacy, and sent to the patient's room? That way, the patient's family wouldn't have to waste time and energy waiting around or dealing with billing problems. Wouldn't that make sense? Of course. And that's how hospitals used to do it, but not anymore. Not since they became so bureau*crap*ic. This is progress?

Anne arrived in Jolly's hospital room and joined the packing and moving-out process just as I discovered that the UCLA patient-liaison people and/or hospice people and/or medical-supply people had screwed up yet again: Jolly's special-order, extra-large wheelchair and extra-large portable commode had been delivered to the *hospital* instead of the *house*. Swell. Now what would we do? I eyeballed the jumbo commode and hoped that I could fit it into the backseat of my rental car, so I lugged the damn thing down to the parking garage to make sure.

Ever bring a commode into an elevator full of people? You know they're all thinking, *That thing sure as hell better not be loaded!* and, *How long can I hold my breath?* Nobody looks at you. Nobody talks. Eyes start to bulge. Everybody gets out much sooner than they'd planned, just in case.

Luckily, the thing did fit in my car, so I didn't have the pleasure of dragging it back up to the ninth floor of the hospital and making other arrangements. As for the wheelchair, I just hoped that the ambulance people who were scheduled to transport Jolly back to the house would bend the rules a little and take it along with them. Thankfully, they did.

At around 2:00 PM, two beefy guys from the hospital's transportation department arrived in Jolly's room for the removal chores. With some huffing and puffing on their part, and grimacing and groaning on Jolly's, they muscled him out of his bed onto a gurney, then trundled him down to the ambulance bay, where two different people transferred him into their waiting ambulance. We were ready to go.

So we had a parade: me in my rental car, with the commode crammed into the backseat along with several grocery bags full of medical supplies (bandages, syringes, suppositories, prescriptions); and then Anne, driving Dad's black Caddy loaded with Dad's suitcases and more bags of medical supplies; and then the ambulance, containing the main attraction himself. We slowly wound our way through the maze of UCLA and Westwood Village, and headed toward home, about a mile away.

When we got there, I got out of my car and tried to guide the ambulance driver up our steep, twisting driveway, but instead of slowing down and listening to me, he zoomed right past me and gunned his rig straight up the hill. I can only imagine how that played out in the back of the ambulance, where Jolly must have been cursing himself, one last time, for buying a house with such a tricky driveway.

At the top, however, the driver finally listened to my instructions on how to maneuver properly so they could deliver Jolly and get their vehicle back down the driveway without getting stuck (a common problem for visitors who didn't listen). Once they'd angled into the right spot and unloaded their well-jostled passenger, their only remaining obstacles were the three steps up from the driveway to the front porch. Good thing I was there. The ambulance driver was big, but his helper seemed a little undersized for this particular job. She meant well, I'm sure, but she literally couldn't hold up her end of the bargain, which happened to be the foot of the gurney with Jolly on it. If I hadn't jumped in to help, Jolly might have rolled right back down the driveway and introduced himself to a passing Plymouth.

As Jolly was bounced from the ambulance into the house, I wondered if he saw the beautiful poinsettias that had just been planted along the front porch. He loved poinsettias and always sent them to people at Christmas, and brought home plenty as well. But this year he'd had a few other things on his mind, so Mom had had the gardeners replace the shrubs out front with several dozen big, bold, blood-red poinsettias. I hoped he caught at least a glimpse of them.

My next tasks were to get Jolly settled in his bedroom and then deal with the hospice people, who were waiting in the living room. I buzzed around, trying to do a little of everything, as did Norma— K's best friend and my godmother, visiting from Portland, Oregon, and helping K.

Poor K. She knew she couldn't help, and that even trying to help would have had the opposite of the desired effect. It must have been awful for her. She'd always been so good at this sort of thing, organizing and directing all the major productions in our family with great precision and success. But the Alzheimer's had robbed her of those skills. Now, when she faced complicated or otherwise stressful situations, she became fearful and anxious, overwhelmed, so much so that she'd start huffing and puffing—panting, almost like a dog. And her worsening emphysema certainly didn't help matters. She'd quickly get light-headed and have to sit down and catch her breath. All she could do now was watch the action from the sidelines, and worry.

The hospice people were easy to deal with: Margo was the main administrator and liaison nurse; Letty was the twenty-four-hour, on-site person. Letty was rather new to hospice work, attentive and eager to make a good impression, but she was tiny. I wondered how she expected to do all the bathing and other chores that Big Jolly would need. But then, of course, I remembered: She wasn't going to have to do any of that. Not for long, anyway.

Suddenly, Jolly announced that he felt a somewhat pressing need to test-drive the commode. So I dashed off to get the thing out of my car and hiked it up the driveway and then . . . well, it was clear that little Letty was not going to be able to take care of this particular task on her own. Luckily, Margo and I were still there.

And so it came to pass that all three of us found ourselves appointed to facilitate the Great Movement. The commode was basically just a removable plastic bucket placed under an extra-large plastic toilet seat, all of which fitted into a gigantic, adjustable, tubular aluminum frame. Letty, Margo, and I maneuvered Jolly to the edge of his bed and into a standing position—not an easy thing to do with a man who is six-foot-three and 250 pounds of injured flesh and fragile bones. And he couldn't help much. It was horribly difficult for him to stand up or move around on his own because of the pain from the hip surgeries and the widespread cancer, plus the nausea from the cancer treatments—one hell of a trifecta. There was much gritting of teeth all around. All four of us were afraid we'd drop him, and we could imagine the agony and humiliation that would ensue. Once we got him standing, we had to keep propping him up; he hadn't the strength to remain upright on his own. We turned him around and positioned the commode behind him, then carefully guided him down onto the seat.

When we finally got him settled, he dismissed Letty and Margo but asked me to stay. Not exactly my preference, but I wasn't going to abandon him. I looked around for a place to sit, as far away from Jolly as I could get without being too obvious.

He was so relieved to finally be seated on the commode that he actually looked happy for the first time in weeks. Then, with a sad smile, he said, "It's a hell of a thing to be so sick that one can find pleasure in just getting one's ass onto a plastic pot."

He often used formal language when dealing with sensitive subjects. Out of habit, I guess, I replied in kind: "Well, one takes what one can get, I suppose." He grimaced a smile at me and heaved a heavy sigh.

A few minutes passed without much conversation. The sound of some progress came from the commode, accompanied by some more heavy sighing from Dad. I had braced myself for the inevitable unhappy aromatic impact, but it never came. Instead I began to vaguely detect a rather medicinal, eucalyptus-like odor. I didn't know if this was the result of all the different chemicals that had been pumped through Jolly's system at the hospital to fight the cancer or what, but I didn't care. I was just grateful.

I tried thinking about other things to distract myself from what I was actually doing—watching my father sit on a toilet— and found myself remembering an old friend of Jolly's: Norman Cousins, the writer and longtime editor of *The Saturday Review.* Norman had died only a few years before, at a nearby restaurant— while sitting on the toilet. Surely not the exit strategy he would have chosen, but there it was. I remembered Norman's wicked sense of humor and decided he would have been the first to come up with a joke about his own final position: "What a crappy way to go." "I was shit out of luck." "When you gotta go, you gotta go." "I just crapped out." And while I knew that "crapped out" refers to the dice game known as craps, it also occurred to me that the singular of "dice" is "die." I think Norman would have appreciated that irony, too.

I tried not to chuckle out loud, because I didn't want Jolly to ask me what the hell was so funny. I wasn't sure that the humor quotient would ease his dismay at being reminded of Norman's demise, especially when he himself was in such pain—and in the same pose.

Were my thoughts irreverent? Certainly. But black humor is a common and accepted practice in hospitals, foxholes, and other high-stress locales. I'd learned that at a young age from Jolly and K, both by report and by watching them in action, dealing with major crises at work, at home, and elsewhere. And I'd learned it firsthand—while getting shot at by drunken Bolivians when I bicycled across South America, digging out of a major mudslide, working in the public defender's office, and other crunchy situations. I'd learned very well.

As the old saying goes, sometimes you have to laugh to keep from crying. In order to keep your wits and be effective (or at least keep your snout above the surface), you brush past, rather than grab on to, certain emotions—the serious, powerful, heavy emotions—so they don't drag you down and keep you from taking care of business. You still have the feelings, of course, but you don't indulge yourself by wallowing in them. Maybe later, but not now. Now you have to stay sharp, and it's easier to stay sharp if you're detached, and humor is the great detacher. You can always get reattached to your feelings some other time.

My reverie was interrupted by Jolly's notifying me that he'd finished. He asked me to call in the hospice workers to clean him up. He didn't have to ask twice. I fetched Letty and Margo, then went outside for a little fresh air. When they were done with the cleanup, I went back inside to help Jolly off the commode and back into bed. This time things didn't go so well.

We started to lift him, but about halfway up he lost his balance and started wobbling and flailing his arms. "I'm falling!" he shouted, and we all surged forward and pressed our bodies against him to keep him upright. I was the strongest one there, and it took all I had to keep him from collapsing, my chest pressed against his back, my hands braced under his arms, trying not to exert too much pressure against any particular point and perhaps break a bone in his shoulder or a couple of ribs. But I had to prevent him from falling onto the hard plastic and metal of the commode. If he fell, I knew he would shatter many bones, which would be excruciatingly painful and absolutely demoralizing, not to mention degrading because of the injuries' cause. Fortunately, we managed to stabilize him and get him back upright. We all caught our breath and slowly maneuvered him to the side of the bed, gently lowered him onto it, then gingerly nudged and slid him into the center of the mattress and propped his head up on the pillows. Safe at last.

Jolly's bed was a story in itself: The frame was standard hospital issue, but it had a high-tech, air-flow mattress—with thousands of pinhole-size openings on the top surface, and air pumped into it by a small compressor at the foot of the bed. The openings allowed air to circulate underneath the bedding, creating a sort of floating-on-air situation that helped prevent bedsores and relieve general discomfort.

Another thing about the bed, an important thing: It was noisy. The compressor ran all the time to keep the mattress inflated, and the air moving through it created a strong white noise—like the *shush* noise one makes to get people to shut up, only louder and deeper. The perfect sound to absorb other sounds, it would muffle any conversation between Jolly and me later. That night, the noise of the compressor would prove quite useful as a mechanical accomplice.

DRUGSTORE MADNESS

After Jolly got settled in bed, other family members arrived to visit with him and welcome him home. I went out to the kitchen and got on the phone with the Horton & Converse pharmacy in Brentwood to submit that rewritten prescription for Jolly's Seconal. I dialed the number, the phone rang, and their answering machine picked up. They were closed.

I collapsed onto a chair in disbelief. I heard the recorded voice telling me that their hours were from 10:00 AM to 1:00 PM on Saturdays . . .

Son of a *bitch*! I called them back two or three more times just to make sure I had heard right. I felt a surge of hot, tingling adrenaline flooding my neck, shoulders, and back. What the hell was I going to do?

I took a few deep breaths and forced myself to collect my wits and think. *Think!* Maybe one of the other Horton & Converse locations was still open. I called around, but the only one still open didn't have any Seconal. Shit! The only thing left to do was call every pharmacy in the area until I found an open one that had Seconal. But it was already a few minutes after 4:00 PM, and I figured that 5:00 PM would probably be closing time for any that were still open.

I was nearly exhausted from the day's various snafus and crises, and I desperately needed a break, but there wasn't time. I don't know why I didn't just tell Jolly, "Hey, they were closed. You didn't plan ahead. We'll do it on Monday. What's two more days?" But I didn't.

Norma walked into the kitchen and I asked her to help me. She immediately sat down with the phone book and started calling local pharmacies while I grabbed another phone book and another phone line and started making calls myself.

Brentwood Pharmacy? No.

Westgate Pharmacy? No.

United Pharmacy? No.

Vicente Drugs? No.

Sav-on Drugs? No.

Longs Drugs? No.

Super Drugs? No.

Kerr Drug? No.

Pavilions? No.

Rite Aid? No.

Fuck!

But Norma scored! She found a place: the Airport Pharmacy. And my heart sank. It was already 4:45, and it would take at least twenty minutes to get to LAX—and that was at my personal best warp speed, and knowing exactly where I was going. I'd never even heard of the Airport Pharmacy, so I'd be flying blind, but it was our only chance. I sprinted out the door, yelling behind me for Norma to call and tell them I was on my way, not to close until I got there, it was for a critically ill patient . . . whatever she could think of.

I peeled out of the driveway and floored it down the street. As I careened down Sunset to get onto the freeway, I glanced at the address Norma had given me: 3250 Pico, near Centinela. Odd—that wasn't near LAX. But then I realized that the pharmacy was near the Santa Monica airport, just half the distance. There was hope!

The ensuing drive can be compared only to a chase scene in a slapstick comedy, except there were no crashes or people jumping out of the way. And it wasn't funny. But I did break almost all the traffic laws in the book as I sped and weaved my way toward my destination. I finally caught sight of the pharmacy just as my watch read 4:59. I veered into a parking spot, jumped out, sprinted across traffic to the entrance, and pushed open the door. Yes! I was in.

I don't know how I managed to look casual when I bounded through that door. Maybe I didn't bound. Maybe I didn't look casual. But no one called the cops, so I must not have barged in looking too desperate. I took a few deep breaths, got my bearings, walked briskly to the back where the pharmacist held court, and put in my order.

He looked at me over his bifocals. "Are you L. J. West?"

Ack!

"Uh, no, I'm his son."

He kept looking at me blankly.

Think fast!

"But I have full authorization. I'm also his attorney."

What the hell, it might help.

He looked at the prescription and nodded to himself. Then he shuffled back to his supply room and began rooting around. I sighed and started to relax a little.

The pharmacist came back to the counter and said, "This card doesn't work."

What? I'd given him Jolly's insurance card, and apparently the evil gods of bureaucracy weren't through fucking with me for the day. I managed to compose myself and simply paid for the prescription with my own credit card. The receipt said $48.14 for thirty pills. The difference between agony and peace cost less than fifty bucks. What a concept.

With the Seconal safely in my pocket, I felt a wave of relaxation wash over me, almost as if I'd swallowed a few of the pills myself. I felt so good, I decided to buy a lottery ticket. What the hell—I'd been damn lucky to get my mission impossible accomplished—maybe it would carry over. And I noticed they had Beeman's gum on their candy shelf, so I bought a pack for Dad. I knew it was his favorite.

As I left the store, I noticed a Trader Joe's market next door and thought I'd pick up a bottle of good wine to take back for Jolly's welcome-home party, so I strolled on over.

```
INT. POLICE STATION - NIGHT

                JOE FRIDAY
              (contemptuously)
    So, Mr. West, you bought your father
    his prescription of narcotics and
    then went right next door to buy some
    expensive wine, and that very same
    night your father died with a gut
    full of Seconal while you drank to his
    "health." What should I make of that?
```

```
                    WEST
          (with shit-eating grin)
    Um . . . coincidence?


                  JOE FRIDAY
                (unamused)
    Lock him up, boys, and bring me a
    nightstick. I need some exercise.

    SLOW FADE OUT as West is dragged off to a
    holding cell, thrashing and howling about
    his civil rights and his one phone call.
```

Yow! No thank you very much! You *did* go to law school, didn't you? Use your damn head! So I bought the wine with cash, to avoid leaving an easy paper trail for any baton-wielding detectives, and drove away feeling euphoric. I'd done it! I'd gotten the Seconal: the main ingredient.

When I got back to the house, I went straight to Dad's room and found Letty attending to him. "Hey there!" I announced, smiling broadly. "I got the Seconal, so all the prescriptions are present and accounted for."

Jolly gave me a hard look. At first I didn't understand why, but then I got it: He didn't want anyone to even *hear* the word "Seconal." He wanted to keep its very existence a secret. But it couldn't be: Seconal was right there on his list of medications, and UCLA had given a copy of the list to the hospice people. And if I acted secretively about getting it for him, and if there were any questions later, guess who'd get the hairy eyeball? Better to treat it like just another item on the list, nothing special; hide it in plain sight. Jolly might

have felt better if I'd said nothing, but it was my ass that was potentially in the sling here, so my approach had to take priority.

Jolly told Letty that he was feeling a fair amount of pain and
intended to take more of the morphine, so he asked for an injection
of antinausea medication (Compazine) as a precaution. While she
busied herself with that, I went to the kitchen. Luckily, no one else
was there, so I could easily grab the other items I'd acquired for Jolly's
private party scheduled for later—items only he and I knew about.

A few days earlier I'd talked with Jolly about a stratagem I'd seen
in a suicide self-help guide: Crushing morphine pills into a powder
and mixing it into yogurt supposedly made it easier to consume
more of the drug. The yogurt also helped coat and calm the stomach, warding off the nausea that sometimes comes from ingesting
large quantities of opiates. Jolly had said it sounded worth trying,
so I'd bought some yogurt and squirreled it away in the back of the
refrigerator. Now I dug it out, got a spoon, and put them in a paper
bag that I took into Jolly's dressing room and hid in his closet. Then
I returned to his bedroom.

LETTY FINISHED UP and started to leave. I gave Dad the raised eyebrow and he nodded, so I left the room with Letty and walked her
to the den, her assigned bedroom.

"Thank you, Letty, for your attentiveness to my father."

"Oh, you're welcome!" she said, cheerfully.

"Listen, I think I should also mention—just so you'll know—
that you shouldn't take it personally if he seems a bit reluctant to
have you around. He's an intensely private man, maybe because of
his profession—he's a psychiatrist, you know—but his privacy is

extremely important to him. That's why he wanted me to tell you this: Don't be surprised if you see a DO NOT DISTURB sign on his door. Also, whenever you go to his room, even if that sign isn't up, be sure to knock first, and then wait until he says, 'Come in' before entering. Okay?"

"Of course!" she said. "I don't want to invade his privacy."

Not as much as I don't want you to invade mine, I thought.

I left her unpacking her overnight bag in the den and returned immediately to Jolly's room. He was waiting.

"Let's get started," he said.

"First let me check on everyone else, so we know what's going on."

"Okay, but hurry back."

"Right."

I jogged down the hall to Mom's room. She and Norma were sitting together, talking. Mom looked up at me imploringly, almost desperate to know how Jolly was and when she'd be allowed to see him. I hated making her wait, but it was only for a little longer. I tried to reassure her. "He's fine, but still getting settled. I think in a little while he'll be up to having some face-to-face time with you, and maybe some of the rest of the crowd, but hang loose for now, okay?"

She nodded, but I could see that she was fearful, unsure of what was going on, and unhappy knowing she couldn't do anything to help. So I knelt in front of her, took her hands in mine, and looked up into her face. "It's gonna be fine, Mom. I promise. Only a few minutes. He just wants to get a bit more comfortable, and maybe comb his beard a little so he doesn't frighten the livestock."

She smiled weakly. "Thanks, Johnny," she said.

I looked at Norma. She gave me a wink and a nod, letting me know she had things under control with K. How glad I was to have Norma there—she gave Mom such great comfort, as only a best friend can do.

I went upstairs to tell Anne and Paul that Jolly would soon be ready to socialize a little, and that I'd let them know when the time came. As I left their room, I felt a pang of sadness for my sister Mary. She had left L.A. just after Christmas, acquiescing to her husband's demands, which meant she wasn't here to say goodbye to Jolly. And even though she wouldn't have known that it *was* goodbye, just seeing him home from the hospital and back in his own bedroom, looking peaceful, would have meant a lot to her.

Downstairs again, I double-checked that K and Norma were still in K's bedroom, and made sure that Letty was still in the den. Then I went back to Jolly's room and told him how things stood.

"Lock the door," he said.

"Right." I put his DO NOT DISTURB sign on the outside door-knob, then closed and locked the door.

"Now, let's take a look at what we've got," he said. "Go get me what's under my sink."

I went into his bathroom, grabbed the various pill bottles, and carried them out to him in handfuls. Several choices seemed logical right off the bat: the methadone, of course, and the heptabarbi-tal and phenobarbital, which I figured must be similar to Seconal (which is just another name for secobarbital)—they're all barbitu-rates. There was plenty of Ambien, the sleeping pill he'd been using for years. There must have been at least four or five dozen different prescription bottles in his bathroom drawers and cabinets.

Jolly put together a pile of about twenty pills, most of which I think were methadone, put them all in one bottle, and set it on his side table. I put the other bottles back in his bathroom, approximately where I'd found them, and went back into his bedroom.

Oops! What about my fingerprints on all those pill bottles? Forget it—I'd have time to deal with that later.

Oops again! I hadn't given Jolly any of that yogurt yet. A little earlier I'd tried crushing one of the morphine pills into powder and hadn't had much luck. So the yogurt would just have to act as a buffer, along with Letty's Compazine injections, to calm his stomach and help suppress the nausea. The yogurt needed to be eaten before Jolly took the pills, of course, so we had to jump on that. I got it out of the closet and he ate a few spoonfuls.

"That's enough for now," he said.

It didn't seem like enough to me. "Don't forget, you don't have anything else in your stomach," I warned, reminding him that he'd eaten nothing for breakfast or lunch.

He gave me a dark look. "I know."

Okay, okay. He was the doctor, so I didn't push it.

"Now the visits?" I asked.

He nodded. "First your mother."

I put the yogurt and spoon back in the paper bag and returned it to the closet. Then I unlocked the door, replaced the DO NOT DISTURB sign on the inside doorknob, and fetched Mom. Norma came too. But it turned out to be a brief visit.

After only two minutes, Letty knocked on the door and said it was time for Jolly's scheduled medications. He asked us all to leave, which seemed odd, but later he told me he'd asked Letty to give him

51

another dose of Compazine, this time in suppository form—hence the need for privacy. Unfortunately, one side effect of Compazine is drowsiness, and Letty had also given Jolly an Ambien because he'd told her he wanted to turn in early. That was a big mistake, because he started slowing down almost immediately. Not good for The Plan. Not good at all.

When Letty left the room, Mom, Norma, and I went back in, as did Anne and Paul, who had been waiting nearby. Jolly talked for a while, primarily to Mom, but the whole scene felt awkward: He spoke sluggishly; all the chairs were full of medical supplies, so everyone but K stood hovering around his bed; K sat in Jolly's wheelchair. She couldn't stand up, she was so drained—physically and emotionally—by the stress of the situation.

I wanted Mom and Dad to have some time alone together, but I didn't feel I could suggest it outright because it might seem odd. After all, there would be plenty of time for that tomorrow or the next day, right? And since Jolly didn't ask for it or encourage it, I couldn't do anything. Maybe he was just too preoccupied with what he was about to do, and trying to stay awake to do it. Because he was noticeably fading already, I thought we might have to wait and complete The Plan the next night.

Finally he admitted to being tired and suggested we wrap things up, maybe because Mom had started to cry and he knew he didn't have the energy to cheer her up. K got up slowly from the wheelchair, looking utterly exhausted. She kissed Jolly and they said, "I love you" to each other, and then Norma helped Mom out of the room. Anne and Paul left shortly thereafter. The welcome-home party was finally over.

THREE

———

Make My Bed. Close My Eyes.

Now it is time to help my father die.

I lock the door again and retrieve the yogurt. Jolly eats a little more of it and starts taking the mystery pills from his recently assembled stash, washed down with sips of water from a plastic cup on his side table. But he's slowing down a lot already and I'm getting worried, so I tell him he'd better get a move on, or he might not get the result he wants.

He finally starts on the Seconal, and I'm suddenly hit with the fear that he hasn't started taking his pills soon enough. His movements are already sluggish; his speech is almost word by word. He mumbles something about being "bored to death." Makes sense, actually. Why just lie there, in terrible pain, bored and waiting for it, when you can go and get it? The expression is "meet your maker," not "wait until your maker tracks you down." Right? Maybe that's what he's thinking.

He takes a few more Seconal, but now he's moving in slow motion, and he's taking long pauses and looking around. I guess those mystery pills he took first were pretty potent. I try to get him to pay attention to what we're doing by waving my hands in front of his face and talking fast. I'm very glad for the loud white noise of that air compressor because I feel the need to almost shout to keep him awake. I'm right next to his ear with "Come on! Take more! You're falling asleep and it won't work!" and other urgings that I hope will get him to take more Seconal and start in on the morphine. He hasn't even touched the morphine yet, and he's getting even slower. I'm barking at him now, right in his ear: "Dad! Hey! Don't fall asleep! Come on! Keep going!"

I have an idea. I grab an ice cube from the large cup of ice he'd asked me to get earlier for his water, and I rub it on his face and neck, hoping it'll shock him and perk him up. But it has little effect. I jokingly threaten to put the ice cube down his pajamas if he doesn't get with the program, but he doesn't register it.

Now I'm seriously worried. For the first time I think, *He's not going to make it.* How ironic: In this case, to "not make it" means to live. And living is *not* what he wants. *He really isn't going to get the job done*, I think. *He'll get it only partly done and end up a damn vegetable for the last few miserable weeks of his life until the cancer finally kills him. Dammit! He's waited too long, he didn't plan, he's blown it. Shit!*

And then I realize I have to calm down and let it go. I can't worry about things I can't control. I've done what I can. After all, I can't force the pills down his throat.

But I can't just sit here and do nothing.

I get close, right in his face, and quietly yell (as loudly as I dare under the cover of the compressor noise), "Keep going, Dad! Get it done! Focus!" But he's moving slower and slower, and his eyes are locked. It occurs to me that he might be so out of it that he's operating at brain-stem level and only deeply imprinted stimuli will register, so I lean down into his face again and bark, "Ten-hut! Wake up, soldier! You got work to do!" It feels silly and has no effect, but I have to try everything I can think of.

He's fading fast. Very little time is left before he falls asleep and can't take any more drugs. I'm almost frantic now, twitching with impatience to keep him awake and swallowing pills. He hasn't even finished the Seconal, let alone taken any of the morphine. And then something occurs to me. It's bad. It's very bad. But I figure I have to do it: I have to hurt him. But how? Slap him in the face? No, I can't bring myself to do that. I try a little whack on his arm, but I can tell that's no good. To rouse him, I'll have to hurt him a lot. What can I do? And suddenly I know what to do. It's more than bad—it's ugly. He's just had hip surgery, right? I hate to do it, but there it is.

"Sorry, Dad, but you gotta take more of this stuff." I shake my head and do it. I push on his leg. Hard. More like a jolt, a shove, right at the knee, twisting it and rotating it inward. And I think it works, because I hear him groan and his body shifts forward, and he seems to come out of his fog a little.

Man, I hated doing that! The whole point is to stop the pain, not make it worse. But I know that our only real chance is *now*. If we blow this one, the doctors will get involved again and we won't get another shot. Besides, most of the Seconal is gone, and there's no way he can get a refill anytime soon.

Jolly emerges a little more from his fog, shakes his head, and looks around. I grab the pills and put them in his right hand, then pour more water into the plastic cup he's been clutching in his left.

He drops a few pills onto his chest, and they scatter on the bedding. He looks around for them but I say, *"No!"* and he stops, looks up, slowly raises his right hand and puts the other pills in his mouth, then slowly, slowly raises the cup with his left hand and drinks. His eyes stay focused on a point right in front of him, but I can tell he's seeing something very far away. And then, in extreme slow motion, he lowers the cup, closes his eyes, sighs a deep long sigh, and leans his head back against the pillow.

He's asleep.

I STOOD THERE, just looking at him, for what felt like a very long time. He seemed peaceful, finally. A welcome change. He'd looked so pained for the last few weeks—knitted brow, gritted teeth—but not anymore.

Everything was perfectly quiet. And then I slowly grew aware again of the noisy hushing sound of the air compressor, which made the room seem both active and still. I looked around the room—at everything, seeing nothing—then looked back at the bed. He was still there, sound asleep. This was real. The clock said it was only 11:00 PM, but it felt like 3:00 AM. After a bar fight and a car wreck. But I still had to get us home.

All I could do now was tidy up and wait. And hope he'd gotten enough of the right chemicals into his system to shut it down. Honestly, I didn't think he had. I even thought of the odds, which for some reason I put at thirty-to-one. If only he'd started sooner, or . . .

This bit of wishful thinking reminded me of something Jolly had told me years ago, that most suicide attempts are only cries for help—

that anyone who *really* wants to commit suicide can do so easily. Even if someone doesn't have access to pills or guns, there are always railroad tracks, the tops of tall buildings, and other readily available sure-thing methods. But these all require mobility, something Jolly had lost—it was a factor he hadn't taken into account. And none of them offer much dignity. So, for people with disabling illnesses, there really aren't readily available options. Such people need help if they want to die, and that places a double burden of medical and legal worries on the loved one who helps. And although I was willing and able to shoulder that burden, it shouldn't have to be this way.

I looked around the room again and thought about how to set the scene. Jolly had wanted his death to look natural, as if he had simply died in his sleep. He didn't want to leave any clues to suggest he'd done anything to speed up the process. Me neither. The decoy letter was in place, if I needed it. But I really didn't think it would seem strange for him to have come home from the hospital, relaxed his grip, and just let go. People do that all the time.

There were a lot of pill bottles lying about, both legit and otherwise, so I decided to clean up. That way, when it was all over, there would be no loose ends. But then I heard something that made me stop. Was something wrong with the air compressor? Then I recognized the sound: Jolly's breathing, getting throaty and thick. I took his pulse: 110. That seemed awfully fast. Why would that be? I timed his breathing at between six and seven respirations per minute. Shouldn't things be slowing down a little? I double-checked his pulse: 90. That was a little more like it. Maybe I'd miscounted before. Then I noticed that he was starting to breathe more slowly, more deeply, making a grating noise as he inhaled. Was that important? What could that be? And then it hit me: He was snoring! I had to laugh—it was just so . . . normal. Then his breathing changed again and became more obviously labored. Long pauses between each breath—deep, rasping, gasping breaths. Further and further apart.

And then I could hardly find his pulse. Was this the end? Had he done it? His breaths were shallow now, and so far apart that . . . had they stopped?

I listened carefully. No breathing.

What about a pulse? I checked, and it was still there, but just barely. And then he heaved a deep sigh, a profound last breath— what's called the death rattle. I checked the clock: 11:15.

He was perfectly still. I couldn't feel a pulse at his wrist, so I put my hand on his neck and then his chest. I couldn't feel any heart-beat or movement, so I leaned over and put my ear on his chest to listen. And just as I did that, he heaved another deep sigh.

I jumped back so fast, I almost gave myself whiplash! But once I'd found my heart and shoved it back down my throat into my chest cavity, I started to laugh at myself. Jesus! The man almost killed *me*! Some thanks I get! Maybe it was payback for when I'd pushed on his leg. Okay, Dad, we're even.

I learned my lesson and did no more direct listening. Checking his wrist pulse was close enough. And it told me all I needed to know: no pulse. No more breathing, either. Fingernails turning blue, skin cooling off. Hard to mistake those signs.

It was over.

I slowly caught my breath from the scare that Jolly's final spasm had caused me, and I stood and just looked at him. It felt very different from a few minutes before, when he'd fallen asleep and I'd noticed that he finally looked peaceful. He still looked peaceful, but now it was deeper, truly final. He was dead. It didn't seem real, somehow. I had expected to feel so many different things—loss, relief, sorrow, maybe even the exhilaration of successfully completing a difficult and dangerous mission, but instead I only felt numb. My mind, my heart, my body—everything seemed fuzzy and quiet, on hold. The air felt thick and heavy; I moved slowly, as if underwater. Maybe the synapses in my brain and spine were overloaded. I made myself take a deep breath, and I shook my head to try to snap out of my daze. And then the world slowly began to resolve itself and return to normal.

I checked the clock again and was surprised to see that it was only 11:20 PM—a mere twenty minutes between Jolly's falling asleep and his achieving respiratory/cardiac arrest. That was fast. He certainly beat the odds I gave him—by a mile. As I thought about it, though, it made sense: He'd been full of the morphine from his intravenous drip bag, and his body had already been devastated by cancer.

I still had to straighten up the place. I started to wipe off the pill bottles, and then it occurred to me that lots of people had been in his room that evening, handling things, moving things around. There was no reason that my prints, and other people's prints, shouldn't be all over the place. With one exception: I wiped off the methadone bottle and put it back in Jolly's hand, so that only his prints would be on it. Just in case. And then I put it and all the other pill bottles that weren't supposed to be out and about back into his bathroom cabinets where I'd found them.

That done, I took stock, walking slowly around his room. There was nothing left to do, but I didn't want to leave. Somehow, it just didn't seem right. And, of course, it wasn't right. Instead of savoring a few last quiet moments together, Jolly and I had had to skulk and scheme—and work. And now, instead of being allowed to mourn, reflect, and share my feelings with my family, I had to hide my feelings and keep working. Not really death with dignity, for Jolly or for me.

I couldn't bring myself to leave the room just yet. I still needed something, but I didn't know what. A transition period, at least, a little time to decompress from the intensity of what I'd just been through. I looked through a box of old family photos I found on one of Jolly's bookcases, but felt nothing special. Maybe I had suppressed my feelings so deeply—in order to do the job Jolly had asked me to do—that they weren't able to resurface yet.

I'm sure they were there, though. Relief—about the end of Jolly's pain, as well as about the end (almost) of my nerve-wracking chores. Sadness—for me and the rest of the family. Many other feelings, surely, but all too subtle to distinguish in this compressed jumble of time. I wondered when they would emerge. How would I deal with them when they did? How would I digest the fact that I had caused Jolly pain by pushing on his leg? Would that be his last memory of me? Or mine of him? Were there hidden Oedipal issues here? Hell, I didn't know what any of it meant—I was still too stunned by it all. This was still the foxhole. But now Jolly was dead. Which was what he wanted.

I took a deep breath and let it out slowly as I tried to focus and regroup. I surveyed the room; It was the last time for a long time that this room would be peaceful. I wondered how the next series of events would unfold, and realized I still had more planning and staging ahead of me. That thought made me notice how tense my neck and shoulders were, and how incredibly weary I felt. I also realized that I seriously needed a shower and some food, and at least a few stiff drinks. Not necessarily in that order.

It was time to go.

I walked over to Jolly's bed and took a long, quiet last look at him. Finally I said, "Well, Dad, we did it. *You* did it. You got what you wanted."

And then, knowing it would be the last time, I said, "Goodnight, Dad." I kissed him on the forehead. Then I left.

THE HOUSE WAS QUIET. Good. I didn't want to have to deal with anyone else. I could see a light on under Mom's door. She and Norma were probably talking and getting ready for bed. I went into the kitchen and got a glass, some ice, and some Jameson's. Not too much—I still had work to do—but I did think it was finally time for a little something to cut the adrenaline. As I sipped my whiskey, I realized I'd forgotten all about the wine I'd bought at Trader Joe's. Oh well. It would keep.

I went outside to the patio. How good it felt to breathe the crisp night air! And to sit down, finally. What a relief it was to be out of Jolly's room. But as I sat there in the deck chair, slowly unwinding, I realized it was the constant noise of that air compressor that I was happiest to get away from—not Jolly, or what we'd done, or what I'd done. All that seemed . . . natural. It *was* natural—the death of a dying man. My conscience was clear.

The sky was clear, too, as I leaned back in the chair and gazed up in the traditional direction of heaven. I looked into the starry stillness, letting my mind relax, and suddenly I recalled a frequent scene from childhood: My sisters or I would be making too much noise, and Jolly would implore us for "a little dod-rotted peace and quiet!" I smiled and said, "You've got all the peace and quiet you want now, Dad." I took another deep drink of the cool air, and of the whiskey—the first toast to Jolly's memory—and went back into the house. Time to wrap up.

I walked to the front hallway to check on the den, where Letty slept. No light under the door. Good. Wouldn't have to worry about her for a while. I turned off the kitchen lights and headed upstairs to take a shower. As I passed by Jolly's room, for some reason I stopped and listened. Just the air compressor. But I couldn't resist: I opened his door and flicked on the light. I wasn't expecting anything weird, but I figured it would be best to put my mind at ease. No movement. Okay. No need to freak out. I closed the door and padded down the carpeted hallway, toward the stairs and the doorway to Mom's room. I could still see light under her door, and I thought about going in, but I listened and couldn't hear her and Norma talking. I considered checking in, but decided I'd let them have some private time. It was damn hard to get any privacy around this place—didn't I know it! So I went on upstairs. I checked the doorways on the landing. I saw light under the studio door, which meant that Anne and Paul were still awake. It was dark under the door to the room of Maria Luisa, the housekeeper. Good. She was sound asleep and had no idea what had just happened in the room below hers. Thank you, air compressor.

I tossed my ripe clothes into a corner of the bathroom and stood gratefully under a long, hot shower. Later, dry and downstairs again, I chose the larger of the two sofas in the living room as my temporary bed. (The den had been "my" room until Letty arrived.) I wasn't sure if I could relax enough to fall asleep, but figured I'd at least collect my thoughts and rest. It would be morning soon enough, and the place would get crazy.

As I settled down on the sofa, it occurred to me that there was an unexpected advantage to my living room location: No one could get to Jolly's room without my hearing and accompanying them. That way, I could manage the information flow about Jolly's death so that no one got the "wrong" idea. My main concern was Letty: If she got up in the middle of the night and checked on him, she'd probably raise a ruckus. I saw no point in that happening until morning, after everyone had had a good night's sleep. Everyone but me, of course. But then I remembered that Letty knew not to disturb Jolly except to give him his scheduled medication, and I believed she would heed that instruction. Just in case, though, I got up and went to Jolly's door, opened it, reached in for the DO NOT DISTURB sign, and hung it on the outside doorknob. It had been there earlier, so it wouldn't surprise Letty, or anyone else, to see it there again.

I settled back onto the sofa and thought about how things stood. The Plan was done; Jolly had gotten his wish: no more pain. I'd arranged things in his bedroom so there were no signs of Self de-Termination. Unless I'd been seen skulking in and out of his room after everyone had gone to bed (and I'd been careful about that—no one had seen me), there was nothing to connect me with being in there unchaperoned. And even if I had been seen coming or going, no one knew what we'd been doing in there, so people could only speculate, and that was insufficient evidence to send me to prison.

I looked at my watch: almost 4:00 AM. I stared into the darkness a little longer and then told myself to knock it off. I'd been asked to do a tough job, and I'd done it. But there would be plenty more work to do in the morning, so now I needed to get some shut-eye.

FOUR

———

The Morning After

I woke to the sound of Letty entering the front-hall bathroom and starting her shower. I checked my watch: 5:30 AM. Oof. But I had to get up. This was the next phase of making The Plan succeed: managing the information flow and arranging for it to have the proper spin.

I put my clothes on, struggled into the kitchen, made coffee, and drank a cup. When Letty emerged from her ablutions and came into the kitchen, I poured her some coffee and sat down at the table with her. We exchanged a bit of small talk, and then I waded in.

"I have bad news," I said. "I woke up when I heard you start your shower, so I got up and went to check on Jolly, and . . . he's passed away."

She was so stunned that she froze—her face blank, her mouth hanging open. To fill the silence, I kept talking—practicing what would become, as the day wore on, The Official Story. "I peeked into his room and he seemed awfully still, so I went in to check more closely. I didn't see any movement, so I checked his pulse and his skin was cold."

She stared at the table and shook her head and said, "I can't believe it," over and over, her hands clasped tightly around her coffee cup.

I thought, *You'd better believe it!* but all I actually said was "Would you like to check on him for yourself, to make sure?"

"No," she said quickly. "Maybe in another minute. I'm not ready yet." And then she started to cry. Swell. Now I had to be a therapist for the hospice worker.

I didn't know what to say to calm her down, so I just went on talking in generalities, further establishing The Official Story: "Jolly was lucky, really. He went to sleep and simply never woke up. He just 'let go' during the night. Not an uncommon thing, I guess, to come home from the hospital and feel so relaxed in the familiar surroundings of your home that you simply stop fighting and let go, and then . . . "

This seemed to work, because soon she stood up and said, "I guess I'd better look in on your father, to make it official." I accompanied her as she timidly entered his room, briefly looked at him, and quickly checked for a pulse at his wrist. She didn't linger.

"I'll be in my room if you need me," she said, and promptly retreated to the den.

I shook my head with relief, shut Jolly's door, and headed back to the coffee pot.

Norma came into the kitchen a little later. I waited until she'd had her coffee, and then I told her the news, too. She was startled at first, but then she sighed and shook her head, and we sat and reminisced about Jolly, who'd been her close friend for forty-five years. Then her strong, practical streak asserted herself: There would be a lot to do today, she said, especially to support K, so she volunteered to help me handle any chores.

How glad I was to have her around—someone solid and strong, who could help me deal with Mom and Anne when they heard the news.

At about 8:00 AM, Maria Luisa ambled into the kitchen. She took the news hard—she'd been with our family for ten years—but eventually she stopped crying and started cooking herself breakfast. Norma and I were content with our cereal and coffee.

Just as I began making a list of people to phone and notify of Jolly's death, I noticed the picture on my coffee mug: an Edward Gorey drawing of two suspicious-looking Edwardian characters at a café table, under which lay a dead body partly obscured by the tablecloth. Ah, the good ol' subconscious. Of all the mugs in the cupboard, I had to choose this one. I couldn't suppress a chuckle as I thought of how much Mom would enjoy hearing about this Freudian slip when the appropriate time came. Not today. But I would tell her eventually. After all, I'd inherited my macabre sense of humor from her, and she'd bought the mugs.

Norma and I agreed to wait to make the notification calls until the whole family was awake and knew what was going on. We also agreed to tell K the news together, and were about to do that when Paul appeared. I told him the news, and he agreed to tell Anne when she woke up. I was grateful. I knew that would take a lot of time and energy, and I had to conserve both.

After Paul left, Norma and I went to break the news to K. We paused at her bedroom door and looked at each other for encouragement, and Norma gave me a big hug that helped tremendously. I hadn't realized until then how much I needed support—some kind of recompense for the steep emotional cost of the previous night's secret activities—and I was grateful that she was there to provide it.

K's soft snore greeted us as we went in slowly, took our places on either side of her bed, and sat down next to her. She awoke bleary-eyed, as she usually did, and noticed that there were two of us. "What's happened?" she asked as she sat up.

We answered gently. Norma said something like, "He's gone," and I followed up with "He passed away in his sleep last night."

Mom said, "I knew it." And somehow, I'm sure she did.

She lay back down and cried—not a tortured, wracked kind of crying, but a simple release. She made very little noise. Tears seeped from her eyes and rolled down her temples as she stared up at the blankness of the ceiling, probably seeing images of the man she'd loved and shared her life with for fifty-five years.

Norma and I stayed beside her. From time to time she'd reach for a Kleenex, wipe her eyes and blow her nose, then cry some more. Norma and I just sat there, occasionally murmuring a comforting word, although we knew that was like offering a Band-Aid to someone with a knife in her heart.

After we had been with K about ten minutes, Paul and Anne came in. Anne was crying, but seemed beyond sad—almost disoriented. I wondered if she was on some kind of medication. She lay down on the bed next to Mom and clung to her and cried until Paul finally peeled her away and took her back upstairs.

I COULDN'T PUT OFF the inevitable any longer. With Norma taking care of K, Paul taking care of Anne, Letty fretting, and Maria Luisa praying, it was finally time for me to call Jolly's doctor, Jim Davis, the man who would decide my fate.

The only quiet place in the house was Dad's room. The air compressor noise distracted me, but I didn't want to turn it off until after the mortuary folks had come and taken care of business, because I didn't want people in the house to see Jolly's body sunken into and enshrouded by the folds of the uninflated mattress and bedding. That would look too terrible. So I left the compressor on and went into Jolly's bathroom to call Dr. Davis.

I dialed his number. An eternity passed. I reminded myself to breathe. Finally, he picked up the phone and I started my performance. "Hello, Dr. Davis, this is John West. I'm calling because Jolly has passed away, apparently sometime in the night, and I thought I should call you to find out what to do . . . "

Dr. Davis offered his condolences and asked only a few questions: Had I noticed anything different about Jolly when he went to bed? Not that I remembered. Did Jolly seem to have any trouble breathing? I didn't think so.

In the back of my mind I could hear Jolly's last, rasping breaths. I was grateful that this conversation with Dr. Davis was over the phone, so he couldn't see me grimacing.

I answered a few more questions that way, telling Dr. Davis what I needed him to hear while simultaneously thinking of how different the reality had been. Then he asked if we had a mortuary lined up. I said we did. "Well," he said, "just have the mortuary send me the death certificate and I'll sign it."

What? Wow!

Then he asked after K and said I should feel free to call him again if there was anything else he could do. We said our goodbyes and hung up.

Amazing! I could hardly believe my good luck. No examination of the body, no checking the pill supply, no coroner's inquest, no Joe Friday . . . I'm clear! After all this time, walking around feeling as if I had a flashing neon sign over my head and a two-ton transformer on my shoulders, it was finally over. No more scrutiny. What a relief!

I tried to get myself into the proper frame of mind. I couldn't exactly come skipping out of Jolly's room with a big-ass grin on my face. But I kept breaking out laughing—I couldn't help it. I couldn't contain my relief; I was ecstatic! But I had to calm down and get back to the others, so I paced around the room, did some deep breathing, and splashed cold water on my face. A glance in the mirror finally settled me down—I looked like hell. I desperately needed a shave, at the very least.

As I put my serious face back on, I looked around at the vast array of pharmaceuticals covering the counter. It occurred to me that Mom would need a few of these, assuming that she actually did want to follow through on her stated wishes. So I gathered the "serious" items and put them together in one place, out of the way, in the back of one of the lower cabinets. For future reference. Then I felt ready to rejoin the others and start making notification calls to relatives and friends.

With each call, The Official Story became more refined and effective. No one questioned anything. Most people don't really want to know the details of death; they're much happier if you give them the familiar platitudes. My simplified version of events fit the bill. But every time someone asked me how I was feeling, I got a cold twinge. How could I answer? I certainly couldn't tell them I felt a mixture of relief and fear. And when they said, "How sad for you," I couldn't tell them that I didn't feel sadness so much as a constant urge to finish my secret work and cover my tracks. So I gave people what they expected and said something appropriate, like, "I'm holding up, thanks for asking."

It felt awfully strange.

The doorbell rang. Two men from Hillside Mortuary had arrived to collect Jolly's body. I filled out their paperwork and watched as they expertly wrapped Jolly's body in a white sheet and then slid the mummy-like shape onto a gurney. They draped a light blue sheet over the gurney and wheeled it and Jolly out of the room, out the front door, into their waiting van, and drove off.

The next arrival was Chuck Heston. The deep rumble of his Corvette's engine entered the house before he was halfway up the driveway, as if his own famous deep voice were preceding him onto a stage. I went out to greet him, squelching a smile at his still driving a Corvette when his knees and hips were so creaky that he had to fold and unfold himself slowly to get in and out of it. He dragged himself from the low front seat and wobbled toward me. I could see that he was trying hard to keep his composure, and when I got close to him and said hi and gave him a hug, he broke down and sobbed into my shoulder: "He was my friend."

That got to me. I'd known Chuck my whole life and had seen him emote quite a bit, both onscreen and off, but this was real and raw. Jolly had indeed been Chuck's closest friend, despite being his political opposite, for almost fifty years. He didn't stay long, but he came back that evening with his wife, Lydia, and daughter, Holly, for the official gathering. Mom didn't want a deluge of people, and neither did the rest of us. So we kept it small—just a few close friends and the local relatives.

After the visitors left, I took my glass of wine out to the patio to decompress and get a breath of fresh air. As I stepped outside, the chirping of crickets greeted me. What a sweet, soothing sound—an auditory massage. Of course, I know that crickets "chirp" by rasping their scaly legs together to attract a mate, but it's a peaceful sound if you don't think about it too much.

Ah, not thinking too much. Maybe I'll get to do that again someday.

THURSDAY, JANUARY 7

An odd sensation, seeing your father's obituary in the paper. And there it was, in today's *L.A. Times,* along with a picture of him from 1983. Unreal. I knew he was dead, but I could still imagine him walking through the front door. He'd done so much work-related traveling when I was a child that his absences from home were a normal part of my life. This felt like just another one of his business trips. Except that I was the one working this time, and he wasn't coming back.

We got word that UCLA was going to fly a flag at half-staff to honor Jolly, and on the appointed day I took K to the campus to see it. We found a lonely flagpole in an out-of-the-way place near

Pauley Pavilion, with a card on the pole imprinted with Jolly's name and title. K and I sat on a bench and looked at the flag and reminisced as students scurried by, oblivious to the lowered flag or the two grown-ups sitting there in the sunshine, looking up.

SATURDAY, JANUARY 9

Jolly's obituary in the *New York Times* appeared today, with an even more outdated photo (from 1976) than the one that had appeared in the *L.A. Times*. But Jolly wouldn't have minded. He'd have shrugged, shaken his head, and said something corny, like "Well, at least they got my name right."

SUNDAY, JANUARY 10

Ridiculous weather. Here it was, midwinter; the patriarch had died, and his memorial service loomed. But the sun shone, the temperature hovered in the seventies, and a few straggling Rose Bowl revelers from Wisconsin still wandered shirtless around Westwood Village, getting their bratwurst-and-beer bellies nicely sunburned.

Flowers bloomed everywhere. Our house was surrounded by a veritable bouquet. L.A. weather doesn't cooperate with the traditionally bleak mood of death and mourning—no dismal gray skies, steady cold sleet, or bare black trees. But it does work well with the more uplifting feelings of life affirmation and moving forward.

A FEW DAYS AFTER the memorial service, Mom and I found that we had the house to ourselves. She asked me point-blank about

Jolly's death: "What help did he get?" (Not "Did he get help?" She still knew a hawk from a handsaw when it came to the important issues.) I didn't want to tell her too much—I worried a little about what she might let slip, given her Alzheimer's. But I did say that I'd had to scramble to get the Seconal, and that Jolly had almost waited too long to swallow it. K gave me a stern look and said, "That won't happen to me."

I had to smile. She still had her pride; she still was determined to be successful at whatever she did.

She also was determined not to lose what remained of her privacy and autonomy. We discussed her options and agreed that she should continue to live at home—not move into an assisted-living facility, as someone who didn't really know her capabilities had recently suggested. And we also discussed finding her a secretary or a personal assistant, someone who could help her on weekdays with mail and phones and scheduling—tasks that Jolly had been doing for her until he'd gotten too sick. Then family and friends could spend time with her on the weekends. I knew I'd be visiting frequently, and it made sense to plan now for other people to pitch in. K knew she needed the help but felt terribly uncomfortable about the prospect of having somebody new in the house, so she said she wanted to wait a while and see how she could manage.

What an ugly irony: K, the accomplished professional, scientist, teacher, clinical psychologist—so proud of her intelligence and independence, her professional identity. She'd established her reputation by being sharp, organized, competent, and capable. And now this: dependence—first on Jolly, and now on family, friends, and hired help. She loathed feeling dependent. Slowly losing her mind was the cruelest disability imaginable.

SATURDAY, JANUARY 23

After a week in Seattle, plowing through stacks of mail and files at my office, as well as stacks of mail and laundry at home, I returned to L.A. to continue helping K adjust to her new situation. She seemed particularly glad to see me, perhaps because, now that Jolly was gone, I was the one person she knew she could rely on for absolutely anything.

Cousin Dave handled the mundane household business matters now, as he had since Jolly had become incapacitated last fall. It became a weekly routine: Dave would visit for a few hours on the weekend, look through the mail, pay bills—do the workaday chores that had been K's job in our family forever. But now she couldn't comprehend finances, much less manage them. The first sign she'd had of her declining faculties, about three years before, was the loss of her ability to do simple arithmetic. It just vanished one day: She opened her checkbook and couldn't remember how to subtract. She promptly made an appointment with a neurologist and soon learned the bad news.

While Dave and K did desk work, I went outside to bask in the Southern California sunshine on the patio, to bake that Seattle moss off my north side. When I came back inside, I joined Mom and Dave at the kitchen table for a snack. Suddenly K began to cry. "There's so much that needs doing around the house," she sobbed. "I can't do it anymore. I just want to end it all." Dave and I hugged her and tried to comfort her, and she recovered her equanimity after a minute. Dave went on and on about how much she still had to live for, like family and friends, travel, and class reunions, but K just shook her head and rolled her eyes.

After a while K settled down, and she and Dave returned to their bills and papers. I heard Dave mention needing old financial records for Jolly's estate-tax calculations, so I went out to the garage and did some spelunking. There must have been seventy or eighty storage boxes crammed with old files and family stuff from over the decades—ancient books that had belonged to Jolly's father; my sisters' and my school files from kindergarten on; packets of maps and itineraries from trips Mom and Dad had taken over the years; correspondence going back more than sixty years; school yearbooks and diaries of K's and her mother's; even needlepoint done by K's grandmother. Our garage hadn't covered a car in years. It had become the archive for four generations and several branches of the family tree. K called it all junk, but she was the worst offender and she admitted it; she'd always been a dedicated pack rat.

After a couple of hours of box rummaging, dust stirring, and spider dodging, I'd found about seven boxes containing old financial records, and I dragged a couple of them into the house for Dave to digest. Just a glimpse of those old documents was too much for K. She decided to take a nap while I showed Dave the rest of the cache in the garage. When he saw the extent of the clutter out there, he wished me luck. We both knew it would fall on me to deal with all this stuff when the time came to settle the estate; neither of my sisters could cope with the sorting and decision-making that would be required. Mary meant well, but tended to be so scattered that she could (and ultimately did) spend an entire day sorting through just one small box. And Anne would see that first childhood letter, report card, or ceramic figurine and become so overwhelmed that she'd be virtually unable to function. Everything would suddenly be a sacred relic. She'd found it almost impossible to let Jolly's old clothes go to charity, so I knew she wouldn't do well with the vast quantity of memorabilia she'd find in the garage.

That evening, an old girlfriend of mine named Cynthia dropped by for a visit, and she joined K and me for dinner at Guido's, a passable Italian restaurant nearby. Recently K had developed anxiety about going to restaurants—and leaving the house in general—which seemed to be another symptom of the Alzheimer's. It hurt to see her so timid in a milieu she used to relish. And now she needed assistance in public restrooms—all those unfamiliar doors and strange locks—so I was particularly glad for Cynthia's presence and willingness to help K when the need arose.

FIVE

——

The Next Beginning

I slept until almost noon. I guess I was still wiped out from everything the new year had brought me. But once I'd had my coffee, I
went out to the garage and began rooting around again. A small box
of old Christmas cards caught my eye, and I took it inside to show
K, who had a great time looking through it and reminiscing. I knew
that long-term memory is more accessible to Alzheimer's sufferers
than short-term memory, but still, it took her almost four hours to
get through a box that contained only about a hundred cards. This
experience made me realize how important it would be to "edit"
the garage for K and give her only the real treasures to review. Too
many objects and memories would overwhelm and upset her, and I
wanted her to enjoy an easygoing stroll down Memory Lane.

As I rummaged in the garage, I realized that I needed an organizing system. I'm my mother's son, no question. If K hadn't been af-
flicted by the damn Alzheimer's, she would have already established

a schedule, posted a color-coded chart, plus a list of chores (all in her impossibly neat handwriting), and been delegating tasks left and right. How I wished it could have been that way.

That evening, after a dinner of pizza and red wine (appropriately), I introduced K to the TV show *The Sopranos*. She got a real kick out of the female shrink treating the male Mafia boss. Interesting power dynamics *there*! She wasn't entirely clear on the plot, but she enjoyed the actors and situations—the entertainment *gestalt*, as she might have said. After the show, we treated ourselves to Pralines 'n Cream ice cream from Baskin Robbins, K's favorite.

And then we talked. We finally had a real heart-to-heart about her thoughts and feelings—and her stated intention—regarding choosing to end her life. She still felt as she had on Christmas Eve, when she'd made her wishes clear to my sisters and me: determined, unafraid, serious, and practical. She said her timetable was soonish, but not *too* soon—perhaps in the summer. We talked about her rate of decline, and the sad and tricky task of balancing going too soon versus waiting too long. And I told her more about Jolly's problems at the end, his not having organized his drug stash in advance, and his last-minute need for the Seconal and morphine in pill form. K listened so attentively, almost hungrily, that I found myself wanting to tell her Jolly's whole story. But could she keep a secret?

Jolly hadn't thought so. Maybe his own illness and worries had colored his perceptions of K, but he'd feared she might blurt out something in front of other people, which would have ruined The Plan for him. How sad: He couldn't talk freely with K during his final days. His final months, actually. Which meant, among other things, that he hadn't been able to say a proper goodbye.

But now that all the jumble and trauma of Jolly's illness, death, and memorial service were behind us, I'd been able to focus on K, and I felt I knew her capabilities. Unlike Jolly, I thought she was still pretty damn sharp and could keep a secret. I couldn't be entirely sure, and that made me worry, but I thought she deserved the truth, so I decided to plow ahead. I swallowed my concerns, took a deep breath, and told her the whole story.

K's eyes focused intently on me as she concentrated on what I said. She leaned forward and angled her body toward me but otherwise remained perfectly still, like an antenna locked in the best position to receive the signal clearly.

The more I told her, the more relieved and confident I felt. It was the first time I had spoken aloud of these things, and now that they were emerging, a deep tension within me began to subside. I even felt a bit light-headed as my brain relaxed its instinctive prohibition on revealing the information I'd kept locked so deeply inside it, the burden of my many secrets reduced by the sharing. At times I felt almost giddy as I related details that seemed odd or ironic, but at other times I felt as ancient and world-weary as the Parthenon, particularly when I described the last moments of Jolly's life.

K was so relieved to finally know what had happened that I could almost see the stress flowing out of her. As I came to the end of the story, she seemed to slide down into the sofa, her head resting against its back ledge, her face toward the ceiling.

"Oh, Johnny," she sighed, "I'm so glad you were there for him. I was supposed to . . . but I can't do it . . . I'm not . . . oh, you know." Then she cried, letting go of all the frustration and anxiety she'd been holding inside and beating herself up about. She had always believed it would be her responsibility to assist Jolly at the end, should he need it, and she felt she had "failed" in her long-anticipated duty. Both Jolly and K had been confident that *she* would be the first one to become seriously ill—she'd smoked and drunk heavily for decades—and that he would help her at the end, just as he had helped her mother, and others over the years, as physician and friend. Neither of them had imagined that they might become disabled at the same time, and that neither would be able to assist the other.

I wished I had put Mom's mind at ease about Jolly much sooner. She didn't seem at all confused, although I went into a lot of detail. I even told her about the secret letters Jolly had written, to be "found" if the need arose, and gave her the one he'd written to her. She cried over it but repaired herself quickly. "I want to talk about *you* now," she said. This surprised me, although it shouldn't have. I had taken on the role of her caretaker, but she was still herself. She was still my mom—the *original* caretaker. And even though Alzheimer's, emphysema, and osteoporosis were slowly destroying her, she could still pay attention to her loved ones. And she still had her professional psychologist's savvy: She knew I'd been through quite an ordeal, and she was concerned about my emotional health.

"I'm fine, generally," I said. "Sometimes, though, when I catch myself remembering details of Jolly's death, I'm still a little amazed. I don't feel guilty at all, but there are moments when I still feel anxious about potential legal jeopardy. I know that's irrational, really, because there's no legal proof against me, but . . . I still feel twinges once in a while."

She nodded thoughtfully. "I'm sure you do."

"I suppose there are other things going on in my subconscious that I haven't addressed yet," I added. I wondered what kind of deeper feelings, what weird and strange thoughts, might emerge from my psyche in the future. After all, it wasn't every day that I witnessed a death, much less assisted in one. But those questions would have to wait for another time and place. I didn't want my musings to worry Mom, so I continued quickly, "But really, Mom, I'm not concerned, so you shouldn't be. I'm fine. And I want you to know that I'm willing to assist you, too, if you want me to."

She smiled and said, "Of course I do."

That took my breath away for a second, but part of me had been expecting it, so I wasn't entirely surprised. She reached over and squeezed my hand reassuringly while I paused to think before I continued.

"I have to tell you, Mom, it'll be much harder for me to do this with you than it was with Jolly. You're in a lot better shape than he was, and I really don't want to lose you any sooner than is absolutely necessary. I will miss you profoundly. And there's always that billion-to-one chance that an Alzheimer's cure will be discovered the following week, and that would absolutely break whatever was left of my heart."

She squeezed my hand again, and gave a small shrug and a wry smile that told me she understood my dilemma.

"And, on a more practical level," I said, "the logistics will be far trickier with you than they were with Jolly, and that'll be an elephantine load of stress on me. I can handle it, but it'll be rough."

K patted my arm and nodded. She was following what I said very closely.

I continued, "I have to admit, it pains me to see you in a de-bilitated state, and to watch you slowly deteriorating, but I'm deter-mined to avoid any 'improper' motives. What I mean is that I won't be assisting your suicide in order to ease any pain of *mine*. This isn't about me; it's your choice. I'm just here to give you what you want when the time comes. But frankly, I want you to stick around!"

She rolled her eyes and clucked at me.

"Really!" I said. "I'd rather look after you and make sure you get all the best care—even if you start thinking I'm the milkman—and hold on to the chance that we could get you back someday. Besides, there would still be times when you'd remember me and other people, and that would be good, right?"

She shot me her famous mock glare and said, "Yes, but then I'd remember what was wrong with me, too."

What could I say to that still intact, impeccable logic?

THAT CONVERSATION was the first of what became a regular testing program for us. During the following months, whenever we talked about her choosing Self de-Termination, I'd stop and ask K if she still felt sure about her decision, and remind her that I'd rather have her around if she wanted to stay. But she always said no, she wanted to go. Always.

After we finished our conversation about Jolly's exit and K's de-termination to follow suit, she went off to bed, but I stayed up late with a large glass of Jameson's, contemplating the way things were. And how they were going to get. And what it all meant. I could only guess how much more heartache, stress, and complication lay ahead of me. Probably off the charts—like the unnumbered red zone at the top end of a speedometer. I knew I was heading to a place that was faster, farther, harder, more dangerous than any place I'd ever gone before, where even the tiniest action could have gigantic consequences. But I had to go there. K needed me to go there with her.

And so it began: The Plan, Part Two.

Monday, January 25

I dragged myself and my hangover out of bed and into the kitchen, and there sat Mom, eating her usual breakfast of Grape-Nuts and raisins and looking at the newspaper. Today we had a rather delicate mission: visiting Jolly's office.

It was the first time either of us had been there in ages, but it looked exactly the same. His white lab coat still hung on its hook behind the door; his correspondence still sat piled on his desk. I think we both expected him to walk through the door at any moment. We looked through his desk for personal items but found only a few photos, a Chapstick, and several packs of gum. We didn't stay long.

Later that afternoon I found Mom sitting at the dining room table, which we now used as a sort of communal desk, looking through several boxes of greeting cards. She said she couldn't remember which boxes were Christmas cards and which were sympathy cards we'd received after Jolly's death, and she vowed to "look through them again." Uh-oh. Whenever she did that, she got upset. I wanted to find a way to keep her from falling into that trap again, but it would have to wait until my next visit. I had to get to the airport.

THURSDAY, FEBRUARY 4

From my Seattle office I placed my now daily call to K. When we were wrapping up our chat, I heard Anne talking in the background and asked Mom to put her on the line. She set the phone down and called out, "Johnny! Johnny!" (instead of, "Annie! Annie!"). This was another example of her progressive neurological damage, and not all that different from what happens to many elderly people, but usually it affected people much older than K—she was only seventy-five. It was too soon for her—she was still so with it in other ways.

I found it hard to be away from Mom, given all that had happened and all that was planned. When I told her so, she said she felt the same and looked forward to seeing me as soon as possible. I reminded her that I'd be back in about a week. After all, I had to spend Valentine's Day with my number-one valentine, right? She chuckled and said, "You bet!"

TUESDAY, FEBRUARY 9

My new routine at work—struggling to concentrate on clients while thoughts about Mom and The Plan zoomed through my head— was interrupted by a phone call from Norma in Portland. She had just spoken with K, who'd said that she and Anne had quarreled the night before.

Damn! Desperate to know what was going on at the house, I forced myself to calm down before calling. I talked with both K and Anne and sensed that last night's storm, whatever it was, had passed. But still, it made me nervous to think about Mom, in her weakened condition, trying to cope with Anne's volatile moods.

Because Cousin Dave lived much closer to the action, I called him next. He said he'd also heard from K about problems with Anne, and he also felt that something should change. I reminded him that we'd discussed hiring a personal assistant for K, and that perhaps the time had finally come to start interviewing candidates. K had been mildly resistant to hiring someone before, but now she might be more receptive. If she had an assistant, Anne might not feel the need to visit as often. That way, there would be fewer occasions for trouble to arise. He said he'd look into it.

Then I thought to call Dr. Davis; perhaps I could learn something from him about K's various medical conditions that we could use to help pry Anne away from K. Unfortunately, Dr. Davis had bad news. He said that K's physical problems were worse than we thought: She had kyphosis, a degenerative spinal condition, in addition to the osteoporosis she'd been battling for years. She needed an exercise program and a special back brace, as well as rehabilitation therapy to strengthen her back and improve her posture. Furthermore, her almost chronic breathlessness might mean that her emphysema had started to snowball.

This news caused me serious heartache, so, for a large helping of friendly-voice relief, I phoned Toby Cronin, an old family friend at UCLA who not only lightened my mood (as usual), but also told me about respite care, a service that provides temporary help for the caretakers of Alzheimer's sufferers, so they don't get exhausted by the job. That gave me an idea: We could tell Anne we were getting K a helper for *Anne's* benefit. (That way, Anne could feel like an appreciated Florence Nightingale, not like she was getting the heave-ho.)

I actually felt sorry for Anne. She was completely oblivious to the negative effects that her unstable behavior had on others. I'm sure she believed she was helping Mom, but the reality was that her efforts usually added to the problem. And she was the only one who couldn't see it.

SATURDAY, FEBRUARY 13

When I arrived in L.A. for Valentine's Day weekend with Mom, Anne had already returned to New York. We knew she'd be back, but we never knew what mood she would be in when she arrived. These uncertainties caused Mom a great deal of anxiety.

Mom gave me the usual big hug when I got to the house, and our first order of business, also as usual, was to sit on the sofa and catch up on each other's news. Hers was bad: She said she felt trapped and afraid.

"Anne is so difficult to live with. Impossible. I have been able, better recently, to calm her down. The extremes . . . oh! A large part of my depression is due to the waiting around and having to deal with Anne. I don't want to 'get things lined up' . . . just . . . go!"

Obviously, things were much worse with Anne than I'd thought. I'd had no idea she was making Mom so miserable. Something had to be done, and soon.

VALENTINE'S DAY

I hoped I could give Mom a pleasant day and improve her mood. I'd planned a visit to the home of a dear family friend named Genevieve, for a musicale. K always loved these living room concerts at Gen's, but she felt so much emotional carryover from the previous day's talk about her problems with Anne that she stayed in bed all morning, crying and dozing. Whenever I checked on her and tried to cheer her up, she waved me off. I finally got her into the kitchen to eat something, and she perked up a bit. But when it was time to drive to Gen's, she relapsed. More tears.

She looked at me forlornly and snuffled, "I don't want to go."

I gave her a hug, hoping it would help. When I asked why she didn't want to go to Gen's, all she could talk about was Anne.

"How can I tell my own daughter not to stay here at the house? And if Anne doesn't stay with me, what will happen? Will I have to go to a nursing home? Jolly's being gone . . . and Anne's being here . . . the house is unpleasant for me now."

This was not good.

"I just wish I could go to sleep forever," she sobbed. She leaned her head against me and kept crying.

I held her until she finished, then gently reminded her that I would take care of all her concerns, about Anne or housing or anything. Cousin Dave would help, too, and Anne seemed to listen to him. But I would make doubly sure that all of K's worries were dealt with promptly. No waiting. No appointment necessary. No need to take a number.

K smiled, finally responding to my assurances and attempt at humor. And when I mentioned that Genevieve loved her very much and would surely have some sage counsel for us—another good reason to visit—K seemed to come around. After a bit of nose blowing and deep breathing, she agreed to go.

Once she had decided, her mood improved rapidly. She got cleaned up and dressed, and she looked terrific. She said she felt a lot better, too, and as we drove up the coast she happily rubbernecked, commenting on the scenery. And when we got to Gen's, the beautiful setting overlooking the ocean worked its own therapeutic magic.

The music was delightful, and the audience of about twenty people wasn't so big that K felt overwhelmed. She thoroughly enjoyed herself, and my heart felt light for the first time in months. Afterward, as the guests began leaving, Gen invited K and me to stay for dinner. She also asked a woman named Carol Snow to stay. Carol turned out to be a professional personal assistant who worked for Gen part-time, and Gen wanted us to get acquainted because she thought K might be able to use Carol's help, too.

What a stroke of luck! It's always hard to find the right person for any job, and the difficulties are magnified when the work is as intimate as assisting someone in her own home. The assistant becomes part of the family, a tricky role in the best of circumstances. And when Alzheimer's is part of the equation, good luck! Which we'd just gotten.

Over the course of our dinner conversation, it became clear that Carol was superb, exceptional. She had owned and operated a small construction business in Malibu, then had worked for sixteen years as Bob Dylan's personal assistant. Smart, sensitive, patient, and intuitively helpful, she seemed ideal. Best of all, K and Carol had the right chemistry and became friends almost instantly.

Gen's personal reference was golden. K could no longer assess someone's work, much less teach someone what she needed. But

Gen knew K and our family quite well, and she'd already tested Carol for us, so to speak. We were very lucky indeed.

Carol had to leave right after dinner, so K and Gen and I sat by the fireplace and talked. K seemed inspired by the prospect of Carol's help, and relaxed by the comfortable, familiar surroundings of Gen's living room, so it came as no surprise when she started talking about her problems with Anne. Gen encouraged K to stop being Anne's emotional caretaker, and I knew that Gen's advice would register with K in a way that mine never could. (The advice of a wise old friend—who also happens to be a psychoanalyst—almost always carries more weight than one's youngest child, no matter if he's a fully grown lawyer.)

K seemed relaxed and relieved on the ride home, happy to have gotten Gen's support and perspective. As we drove along, she admitted that her worries about Anne conflicted somewhat with her feelings about The Plan.

"I definitely want to end it sooner, not later," she said. "And sometimes the pain and frustration—Annie's behavior—make me want to go right away. But other times those same feelings make me want to hang on longer, try to help her somehow."

"Listen, Mom, you're not exactly in the best of shape for performing psychotherapy, you know?"

She chuckled. "Yes, I know. But I can't escape feeling like I could do something more to help Annie. Maybe if I'd done more, years ago, she wouldn't be so . . . You know what I mean."

"Yeah, I know. But Mom, listen, you're probably just feeling what all parents feel—a lifelong concern for the well-being of their kids. It must be almost impossible *not* to feel a desire to 'do more' for your children when they so obviously need help."

"That's right," she said, nodding emphatically.

Given the late hour and the full day, I felt we should ease off the intense topics, so I changed the subject to the beautiful evening— the night lights of Santa Monica glittering in the near distance, the occasional open stretch of beach showing off its surf and spray illuminated by the lights of beach houses. It was a lovely night. And I was a lucky man: cruising down the road with my number-one valentine.

Monday, February 15

The sad, confused, bleary look in Mom's eyes in the mornings always broke my heart. Sometimes she stayed bleary until well into the afternoon, and sometimes into the evening.

After breakfast she shuffled back to her bedroom to dress for the day. When she reappeared at the kitchen table, however, she was wearing only a sweatshirt, underpants, and moccasins. Uh-oh. She seemed to be searching for something. (Her pants?)

"Hey, Mom, whatcha looking for?"

"My watch. My watch is missing."

"Okay . . . uh, how about I look around for it out here while you go back and finish getting dressed?"

She didn't seem to get my hint, but she did wander back toward her room. Oh, man! I hoped this was just a temporary dip in her awareness, not a sudden, permanent downturn. Cross those fingers.

The rest of the morning was peaceful, but in the early afternoon she worked herself into a lather: Where *was* her missing watch? She became almost frantic. But suddenly she remembered removing it in her bathroom before showering. We walked back to her room, where, sure enough, the watch lay right in the middle of her bathroom counter. While relieved to have found it, she was mad at herself for getting upset over such a small thing.

She decided to take her afternoon nap then, to recuperate from the excitement of the day so far. Good idea. And I had a long, hard workout—a good stress buster.

Her nap helped. At dinner she was in excellent mental shape, so afterward we went into the living room, sat on the sofa, and had a long talk, reviewing what we'd discussed at Gen's, including the Anne business, and what effect it might have on The Plan. I felt I should "test" K again and see if she was still sure about her choice to end her life. As always, she said she was sure. I also told her that while I didn't want my views to affect her decision, I did have one strong opinion: I didn't feel that she should spend the last months of her life in a frustrating attempt to achieve a therapeutic breakthrough with Anne. Of course, it was entirely K's choice—after all, it was her life, and she could live it and end it as she chose. But my greatest hope, I said, was that she could enjoy, rather than dread, her remaining time. I wanted her final chapter to be smooth and peaceful, not stormy and painful.

My worries weren't just about K. I had my own list. I felt that The Plan required a near perfect effort on my part, which I feared I wouldn't be able to achieve. That made me feel guilty in advance. Not because I was doing anything wrong by helping K—not at all.

I just needed to be absolutely sure that it was what she wanted. And despite all the clinical detachment I could muster—following Jolly and K's lead—the enormity of what I was doing sometimes rose up in front of me like a huge wave. Would it drown me? Would I be able to live with this?

There was only one person I could talk to about these feelings, someone who was better suited than anyone else to be my consultant: K herself. After all, she'd been my trusted advisor my whole life, and she knew me better than anyone. So I explained my fear that we'd go through with The Plan and somehow, despite all my double-checking and all her repeated confirmations, there would be a mistake and it would turn out *not* to be what she wanted. How could I ever forgive myself? How could she ever forgive me?

She solemnly and seriously assured me that she wanted to go through with The Plan. But I kept going. I said that if I wasn't *absolutely* sure it was what she wanted, I would be in agony for the rest of my life.

"*I am absolutely sure,*" she said.

But something inside me needed more than that, and it just jumped out: "Well, will you forgive me in advance?"

She turned and faced me, looking straight at me, so focused and clear that I felt I was seeing the face of Truth itself, and then she said in a calm, steady voice, "Not only do I forgive you, I thank you."

Well. Right. That was what I needed.

So I heaved a huge sigh of relief, K smiled, we hugged, and then we did what seemed like the most appropriate thing: We went to the kitchen and had a bowl of ice cream.

Tuesday, February 16

At breakfast Mom said, "The funnies aren't funny anymore, and I don't understand most of them. Argh!"

Well, *that's* not a great way to start the day. Her awareness of her condition was considered good by the neurologists, which simply goes to show how relative the word "good" can be. What was inescapably *bad* was that her overall condition, of which she was so unhappily aware, was definitely going south.

She fought it as best she could. One of her techniques was to stay as organized as possible. She made a ritual of preparing breakfast: First, three scoops of Grape-Nuts went into the bowl, then one scoop of raisins, then she dutifully put the raisin container and cereal box back in their proper places in the cupboard, then she carried her bowl to the table, and then she shuffled back to the refrigerator to get her small pitcher of milk.

She'd taken to keeping her breakfast milk in the creamer of an old stainless steel cream-and-sugar set, vintage 1960, because her osteoporosis made managing larger milk containers impossible. Forget the gallon jugs; even the quarts were difficult.

Another of her elaborate rituals was to sort the newspapers every morning—throwing away the classifieds, stacking the readable sections at the far end of the table, and opening the funnies so she could look at them while she ate breakfast. At night, just before going to bed, she'd round up and throw away all the newspapers. This daily routine gave her a sense that she still had a modicum of control over her surroundings and could still accomplish something useful.

I had my own paper-organizing project in the works: Jolly's personal papers and files from his office. Luckily, the UCLA Archives people wanted all of his professional papers (there were literally tons of them). Mom showed interest in the more historical items I'd retrieved, such as letters between Jolly and his parents, but felt inundated by the quantity, so I put the dozen or so UCLA "personal" boxes in the garage with all the other boxes of old family stuff.

That afternoon, Carol Snow came over for an "interview" with Cousin Dave, Mom, and me. I had told Dave that we needed to move quickly, given the high quality of the candidate and the fact that she'd come so highly recommended by Genevieve. After Carol had dazzled Dave—she unquestionably had that indefinable "it"— he agreed that we should hire her right away.

So Carol started coming to the house on Tuesdays and Wednesdays from midmorning until dinnertime, and on Thursday afternoons. At first she and K just sat and talked, getting better acquainted. These discussions gave Carol a better sense of the situation, and an idea of what K intended them to do together, like organizing K's old home office upstairs, "the studio." The two of them quickly became close and worked easily together. Carol's patience and calm were exactly what K needed.

SUNDAY, FEBRUARY 28

After a week and a half in Seattle, catching up at my office, I returned to L.A. Mom and I were having one of our usual sit-and-talks on the sofa, but she seemed unusually groggy, especially for that time of day. "I don't know where things are anymore," she complained. "I don't want to take antidepressants. I just want to die. But I don't want you to get in trouble. And I want to do it right—no vomiting."

I wondered if her grogginess came from Zoloft, the antidepressant she'd recently been prescribed, or from Aricept, her Alzheimer's medication, which she occasionally took by accident in the morning instead of at bedtime. When she did that, its soporific effect messed her up for most of the day. Did she now have *two* medications that made her bleary? This was not what she wanted.

K complained a little about Anne, and I assured her that Dave and I were working on a solution—and reminded her that Carol was part of that solution. She perked up when I mentioned Carol. The more Carol got established in the house, I said, the more Dave could suggest that Anne keep her distance.

Mom also mentioned that "the cards" had been worrying her. Apparently, it is considered Proper Social Etiquette for the family of a deceased person to send thank-you cards in response to the sympathy cards they have received. At first I thought this was just a bunch of hooey concocted by people who don't have to work for a living. But a savvy friend of mine told me that the mere process of writing these response notes can actually be therapeutic, and after thinking about it, I realized how it might help some people deal with their grief.

But for K, whose illness made it so difficult to focus and organize and do things outside her regular routine, this new "obligation" became a huge burden and a source of great unhappiness. She said she was desperate to finish with the cards so she could move on to other things. Since her remaining time on the planet was extremely limited and precious, it seemed ludicrous to me that she should spend any of it on esoteric social niceties. I asked her how the card business had come about.

She gave me a dark look and said, "Annie . . . and Chuck."

I could only shake my head in frustration.

But Mom, always able to find a little humor in a tough situation, shrugged and said with a sly grin, "You know how it is." Then she sat up very straight, lifted her head, arched her eyebrows, looked down her nose at me, and said airily: "*It's what we rich people do.*" She shook her head and laughed disdainfully, and I joined her.

She was still so sharp sometimes! With that one dramatized sentence, she captured the essence of the thing: Anne getting carried away by an old-fashioned custom presented to her as a Rule of Proper Society by her old-fashioned godfather, Charlton. Anne had initiated and pushed the project but then had quit, saying she found it "too stressful" dealing with Mom. Of course, Mom couldn't do it alone because of her Alzheimer's, so we'd ended up hiring someone to help.

But K's sense of humor was still intact—laced with black, as always—and she took to calling them the Sorry We're Dead cards. She laughed every time she had occasion to use the phrase, or when she heard others use it. And most of us did, with great pleasure. Underneath it all, K was still her old self. For now, anyway.

THE PLAN OCCUPIED my mind more and more. For some reason, my instincts told me to find a safer place to hide those drugs—the "useful" ones I'd stashed in the back of Jolly's bathroom cabinet.

I found a great hiding place in Mom's studio, in the bottom of a filing cabinet. But then she started getting into what's called "wrapping up behavior": In anticipation of her death, she began simplifying, closing her life—emptying desk drawers, cleaning closets, giving gifts. Many people do this subconsciously, but K was on a conscious mission. And Carol was helping her, which meant that every corner of the studio would get checked, so I had to move the stash again. I looked all over the house but couldn't find a place that felt right. And the detached garage often got extremely hot, which I thought might affect the drugs' potency, so that wouldn't work. I considered taking the stash home with me to Seattle, but how could I explain a baggie full of narcotics if my luggage were searched at the airport?

I finally found a place I thought no one would ever disturb. At the bottom of a hall storage closet squatted a large piece of defunct telephone-switching equipment, with four or five partly used gallon cans of paint stacked behind it. Judging by the dust on the paint cans, I could see that nobody had been in there for ages. So I put the plastic baggie of pills into a paper bag and crammed it behind the old paint cans: surely the safest place in the whole house.

Still, what if Maria Luisa suddenly decided to clean out that closet? I could never be entirely sure about the security of anything in the house. But I had to live with all the uncertainties, the chronic stress of everything about The Plan.

As I grappled with the complexities and pressures of Mom's situation, I reflected on how different it was from Jolly's. Particularly troubling was the fact that her health wasn't failing as obviously as his, which meant that more questions might be asked when she died. What would people think? What would Dr. Davis think? Would he order an autopsy? If so, what would happen then?

Not a day went by without my chewing on the various options, running different scenarios through my head, imagining what I might say to Dr. Davis, or my family, or Joe Friday.

Where's that Jameson's?

TUESDAY, MARCH 2

Unexpectedly, Mom joined me for brunch with Walter and Mickey Seltzer—very dear and longtime friends of the family. She usually didn't like to be out and about until at least noon, because it took her most of the morning to get her synapses running smoothly and to feel that she had herself together. But the Seltzers were among the few people K felt comfortable with anymore. She could relax and be herself with them.

As we drove over the hill into the San Fernando Valley to the Seltzers' house, I told K that I remembered her driving me to school a few times along this very same route, years ago. She looked out her window and didn't say much. Mornings weren't her best time of day for talking, so I figured she was saving her energy for brunch conversation. But perhaps she was thinking of those times she'd driven me to school or hockey practice, or when she ran errands along Ventura Boulevard, because she said wistfully, "I'm losing my abilities." I couldn't contradict her and I didn't want to agree, so I just drove.

Brunch with Walter and Mickey was wonderful. There's nothing like sharing a meal with great old friends to make everything seem right with the world again. At one point, just after Walter and I had finished an animated back-and-forth about the politics of the day, Mom said, "When you two were talking about all those things, I just started to drift off with thoughts of *I don't understand any of this.* Oh well; I don't have to care anymore."

She often said surprisingly honest things about her deteriorating condition, which showed me how brave she was. She certainly didn't like what was happening to her, but she didn't fear the truth of it. It showed amazing strength of character for her to admit that she knew she was slipping away. We all could learn from her example.

AFTER DINNER THAT EVENING, Mom and I sat in the living room, talking and basking in the comfort of each other's company. For so many years, I realized, whenever I'd visited home, other people had been around: Dad and Maria Luisa coming and going, or holiday guests and other family milling about. Only rarely could I sit and really commune with this amazing woman, this deep and smart and savvy, and also kind and gentle and just plain nice, woman.

Now that we had a lot of time to ourselves, we talked and talked, about anything and everything. Mostly about family, of course—lots of reminiscing about K's parents and brothers, train trips we'd taken when I was little, school plays, pets we'd had over the years. I even learned a few things about her that I hadn't known before, such as her controversial political views in high school (she lived in a largely German immigrant small town in 1930s Iowa, but she was *against* Hitler!); humorous, behind-the-scenes details of her professional life; and how close she and Jolly had come to getting divorced in 1969. I learned a lot from just sitting on that sofa with K and listening.

Despite her debilitating illnesses, this was a golden time. She was still wonderfully rich, a deep mine of valuable ore—some of it easily gathered, some requiring a bit more digging, now that her verbal skills were damaged, but well worth my effort every time.

SIX

March Madness

L.A. can't be real. How can there be such sunny warmth and greenery and flowers bursting with color and aroma in early March, the deep end of winter? The neon orange of poppies opening their faces to the sun, the pale yellow and deep purple of pansies, the moist pink and white of camellias; alyssum's clover fragrance, jasmine's spice, and orange blossoms' sweet scent wafting over from a neighbor's yard. While Seattle (like most of the nation) was a cold, soggy, muddy, cruddy, dark, damp, and damnable place, L.A. was bizarrely beautiful.

I was on a mental-health break, soaking up sun on the patio and letting my mind float, when I heard a crunching sound over the hum of the pool filter that made me open my eyes and look around. As I squinted into the glare of the afternoon sun, I thought I saw something move on the hillside behind the house. I got up and crossed the patio to a better viewpoint, and peered up the hill.

Hey! A deer! A large, stately doe, munching on the underbrush, peacefully going about her business.

I watched her for a few minutes as she grazed and moseyed slowly across the hillside, and then it occurred to me that Mom would get a kick out of seeing this. I slowly eased into the house so as not to startle the doe, but once I was inside I sprinted to K's bedroom. She perked up at news of the deer and followed me outside. Sure enough, the doe was still up there. It took me a while to point her out, but K finally saw her, and we stood there, enjoying the tranquil scene, until K felt a chill and I took her inside. When I came back out, the deer was gone, but I made a mental note to check the hillside the next day around the same time.

I sat down in the sun again and thought about how the deer moved so gracefully, so gently, yet I could sense its great physical power. It had a natural dignity and presence, yet it also seemed fragile, even fearful—and rightly so. For deer, fear isn't weakness but strength; it's smart to fear danger, to avoid harm. In order to survive, you run. It's instinct, the way of the wild.

But humans, because we can think rationally instead of just instinctively, sometimes *don't* run. We have the option of deciding for ourselves. We can stand and face, even embrace, the inevitable—on our own terms—and make it as comfortable as possible. We need not run from death mindlessly, unable to think about anything but our pain and fear. We can be brave, honest, and dignified. Like K.

A FAIRLY ROUTINE EVENING: After dinner, we had ice cream and watched TV in the living room. At one point, when Mom got up to take her ice cream dish into the kitchen, she walked all hunched over and wobbly, clutching the dish in both hands, looking like someone straight out of a documentary on the horrors of osteoporosis. I gave her a friendly holler: "Straighten up!" It had become my habit when I saw her walking like that; if I was near her, I'd pat her back gently as a reminder. She usually didn't object, but occasionally she'd glower at me and I'd say something like "Hey, I'm only trying to keep you from turning into a pretzel!" And then she'd smile and shake her head and sigh. But she'd stand up a little straighter.

About a year before this, K had had several nasty falls, and Jolly had said that either the Alzheimer's or the medicine for it was somehow affecting her balance. Perhaps K's fear of falling made her overcompensate and walk hunched forward; perhaps it made her feel more balanced, more in control of her body. But it also made her look like hell—almost to the "hump" stage of some elderly ladies with osteoporosis and kyphosis. And since she had both of those diseases, I knew she should be careful about her posture. But I also knew she didn't have to be careful, or suffer, much longer.

Once she got into the kitchen and put her dish in the sink, K started her intricate evening pill-taking routine. She leaned over the counter and peered closely at the contents of her plastic pillbox, turning it over in her hands. It had a covered slot for each day of the week, and sections within each slot for different times of day. The lid covering the next day's presorted pills accidentally slid open, and for a second I was afraid the pills would fall out. If they did, I knew that the ensuing jumble would throw Mom into a confused panic. Luckily, they stayed put. Mom fiddled with the two sliding lids for a while; I went to help her but she shooed me away, insisting on doing it herself. Finally she figured it out and got the next day's lid closed and this night's lid open, then put her six evening pills into a little white plastic bowl. She straightened up, sighed, and leaned forward against the counter with her arms outstretched, her head back, and her eyes closed.

Then she looked over at me . . . and laughed! "This isn't how we imagined it would be, is it?" she said.

I shook my head and laughed too, because she was right on the money.

"I walk around this house," she said, "and I talk to myself—actually, I'm talking to Jolly—and I chew him out! 'It wasn't supposed to be like this! I was supposed to go first, not you. You were supposed to help me, like you helped my mother.'" She shook her head, looked at me, shrugged, and said, "It helps to have a sense of humor." Then she grinned. "That way, I can keep going until it's time to blow my brains out."

I laughed out loud at that one. Then I gave her the same kind of mock glare she liked to give me, and growled, "All right, you, knock it off!"

We both giggled and shook our heads. What a world. But a sense of humor *does* help. And sometimes, the blacker the better.

"There's the two things that make me feel bad," she said. "The . . . " she struggled for the word, one hand poised in the air in front of her, as if she might catch the word if it happened to float by.

I don't know how I knew what she was driving at—perhaps she got some of the word out before she lost it—but I offered, "Grief?"

"Yes!" she sighed. "There's the grief over Jolly's death, and I'm over that, or almost over that . . . sometimes a little bit . . . " and she shook her head. "But the other thing is the Alzheimer's, and I guess I can put up with that for a few more months . . . "

The opening was there, so again I took the opportunity to discuss the optional nature of The Plan, and again she confirmed her desire to go forward. I also mentioned that her "blow my brains out" comment made me think of two things. First, The Plan didn't include any gun. She would be ending her life by going to sleep, in her own bed—the most peaceful way to go. And second, choosing to die was probably the most important decision a person could make, and it took a lot of courage. I told her I admired her bravery.

"I'm really not afraid," she said, in a steady voice that sounded almost as if she was reassuring me, which in fact she was. "It's a haven for me," she said. "I look forward to the peace." And she looked completely confident and serene.

But since we were talking about it, she did have a few questions. How long would the process take? I estimated an hour or two, and explained how first she would take an antinausea medication and wait a while, then take the drugs that would put her to sleep, then become unconscious. After that, I said, I didn't know exactly how long it might take to reach respiratory and cardiac arrest and then death. It probably depended on her body's metabolism, the amount of drugs she managed to ingest, and other biological variables. But she didn't seem too concerned about that. She nodded thoughtfully and said we'd have to plan to make it an early bedtime. Ha! She still understood scheduling!

I told her we'd have a timetable worked out well in advance, and that on the chosen evening we would probably sit and talk and reminisce and laugh and cry together, and then she would go to bed and go to sleep, and that would be that. I would call Dr. Davis the next morning, just as I had done with Jolly, then I'd call Hillside Mortuary, and then family and friends.

She said, "If you think it will help, I can start behaving like the woman on *Mystery!*" She leaned back, moaned mournfully, and put the back of her hand to her forehead, remarkably resembling the Edward Gorey character at the beginning of the *Mystery!* PBS TV show. Then she grinned at me hopefully. I couldn't help but laugh, and I promised I'd let her know if any acting became necessary.

Maybe she had a good idea: The more people thought she was "declining," the more likely they'd be to accept her death as natural. But the big question mark was Dr. Davis. If he did with K what he'd done with Jolly, all would be well, but there was no way I could know in advance. Perhaps it *would* be helpful for K to do and say "declining" sorts of things for Dr. Davis to see and hear. Then he might be less likely to question her death. Maybe K would get to act after all.

Only one thing troubled me more than the possibility of questions and problems after K died, and that was the possibility of "screwing it up," as K would say. I'm not a doctor. I didn't know for sure what had killed Jolly, and I could only speculate about the types and amounts of drugs necessary to do the trick for K. I could compare the two of them physically—make allowances for Jolly's advanced cancer versus K's emphysema, his weight versus hers. I could take into account what I'd read about this sort of thing, and hope for the best. But failure was not an acceptable option. If K failed to achieve lift-off and ended up in a damn coma or something . . . that was unthinkable.

It was bedtime. Mom and I made our way to our respective toothbrushes, and then I went to her room to say goodnight and give her a back scratch—what had become our standard end-of-the-evening routine. But our discussion of The Plan had stirred her up, and she was in no mood to go to sleep, so we stayed up and talked.

Nighttime was definitely K's best time. It was amazing how her verbal ability and mental clarity improved over the course of the day. Other than her usual fuzziness right after her afternoon nap, it was basically a straight-incline graph that even curved a bit upward some evenings, when her vocabulary was particularly good.

She told me she'd been thinking a lot about her mother, Harriet, whom Jolly had helped to die with dignity almost twenty-five years before. Harriet and Mom had always been close, and I think it comforted Mom to know that she was, in a way, following in her mother's footsteps. I suddenly remembered that one of the personal files I'd gotten from Jolly's office had Harriet's name on it, so I went to the garage and found it and gave it to Mom. We looked through it together, hoping to find something special, perhaps a long-held secret. We found nothing significant, but still, it felt good to connect with that part of our past.

K also talked about needing to finish the Sorry We're Dead cards. They worried her constantly, and she wanted them out of the way.

I hated seeing her bothered by that boondoggle, so I weighed in. "Mom, let me see if I can get those done more quickly for you, okay?"

"I like the sound of that," she said.

"I'll find a solution, don't worry. You shouldn't have to spend your precious remaining 'good' time on this sort of thing."

"I couldn't agree more," she said. "But I'll try to get through it—the cards and all the other stuff. If it's too much stress, I'll just go sooner."

"Whoa! Not *too* soon!" I jumped in. "Let me try to clear up this card mess before you make any major decisions, okay?" She nodded.

And then it hit me: Of course! Carol Snow—K's new personal assistant—could handle the cards in a snap! I didn't want to say anything to K until I'd checked with Carol, though. The last thing I wanted to do was get K's hopes up and then have to disappoint her.

Then I had an even better idea. I grinned slyly and said, "You know, we could just dump the damn things in the trash." She looked up, startled by my suggestion, but then she started to laugh. She shook her head and sighed. "No, my Scottishness couldn't handle the waste."

But then I reminded her that if we *did* dump them, we'd be saving the cost of a stamp on each one, and that would be thrrrrifty!

She chortled at my exaggerated Scottish accent. It was great to see her smile again.

"So," I asked, "what do think you'll do with all your free time once I get those damn cards off your back?"

She sighed and said she thought she'd want to look at the old family photo albums which she called "pictures of the generations." She sighed again and seemed to deflate a little. Then she shook her head. "My condition . . . I'm so susceptible to stress. I can't understand the complexities, or even simple things, anymore . . . I should just go."

"Well," I said, "that can happen whenever you want it to, as long as you're sure and you're ready."

"Sooner's better than later," she said.

"Yeah, I know," I said. "We've talked about that."

I didn't want her to get sad right before bedtime, so I shifted into a lighter tone of voice and said, "But first you should take some time and have a little fun! What would you like to do that would be just plain fun?"

This new direction I'd taken intrigued her, and she perked up. She thought for a second, then smiled and said, "I want to have some fun with Norma."

"And what about *me?*" I whined, pretending to be devastated.

"I guess I can spare you some time," she replied slyly, and we both laughed. "But I do want to see Norma as much as I can."

"And so you shall!" I proclaimed theatrically, which made her giggle. "In fact, she's coming to L.A. in a couple of weeks, and she can show you pictures from her recent trip to Italy. You two characters can run around and do whatever you want—see an opera, get your hair done, play ice hockey, whatever!"

Shooting me her patented mock glare, she said, "I don't think so. Just talking is about all for me now." And then she grew somber and reiterated that she didn't want to wait around too long.

It was late. Bedtime for both of us. As I got up to leave, she got up too. "I'm so glad you're here," she said. "I'm so glad you're such a good son." She hugged me. She used only her left arm—her right arm was pressed against her side, for balance—but it was still one of the best hugs I've ever gotten.

Thursday, March 4

K went to lunch with a couple of her old gal pals, and when she got back we sat in the living room and talked. "I try to be sensible about things," she said, "but I know I don't make any sense." (*There's* one for Lewis Carroll.) I asked her what had prompted this observation. "During lunch conversation, I just drifted away. But it's nice to not have to worry . . . "

I guess she'd felt comfortable enough among those familiar faces (as she had at brunch with the Seltzers the other day) to not feel anxious about her declining skills. She didn't have to worry about her abilities in front of those women; they loved her anyway.

The phone rang. My sister Mary was calling. I talked with her first, then turned her over to Mom, who picked up the phone and said, "Hi, Johnny!" She didn't get flustered when it turned out to be Mary on the phone, because her mind was still on track, even if the train hadn't stopped at the right platform. She was thinking that she was about to say hi to Mary, but she was probably also thinking, *Thanks, Johnny*, when I handed her the phone, so it came out as "Hi, Johnny." Just a contraction of two sentences, really. No problem.

When Mom hung up the phone, we continued our talk. She said, "It's hard to abdicate all attempts to do things for myself." (As I said, her vocabulary was still good at times. Some of those trains still went to *exactly* the right platforms.) "I can't solicit and succeed when people are trying to communicate with you." (Uh, then again, some of those trains got derailed in the woods.) "I feel vulnerable to my own lack of experience." Here I think she meant that she felt vulnerable due to her *loss* of experience—especially her waning memory. I wanted to protect her from such feelings if I could, and later that evening I made some real progress. I called Carol Snow to talk about the Sorry We're Dead cards, and we got into a deep discussion about K's condition. Carol had already become finely attuned to K's moods, and said she thought K felt particularly vulnerable because her Rolodex was gone.

Aha! So that was it! The woman we'd hired before to help with the Sorry We're Dead cards had taken K's big Rolodex home with her, to use in addressing the envelopes, and just its absence from our house made K anxious. She knew that her memory was eroding, and if this Rolodex somehow disappeared, it would be like losing another huge chunk of her brain.

The solution was simple: Get the Rolodex back to the house, thank the lady for her help, pay her off, and turn the job over to Carol. Then K could see her Rolodex, safe and sound, and could "supervise" the process to her heart's content. Carol would be patient, steady, and focused, and this frustrating chore would soon be finished.

FRIDAY, MARCH 5

When I put down the morning paper and went to rinse my coffee mug, I noticed that Mom's breakfast dishes weren't in the sink, which meant she hadn't gotten up yet. Odd. It was already 10:00 AM. Hmm. I went to her room and found her in bed, crying. "What's wrong, Mom?" I asked, sitting down on the edge of her bed. "The cards," she snuffled.

Apparently, the prospect of all that paperwork coming back to the house overwhelmed her. She was exhausted, and she hadn't even gotten out of bed yet. And although I knew we were actually solving a problem, at that moment I felt like I'd created one.

Luckily, Carol arrived before I had to leave for an appointment, because I didn't want to leave K alone in her current state of mind. Carol quickly grasped the situation and said she'd reassure and calm K as best she could, and then get going on retrieving the Rolodex and finishing the cards, pronto.

When I got home in the middle of the afternoon, K was still in bed. When I first saw her I thought she was asleep, but when I crept close to her bed to check, she raised her head and waved her hand weakly at me, so I sat down and we had a chat.

"Carol knows what to do with the cards," she said. (I knew what to do, too: trash the damn things! But I didn't think K was up for that kind of humor at the moment, so I kept it to myself.) I assured her that Carol would indeed take care of the cards, and her mood seemed to improve. But she still didn't get out of bed. She napped on and off throughout the day while I made phone calls and worked out and seethed at those damn cards and the unnecessary pain and trouble they'd brought into K's life.

She must have recognized the whole terrible card business as an unmistakable sign of her decline; a sign pointing to the time when she would have to have strangers living in her house, feeding her with a spoon, washing her and dressing her and talking baby-talk to her. Which she loathed. Which she knew was coming. Which she was determined to avoid.

For some people, the physical pain is the worst; for others, it's the emotional pain. Who's to say which is worse, and when enough is enough?

Isn't it obvious? There's only one person who *can* say: the person experiencing the pain. No one else.

IN THE EVENING, K finally pulled herself together, got cleaned up and dressed, and came to the kitchen for dinner. Afterward we entertained ourselves with the contents of one of Jolly's office boxes. I sorted through the files and K looked at photos—mostly old ones, and a few that were just plain bizarre: Jolly dressed up like the Frito Bandito? *¡Ay, caramba!* Must've been from a party thrown by medical students or residents. Jolly always did like to entertain the troops, so to speak, and the students revered him. He played the role of Big Daddy very well.

SATURDAY, MARCH 6

When I woke up, I decided to check on K first thing. She was still in bed, still tired, still sad. She told me she'd had a nightmare about the cards. (Fucking cards!) She wanted to write personal notes in them but felt frustrated because she didn't have the energy, and her handwriting was getting worse. (It occurred to me that she might have trouble writing a farewell letter now—another thing we'd have to talk about soon.) I suggested that in lieu of writing personal notes in the cards, she could make phone calls. This idea seemed to boost her hopes, but she said she'd need Carol's or my help.

"You can see how humiliating this feels," she said.

"Of course," I said.

"I'm more and more frightened about not being able to talk. Sooner is better than later, Johnny. I'm gonna wait to see Mary again, and then I want to pack it in. I don't want to get where Jolly was. I don't want to go to the loony bin. I fear that more than anything."

"Mom, you aren't going to any loony bin, I promise you. And your speech really isn't so bad. I can tell what you're saying, even when you get confused."

"Thank you, Johnny. That makes me feel better."

"I understand why this worries you so much, though. And I agree that we need to be careful and analyze your situation regularly. That way, when it looks like you're starting to slide downhill rapidly, we can go forward with The Plan."

"Correct," she said, and she took my hand in hers and squeezed it.

"And I promise you again that no matter what, I will honor your wishes, whatever they are, and handle things accordingly. Okay?"

"I trust you completely, Johnny," she said. She smiled, sat up, and hugged me. "Well!" she said. "I guess I'd better get up and see what trouble I can get into while I still can." So she got out of bed, and we sauntered off to the kitchen to have breakfast.

WEDNESDAY, MARCH 10

Back in Seattle, I felt sad to be away from Mom, and frustrated by the limitations of talking with her on the phone, especially when I called from my office. But she seemed upbeat, and her speech sounded relatively good.

"I don't have a babysitter today," she stated proudly. "I didn't have one yesterday or the day before, either." I knew she hated asking people to "babysit" her, so I suggested that she simply ask them to come by for lunch, or for dinner and a TV show. She said she understood, but just knowing that she needed people around more and more these days—"just in case"—made it feel to her like babysitting.

She also said she had some ideas to share with me the next time I came for a visit and we were "behind docked lors—*no!*" She struggled to get it: " . . . locked . . . doors!" Then she sighed loudly in frustration.

"I understood you the first time," I said quickly. Then, to lighten the mood, I added, "But if you switch over to pig Latin, I'll have to yell for an interpreter." She sighed again, but then she chuckled.

She was still herself, no doubt about it, but for how long?

Friday, March 12

Another telephone talk with Mom. She asked, "Have you met Carol?"

Uh-oh. That's not good. But maybe it was only a small lapse in her short-term memory (typical with Alzheimer's) and not indicative of more serious deterioration. So I didn't panic, just said, "Yes, Mom, I've met Carol. How are you two getting along?"

"I love her!" K said happily.

That *was* good.

I told her I'd heard that Anne might be coming back to L.A. for a visit soon. "Mary too?" she asked hopefully.

"I don't know," I said, "but I'll find out and get back to you."

"Thank you, Johnny," she said. And then she added, "Guess what? I've got some good news."

"What is it?" I asked.

"Carol has finished with the Sorry We're Dead cards!" she said, and I could hear the relief in her voice.

"Hooray!" I shouted. Thank goodness that terrible mess was finally over.

JACK GOES TO THE JOINT

It felt great to wake up to another sunny morning in L.A. I strolled out to the kitchen, sipped my coffee, looked out the window, and smiled at the prospect of sitting outside in the dry warmth and relaxing into the day. It was Saturday, March 27.

As I headed to the patio door, I walked past the kitchen table and there, on the front page of both the *New York Times* and the *L.A. Times*, were the big and bold headlines: "Kevorkian Is Found Guilty of Murdering Dying Man"; "Kevorkian Convicted of 2nd-Degree Murder."

Swell. This was *not* a good way to start the day.

But there it was, staring up at me from the kitchen table. So I did what I had to do: poured myself another cup of coffee, grabbed the sports section, and went outside.

Eventually, of course, I had to read the articles. Dr. Jack Kevorkian, the retired pathologist from Michigan who had made a second career of assisting in various people's suicides, was going to jail for helping to end Thomas Youk's suffering.

Kevorkian had always been acquitted of such charges before, in part due to the juries' understandable unwillingness to second-guess the wishes of the individuals who had requested his assistance. He also had a good lawyer. But in this latest case, Kevorkian

118

had chosen to videotape the assisting. He also had chosen to act as his own lawyer—with the inevitable poor result. So he wasn't going to be in the newspapers again anytime soon, but he certainly had kept the issue on the front pages and in the public consciousness for a long time. His actions had opened a lot of people's minds. And, as the famous bumper sticker says so well: MINDS ARE LIKE PARACHUTES—THEY FUNCTION BEST WHEN OPEN.

TUESDAY, MARCH 30

K stayed in bed all morning, crying. "This will be why I go sooner," she said. "I don't want to go out of the house. I just want to go to bed, crawl under a bush . . . " Apparently, she had forgotten to take her Aricept the night before. I couldn't imagine that she would have such a strong physical reaction to missing only one pill, so I figured that she was upset by just the realization that she'd forgotten to take it. Alzheimer's sufferers commonly have extreme responses to relatively small problems, but this seemed deeper than that. All I could do was hold her and let her cry. I knew that her frustration would eventually ebb and she would regain her composure.

I found it particularly hard to understand her speech when she cried. She said something garbled that referred to "a month." (What did that mean? "Can I last a month?" What a question to ask oneself!) And she said, "I want Anne to feel good about herself first." (Uh-oh, not this again.) "She needs to be with her husband . . . I feel like a part person. The part that's here . . . oh, Jesus . . . I just hate to do this, but I want to be in good shape . . . and you know what I mean." I said I did, but I really wasn't sure.

When she'd calmed down a little and I could understand her better, she told me she'd shown Carol her poetry and pictures of her parents. "I want to look at pictures and say goodbye. Then it'll be okay. I've got to do that." I told her it all sounded quite reasonable, and kept hugging her.

She went on snuffling. "When I was upstairs alone, sorting papers, I got tired but felt if I could do some of that with Carol . . . and talking about the things I love . . . I don't want to hang around much longer . . . How do you think things will work out with the house? I want to talk with you about that . . . If I can help Anne, I want to do . . . whatever I can, but I don't know what it would take . . . " She continued this way for a while, discussing her worries and getting sad, then shifting to practical matters and calming down, back and forth.

Later in the day, just as K seemed to be emerging from her gray cloud, a specific worry hit her: She'd lost her ATM card. She kept rechecking her purse and desk, and Maria Luisa and I rooted around all over the house, to no avail. I finally called Cousin Dave and asked him to cancel the card with the bank, and it turned out that *he* had it! He'd used it to get cash for K when he'd been at the house the previous Sunday, but he'd forgotten to put it back in her wallet before he left. I treated him to several pungent comments.

When I told Mom that Dave had the bank card and would be returning it soon, she looked at me ruefully and said, with a tinge of her classic black humor, "Well, I feel better knowing I'm not crazy." She sat on the sofa, staring off into the middle distance for a few seconds, holding her favorite fleece blanket on her lap, her fingers worrying its edge. Then she said she needed a nap and gathered herself up to go to her room. But the way she did it broke my heart: She slowly got to her feet, but seemed to stay in a seated position (rotated forward 90 degrees)—bent at the waist, bent way over. Then she shuffled unsteadily out of the room, still holding the blanket on her now almost vertical lap, clutching it to herself desperately, as if it were a life preserver, but somehow knowing that it really wouldn't float.

AT DINNERTIME WE WATCHED the news: Albanians finding hell in Serbia. What a sad and horrendous business. I found myself having too much wine again. Was I drinking to deaden the pain of watching K's decline up close? Or was it to relieve the stress of all the planning for her death that I was doing in my head? Probably both. It would be better to intensify my workouts instead.

At one point, Mom got up from the table and went into the front-hall bathroom, but she didn't shut the door. Thankfully, from where I sat I could see only the side of her knees and her pants down at her ankles. She forgot to do certain basic things sometimes, but I couldn't bring myself to tell her, because she'd be so deeply embarrassed. Alzheimer's is humiliating enough without additional reminders.

Maybe I'd have another glass of that wine after all.

AFTER DINNER, MOM AND I made a few phone calls to relatives and friends. I liked helping her with her calls, so she could keep in touch with the people she cared about. She hardly ever initiated phone calls anymore because she was so self-conscious about her diminishing verbal skills. She found face-to-face talks difficult enough, even with their helpful visual cues. But when I was with her, we used the speakerphone in the kitchen so I could jump in—if necessary—and help clarify things.

When Mom reached her phone-call limit, we moved into the living room and watched two of her longtime favorite TV shows on A&E's special *Mystery Night* series: *Law & Order* and *Inspector Morse*. She couldn't follow the plots very well now, or understand much of the bantering byplay, so I had to explain things—which was sad because she used to be so quick-witted. But she still enjoyed the action, and she even teased me about the "mystery" that we were going to create soon ourselves.

After TV we looked at old family photo albums from the mid-1950s, and then went into the kitchen for ice cream. Just before bed, as always, K consulted the big calendar on the wall above the kitchen table to remind herself of what the following day would bring. Then she headed for her bedroom and I tagged along.

"Do you want your back scratched?" I asked, but I already knew the answer.

"You bet!" she replied, grinning.

She climbed onto her bed, stayed on her hands and knees, and growled, playing Mama Bear, and then settled in, face down. I gave her the old two-handed superscratcher, and she grumphed appreciatively. It was so easy to give her a moment or two of happiness each day, and it felt great to be there for her.

When I finished chasing away her dry-skin itches, we said our goodnights. I was glad that her long, rough day was finally over and had ended on a high note. I'd hated seeing her get confused and upset by simple and insignificant things—the low notes of her day.

I poured myself a splash of Jameson's on the rocks, then headed for my personal refuge, the patio. The night smelled fresh, clean. The Santa Ana winds had prowled in and were rustling through the vegetation, stirring things up, breathing warm new life into the city. It felt good.

I noticed that our new next-door neighbors—a pleasant young couple with two little kids—had planted a jacaranda tree in their side yard. I thought of the pine seedling I'd planted in the front yard of a duplex where I'd lived fifteen years earlier. I'd driven by there and seen it again just the other day, and it was huge—bushy and sturdy and at least fifty feet tall.

I felt like planting more trees. Pines. Oaks. Maples. Poplars. Fruit trees, too. Get a big piece of land somewhere and plant a whole mess of trees—establish a giant, generous forest that could nurture and protect all the animals that would surely gather there and thrive—a vital legacy. As I witnessed the end of Jolly's and K's lives, and realized that I was probably closer to the end of my own life than to the beginning, I found myself wanting to do more things of an enduring nature. Creative things. Meaningful things.

Mom and I had looked through our 1956 photo album earlier in the evening. She was only thirty-two years old back then, and she'd just given birth to me. She looked so vibrant in the pictures, so alive—her posture perfect, her eyes bright, her smile confident. And now, suddenly, she was seventy-five and slipping away rapidly, melting before my eyes like an ice-cream cone in that same intense Oklahoma August heat into which I'd been born. It was so fucking unfair! For her, for me, for the rest of the family, for everyone who knew the *real* K. Just a few minutes ago, she was thirty-two. And now she was almost gone.

The Santa Anas gained strength, and I could hear them pushing through the trees and brush of the canyon. I hoped the neighbors had properly staked and secured their new jacaranda. I could see it bending way over in the wind.

Stand fast, young tree; be strong. The wind, the woodsman, the worm . . . they're coming. They come for us all.

SEVEN

―――

Remembering and Preparing

WEDNESDAY, MARCH 31

At breakfast Mom said, for no apparent reason, "I have a smeal on my mouth."

Of course she meant "smile," but I couldn't imagine why she'd brought it up. I thought for a second and responded, "What would Eleanor say?"

She didn't get the joke, of course, and looked at me as if I'd just started speaking Portuguese, so I reminded her that Eleanor Smeal was for many years president of the National Organization for Women, which K had supported wholeheartedly. Then she smealed again. Me too.

Later that morning, as K got ready for her regular Wednesday hair appointment, she seemed agitated. When I asked her about it, she said she wanted to give her hairdresser a wedding present of a hundred-dollar bill inside a greeting card, but she couldn't quite figure out how to do it. So I did it for her and she relaxed. Then we gathered everything she needed for her excursion—her cane, shawl, and purse (containing Kleenex, wallet, lipstick, house key, and the card and money for her hairdresser)—and off we went.

The beauty parlor was nearby, and when we got there K introduced me to everybody. They all clearly thought the world of her and were used to taking good care of her, and she was happy to be there with them.

Maria Luisa would be retrieving K from the salon, so I excused myself to run a few errands. When I returned to the house a few hours later, I found Mom emerging groggily from her usual midafternoon nap, confused about where I'd been while she was getting her hair done. I wanted to believe that this was typical post-nap fogginess, until she got teary and upset with herself for not remembering that I'd told her about the errands earlier.

"I wish I could be the way I was," she sniffed. "There's so much I want to talk about with you."

"Everything will be fine, Mom, once you wake up completely. We'll have plenty of time to talk. I promise."

This assurance seemed to make her feel better. I left her to get her bearings while I went and worked on a few home-fix-it chores. When I reached "Mom's bathroom" on my list, K watched, fascinated, as I moved and reattached the broken towel rack next to her bidet. She'd used the towel rack as a handrail to help herself sit and stand, and it wasn't designed for that. A professional had recently installed a proper handrail on the other wall, but for some reason hadn't fixed the towel rack. I apologized to Mom for the holes I'd left in her wallpaper and said I'd figure out how to cover them up later.

As I kept working she wandered off, and I reflected on how she had alerted me to the towel rack problem. On a Post-It note, she'd written: "Be-Day." It had taken me a second to understand, and then all I could do was shake my head.

I was under the sink, fixing a drip, when K reappeared, smiling and holding an old roll of bathroom wallpaper that had been stored for years in the back of a cabinet somewhere. Amazing! How the hell had she remembered where it was?

"I may be losing my mind," she proclaimed triumphantly, "but I'm not there yet!" She brandished the wallpaper roll and playfully conked me on the head with it. I did my best imitation of a beaten hound's yelp and we both cracked up. She still had a good mind in there, by God, and I wanted to sing and celebrate every time she escaped from her cage and danced again in the better world.

After dinner and the usual TV shows, we looked through more photo albums from the late 1950s, moving forward a few years in our pictorial review of family life. What a kick to see pictures of myself as a toddler, Mary and Anne in their school uniforms, Jolly without a paunch, and K in her very first office—at Casady School in Oklahoma City, where she'd been the testing and guidance counselor.

We came across a picture of my grandma Harriet (K's mother) rocking me to sleep in the white fiberglass Eames rocking chair we'd had in our family room, next to the picture windows looking out onto the wooded back yard. I could almost smell her dusty-floral perfume. Asleep on the floor nearby was our sweet dog Wello, a Welsh corgi who could howl like an opera star and willingly followed me everywhere but the bathtub.

Not all our reminiscing was pleasant, though. At one point I got the impression that something irked K, but she shrugged it off when I asked. Then she changed her mind and pointed to one of the pictures, took a deep breath, and said, "That's the woman Jolly copulated with frequently."

Damn! That was *not* the kind of memory I wanted to reawaken. These sessions were supposed to be fun, not painful. But then K remembered the great story she liked to tell about how this woman had appeared at K's office one day and insisted that K give Jolly up. Why wouldn't K give Jolly a divorce? the woman had demanded. K had smiled patiently at her and replied, "Because he hasn't asked me for one. And besides, what makes you think you're any different from all the others?" Needless to say, the woman fled.

The phone rang, and I went to the kitchen to answer it. It was Mary, who said she needed to talk with me privately but wanted to say hi to Mom first. After Mom and Mary finished their chat, Mom handed me the phone and said she was going to go brush her teeth.

I found Mary's news almost unbearable. She said she'd been afraid to tell me before, knowing I'd get angry, but felt she could tell me now because the incident was almost two months in the past and things seemed to be back under control. She said that the day she'd arrived in L.A. to visit Mom last, Anne had been at the house too, but preparing to return to New York. Anne was behind schedule and packing frantically; Mary hovered nearby. When Mom appeared in the doorway and asked if she could do anything to help, Anne whipped her head around and bellowed something like, "If you confuse me, there'll be trouble!" and went back to thrashing her clothes around. Mom staggered backward from this salvo, slunk out the door, and shuffled to the safety of her room. Mary watched, horrified, and then rushed off to comfort Mom.

After Anne left in a cab, Mary called Cousin Dave and told him what had happened. He said that from then on, Anne wouldn't be allowed in the house with K unless someone else was present, too. He also said he'd ask Maria Luisa to keep a closer watch on things whenever Anne visited.

At the end of this horrible story, Mary reiterated her hope that I wouldn't get angry.

I wasn't angry—I was frozen. I could barely talk. I managed to croak a few words of thanks to Mary for filling me in, and assured her that I was okay. But I wasn't. I think I was in shock. I was standing right next to the liquor cabinet, so I grabbed the Jameson's and took a gulp. After it thawed out my top layer, I asked Mary for more details. It sickened me to hear them, but I felt I had to know about everything that affected Mom.

Eventually Mary and I rang off and I sat there for a few minutes, head in my hands, still in shock and trying to digest the news. No wonder Mom had been so conflicted about Anne recently. That Valentine's Day after-dinner discussion at Genevieve's—about how K needed to stop trying to fix Anne or be Anne's caretaker—would have happened shortly after the awful scene Mary had described. Having just been brutally reminded of how damaged Anne really was, K certainly would have felt a need to help her. But K would also have wanted to avoid Anne, out of sheer self-preservation. What terrible ambivalence K must have been feeling, and how difficult it must have been for her, especially given her Alzheimer's. Damn!

I saw Mom's bedroom light still on, so I went in to say good-night and give her a back scratch. I really wanted to ask her about the incident with Anne, but I bit my tongue. It was bedtime—not the time to stir her up. Maybe after I'd processed it a for a few days . . .

Or maybe not. It would only upset her, and that was the last thing I ever wanted to do.

Thursday, April 1

I headed out for an early brunch with Walter Seltzer. Getting a chance to see him on my quick trips to L.A. was always a delightful tonic. He's always been like a favorite uncle and then some—with a razor-sharp wit and martini-dry sense of humor. We had omelets and an invigorating catch-up session on friends, family, and politics, and once again he proved that he had the most agile mind of any octogenarian on the planet—more agile than most people half his age. Just like K used to be.

I hustled home to make sure K was ready to embark on one of her ladies' luncheons; she appreciated my double-checking that she had all the essentials in her purse before she left the house. I was glad she occasionally felt comfortable in the outside world and wasn't completely housebound yet. She was getting close, though. Very few things could entice her away from the safety of home and her familiar routine.

When she returned from lunch, I took her to UCLA for her neurology appointment with Dr. Jeffrey Cummings: a severe-looking fellow—tall and lean, with a riverboat gambler's goatee—

but gentle mannered. I was glad to see him treat K as more of a colleague, and not just a patient. Certainly, he was used to dealing with elderly folks in varying stages of neurological deterioration and knew what style of interaction would be most effective with whom, but I felt sure, based on how he treated K, that he genuinely liked her.

As Dr. Cummings asked K questions, I watched him scrutinize every nuance of her answers—what she said and how she said it. He also put her through several tests: remembering three words; naming as many animals as she could in one minute; working a basic arithmetic problem; copying a simple drawing.

It was hard to watch K struggle with such easy tasks. At one time she'd been a talented cartoonist, but now that talent had vanished. Cummings showed her a picture of a triangle poking into the side of a circle, and K laboriously drew something vaguely resembling two adjacent rectangles with triangular tops.

The three words that Cummings asked her to remember at the start of the exam were "penny," "table," and "baseball." When he asked her to recall them about five minutes later, she couldn't, but said she thought "there was a 'pig' in there somewhere."

How many animals could she name in one minute? "Cat, dog, wolf, rabbit, horse, cow, reindeer, alligator, elephant, lion, zebra." That was all. No pig this time. And the test-taking alone made her anxious, especially the list of animals because it was timed, and she started panting and puffing from the tension (not helped by her emphysema). Clearly, she felt even more frustrated by *knowing* that she was having difficulty doing what should have been easy for her. Once upon a time.

The simple arithmetic test was too bad to describe.

But at the end of it all, Dr. Cummings said that K had experienced no noticeable decline since her last appointment, two months before. Maybe there was no decline that his tests could measure, but K and I knew what the *real* decline rate was. Cummings also noted that K seemed in a much better mood than she had at her last appointment. (*Yeah*, I thought, *that's because she's finally done with all the smiley-faced bullshit being handed to her about possibly getting better, and she knows what she's going to do about it.*)

"Fluent aphasia" was how Cummings labeled K's speech problems. Apparently it's quite rare, this combination of unusually clear insight into one's cognitive difficulties and unusually serious language trouble. Cummings said that a typical Alzheimer's patient with K's level of verbal impairment would be much further along in the dementia component of the disease; she probably wouldn't know who she was or what was going on around her, and would perhaps already be soiling herself or starting fires or displaying other symptoms of the latter stages of the disease. On the other hand, a patient with K's high level of awareness of her condition usually wouldn't have nearly as much trouble speaking as K did.

Swell. The double whammy: She knew what was going on but couldn't make herself understood—not very well, anyway. She was trapped. Caged. With only one way out, sooner or later. K and I knew which of those it would be.

Dr. Cummings told K to continue with her Aricept and megadose vitamin E, and he mentioned that an experimental drug that his department was studying might be available in a month or two. K said she'd think about it, but as we got up to leave, she caught my eye and made a face. I had to fake a coughing jag to cover my laugh.

Cummings scheduled K's next appointment for early June, two months out. Setting it that far ahead made me think about the time-table for The Plan, and based on what K had been saying and feeling, I doubted she'd be keeping her next appointment.

When we got home, Mom wanted to talk about "matters relating to my death." Not too surprising, given what she'd just been through. Now that she'd recovered from Jolly's death, she said, she was thinking more practically about her situation. "If things go to hell, I want to go . . . But sometimes things are good, and, to stay around for, like helping Annie. Some are not so good; like, if I had to go out to lunch every day, I'd make about ten and then, on the eleventh time, I'd say, 'That's it!'" Not because of the company, of course—K loved her lunch pals dearly—but because the strain of coping with all the differences from her regular routine, and multiple stimuli (especially restaurants' noise and unfamiliar bathrooms). It exhausted her each time.

How bitterly ironic. K used to savor variety and complexity. And now she found it difficult to cope with a luncheon and a doctor's appointment on the same day.

We talked a little more about her trying to help Anne. Mom made a brave effort to explain to me the emotional dynamics between the two of them, and how those dynamics had changed over the years. K had amazingly sharp moments like this, in which she still seemed to be the training director of the psychology service at the Brentwood VA hospital. We discussed how Anne's near chronic anxiety tended to upset Mom, which in turn made Anne even more anxious. What a mess. I suggested to K that the "Anne business" might be one area of her life where she could do that acting we'd talked about before. If Anne were made to believe that Mom had rebounded from Jolly's death and felt much better, then maybe she'd get on with her new married life in New York, visit L.A. less often, and give Mom a break.

My mention of acting reawakened Mom's conspiratorial instincts and reminded her of another part of The Plan. She reiterated her willingness to pretend behaviors that might make things safer for me, and again told me how much she needed to be sure that my helping her wouldn't put me at risk. Here she was, preparing for her own death yet worrying about everybody else. An incredible lady.

But I concluded that, as much as K wanted to show off her acting chops, pretending about *anything* would likely confuse her. Strategic thinking was no longer her forte. Once, I mistakenly mentioned a handful of options I had contemplated regarding The Plan, but she couldn't grasp them and became upset. Her mind could hold only one or two things at a time, and a short time at that. Her brain had become like a sieve, and she could feel it.

When I told her we'd be taking a simpler approach to The Plan, one that would allow her to be herself and not have to do any performing, she looked disappointed.

"I was looking forward to having fun, fooling people. I know I can pull it off."

I hated seeing her deflated.

"Okay, Mom, I promise to keep an eye out and let you know if and when we can use your Bernhardt imitations, all right?"

"All right," she said, smiling again.

Then she wanted to talk about the details of what would happen after she died. *That* came out of nowhere. But I took a deep breath and started describing, without too many gory details, what I thought would happen, based on my experience with Jolly: the call to Doctor Davis, the call to the mortuary, the collecting of the body, the paperwork, the calls to family members and friends, and eventually a memorial service. And I reminded her of the events she had seen and been part of, like going with me to the mortuary to sign the papers necessary for Jolly's cremation.

She listened attentively, nodding slightly in acknowledgment. When I finished, she reflected awhile, then sighed and said, "It's a difficult decision. But the disease is the worst. Maybe death is terrible, but I don't think so."

I said I agreed, but I reminded her that she could always change her mind, that it was her choice. She shook her head and waved me off. She had other things to talk about.

"When I die, things will happen," she said. "It'll have an impact on my kids."

From the way she said it, and the way she looked at me, I knew she was trying to ask a question or raise another issue, so I asked her to explain what she meant. She fumbled a bit verbally, but finally got enough out for me to understand that she wanted to know what I thought each of us kids would do with our inheritance.

I hadn't thought of that. I pondered a bit, then told her I thought Anne and Paul would probably buy a house. I had no idea what Mary might do, so I randomly guessed that she'd do something completely uncharacteristic, like travel around the world.

As for me, I said I didn't have any particular wants or needs—maybe I'd get a sporty new car. K brightened at that. She liked sports cars and enjoyed driving—she'd taught me how. And maybe I'd take a much needed vacation—a week or two of tension-free solitude and tranquility in the mountains. And maybe I'd write a book about this whole business. She liked the sound of that—a lot.

She said, "Everyone should know what it's like to go through this."

"Knowledge is power, right?" I asked.

"Right!" she said forcefully, with a gleam in her eye, and she smacked her fist onto the arm of the sofa. "And change these damn laws that make it so you can't go when it's time!"

Amen, sister. Testify.

AT BEDTIME THAT NIGHT, Mom performed her usual elaborate pill-taking ritual, but I seemed to see it with new eyes, eyes that looked ahead to The Plan—and what I saw worried me. First she got her special cup, a flimsy red plastic one, from its special place on the pass-through counter between the kitchen and the dining room. Then she toddled over to the freezer and put one or two ice cubes in the cup. Then she fetched her pillbox, which she kept in a shoebox in an overhead cupboard. The shoebox also contained the original prescription pill bottles that supplied her pillbox with its well-organized ammunition. She then removed the rubber band she kept around the pillbox for extra security, rooted around in the pillbox, fingering the tablets and capsules she was about to take, reassuring herself—to the extent that she could—that they were the right ones, her evening pills: Aricept, Ambien, a large multivitamin, a small iron supplement, a gigantic calcium supplement, a 500-milligram vitamin C, and a 500-milligram vitamin E.

Once she was satisfied that the pills were the right ones, she shook them out of the pillbox into a small white plastic condiment bowl, closed the pillbox, replaced its protective rubber band, and put it back in the shoebox. At this point she paused and rested, leaned against the countertop, and sighed deeply. (She sighed a lot, probably as much because of her worsening emphysema as because of her increasing frustration about life with Alzheimer's.) Then she poured the pills from the little bowl into her left hand and fingered through them again, double-checking to see if they still looked right, or perhaps to see if any squids or motorcycles had somehow joined the mix, and carefully placed the pills on the countertop.

She took her cup over to the freezer and—oops!—discovered that she already had ice in the cup, then went to the sink for water. Then she shuffled back to the little pile of pills on the counter, looked them over one more time, chose one gingerly, put it cautiously on her tongue, took a mouthful of water, and jerked her head back sharply before swallowing. The motion was so extreme, I had to ask her about it—it looked as if it might actually hurt. But she said it was just how she'd gotten used to doing it over the years, to make sure the pills got to the back of her gullet, where she could be sure to wash 'em down. When she had thrown back and swallowed all seven pills, she drank another half cup of water for a final rinse and replaced the special red plastic cup in its special place on the pass-through, next to her small square pot of African violets.

I wondered how many pills Mom would be able to take when the time came to carry out The Plan. Would she tire quickly from the physical exertion that her pill-taking seemed to require? Would she be unable to take enough to do the job? I decided to voice my concerns then and there: Could she swallow her pills without her head jerking? I asked. Did she need to swallow so much water with each pill? Could she take more than one pill at a time? These were important things to know, because on the final night I didn't want her to fail due to exhaustion, or throw her back out, or feel like a bloated water balloon. After all, comfort and dignity were important aspects of The Plan.

She said she thought she could take two at once, and also use less water, so she tried it with a pair of vitamin pills, and it worked. She was very proud of her achievement, and vowed to practice this new method and get comfortable with it. What a trouper.

SUNDAY, APRIL 4

Cousin Dave came by to do his regular household-management paperwork, and K looked over his shoulder. Watching them made me heavy-hearted, remembering how capable K used to be. I overheard Dave talking, as he sometimes did, about wanting to take K on a train trip to one of her class reunions in Iowa, or on a cruise ship to see glaciers in Alaska. Mom always smiled and nodded when he suggested these grand safaris, but she'd roll her eyes discreetly. The only place she wanted to go was completely away.

While K and Dave did their pencil pushing, I did some of my own. I had to keep up with my office work. But I also managed to squeeze in a workout on the patio, which was doubly good because of the beautiful sunny day. I sometimes found it difficult to stay indoors, talking with K on the sofa, when the weather was so nice, especially compared with soggy Seattle, but I could rarely convince her to join me outside because she got chilled easily. Whenever I got antsy, however, I reminded myself that the sun would still be here in a few months; K wouldn't be. And then I'd forget about the weather outside and simply bask in her warmth.

K was strong all day. She made a point of telling Dave and me that she didn't want Anne around, at least not for any extended stay. "I don't want to babysit Annie . . . want to do my best to get her to focus on Paul." Well! Maybe she was finally serious about enjoying the short time she had left.

After dinner Mom and I had our usual TV session, but she seemed to have trouble with the remote control, so I worked with her a little on its operation when the shows were over.

It was a perfect opportunity to exercise her synapses a little, and she always felt good when she could shore up her eroding skills. So we had a little ego-boosting session as she regained mastery over the channel and volume controls.

At bedtime I told her I'd been thinking about Dave's recurring talk of travel. I said I knew she had absolutely no interest in going anywhere, but my heart still ached whenever the subject came up, because I wanted her to come to Seattle one last time. It had been several years since her last visit, and in the interim I'd finally been able to buy a house. I wanted her to come stay with me for a few days so I could always remember her being in my home, sitting in my living room, walking through my garden.

But even as I talked with her, hoping she'd say okay, I knew it wasn't going to happen. I knew I'd have to content myself with visiting her in L.A. I said I could live with that, but it wasn't the ideal situation.

She smiled sweetly, took my hand, and shook her head slightly. "There is no ideal situation," she said. "We do the best we can. And I love having you here." She smiled again, and I felt completely better.

THURSDAY, APRIL 15

I spent a long day at my office in Seattle, and finally had a chance to call Mom when I got home in the evening. She sounded like she was in bad shape.

"My voice and speech are so bad, and remembering the things I need to do . . . I'm more aware that I'm becoming like a cripple. I don't want to see people . . . just a few special people important to me . . . I *was* grieving for Jolly, and now for myself and my lost abilities. I get mixed up. I can't even get the TV where I want it. I just want to die."

When she stopped and caught her breath, I offered some soothing words, but her mind was still careening among troublesome issues, and it ran into another big one.

"I've thought a lot about Anne," she said. "She called yesterday and referred to visiting here, and I said, 'Don't forget to clear these things with Dave,' and she didn't say anything about it, didn't have a fit."

She went on a while longer about Anne and some other concerns. I didn't say much, just made sporadic comforting and supportive comments, but by the time the call ended she'd completely transitioned from her initial frustrated sadness into a calm, clear state. That's the way Alzheimer's works.

K's verbal hang-ups happened much more frequently now, but I'd gotten good at interpreting her, and my prompts were about 95 percent right. When she'd get stuck on a word, I could usually pry her loose because I paid close attention to the context. For example, when she said something about a particular kind of behavior not seeming "ranesh . . . rashel . . . , " I suggested, "Rational?"

"Yes!" she almost shouted, heaving a sigh of relief and thanking me. But then she couldn't remember the topic we'd been discussing, and I had to remind her.

When I guessed wrong about her meaning, she got even more confused, so I tried not to weigh in unless I felt sure I knew what she was trying to say, or if she was clearly losing her train of thought. I'd let her work at it, though, because I knew how much she wanted to find the word for herself, and because I knew that the more she exercised her synapses, the longer she would stay lucid—the mental exercise would slow the progress of the Alzheimer's. But it was tough to watch her struggle—eyes darting about, searching for cues; mouth twisting and trying to form a word; hands waving, as if to direct the cluttered traffic in her mind. Actually, it was more than tough to watch—it was agonizing.

That night, I dreamed about K struggling with the TV and not being able to swallow her vitamins and crying. I hadn't had such a dream before, and it was so real that it woke me up in a sweat. I thought I'd been dealing sufficiently, on a conscious level, with all my worries and fears about K's worsening condition, but I guess I had so many of them that my unconscious decided to get in on the act and work on them, too.

Things did seem to be getting worse. For K and for me.

SUNDAY, APRIL 18

On the phone, K was having another rough day with her speech. I couldn't prompt her nearly as well over the phone as I could in person, so we were both frustrated. She was trying to tell me something about Jolly's bedroom, but she couldn't find the right words. She spluttered, "Jolly's . . . clothing . . . purple . . . oh, this is getting so terrible! It's, uh . . . *bathrobe*!" She'd finally found it. Then she sighed wearily and continued, "I thought you might want it, and then I thought . . . Oh, Johnny, the words are too hard. I don't know how I can go on like this."

I jumped in: "Hey, now! Don't forget—I understand your speech pretty damn well."

This seemed to calm her down.

Then I said, "As for Jolly's bathrobe, thanks but no thanks. You gave me a bathrobe for Christmas a couple of years ago—all different colored stripes, remember?—and it still has plenty of wear left in it. Besides, I can't imagine Jolly's robe fitting me, and I don't know any sumo wrestlers I could pass it along to . . . but maybe if my sofa ever needed reupholstering, I should have it around, just in case. What do you think?"

She chuckled at that, and I was glad to have lightened her mood.

I told her I'd been thinking ahead a few weeks, to Mother's Day, and wondering if she'd like me to arrange something special—like having Mary join us in L.A. K said she wasn't sure; she wanted to sleep on it. She said that Anne had suggested visiting then and wanted some time alone with her.

Uh-oh.

I knew they wouldn't be entirely alone, because Dave would remind Maria Luisa to keep an extra-sharp eye on things. But just the thought of Anne in the house worried me; she'd already shown us that she couldn't control herself—her anxiety, her temper—around Mom. What else might happen?

MONDAY, APRIL 19

"I don't give a damn about Mother's Day," K said.

I'd called her after supper to talk about the Anne situation and a possible Mother's Day get-together, and she said she didn't feel up to doing anything with a lot of people. That wasn't a good sign. If the prospect of a family gathering made her nervous, then I'd probably have to stay away, and that would be tough. I *really* wanted to spend this Mother's Day with K. I knew it would be her last one.

She said, "I don't know what to do. I'm so grateful to have some time without a lot of people running around. I don't know what people want from me. I don't want to be responsible. It all depends on what we want to accomplish. I'm ready to speak to Anne, alone or with others. But I'm not gonna do direct therapy. I can't be sure I can take care of everybody's notions of what it's supposed to be."

Although she had a lot of verbal difficulty during all this, I thought I could follow it. But the fact that she had so much trouble talking, especially to me, meant she was extremely upset. To calm her, I spoke slowly and concretely, and asked simple questions, like, "Do you want us all together at the same time?"

"Meet at different times," she said. "Might overlap, but be realistic about the different work people have to do. Why can't we enjoy each other separately? The quality of being together is more important than the quantity. It's hard to be therapeutic to our friends if there's other problems that are complicated. I'm more unstrung. What do you think would be best?"

Before I could answer, she was rolling again. "I'm so much more concerned with Mary. She's strong, but dumped on by Annie, and has to listen to criticism. It shouldn't be that way!"

She was getting too wound up now, so I jumped in: "Okay, Mom, tell me if this is right. I think you're saying you're afraid that if all three of us kids are there together, someone might misbehave, right?"

I could hear her sigh long and loud, as if I'd taken the tip off an old-fashioned air mattress. She said, "None of us is foolish enough to go up to Anne and say, 'You're not gonna act like a nut, are you?' We can be more subtle than that and humor her . . . Oh, Johnny, I feel voiceless with you."

"Nah, Mom, I understand. You're worried because some of Anne's visits with you haven't been very good, right?"

"Aha! You understand!" she said.

"Yes, I think so. I think you're worried that if we're all there together, Anne will be more likely to have one of her explosions, and you'll have to act as her caretaker again."

"Yes! Oh . . . I've had to hold Anne when she starts screaming until she cries, and I haven't been able to help her recently. I'll do whatever I can to help her."

"I understand," I said. And, sadly, I knew I was going to have to step aside. "You want some space to deal with Anne, and you think that Mother's Day alone, just the two of you, will be when you can get something accomplished with her."

"Yes! You *do* understand!"

"I hope it works, Mom, for both your sakes. I really do."

I suddenly realized that she'd had so much trouble talking about all this because it wasn't just complicated and heavy stuff—it was *final* stuff. She knew this would be her last Mother's Day and probably her last chance with Anne—her last chance to resolve the conflict that had been such a large part of their relationship for decades.

We'd been talking for well over an hour, and I knew that was another part of the problem for her. It was time to wrap up.

"Okay, Mom, you get Mother's Day alone with Anne, and Mary and I will visit you at other times."

"Oh, yes, that's wonderful, Johnny. You understand me so well."

"Well, I just try to figure things out—you know, like you taught me."

"I'm glad *one* of us remembers how to do it," she said, and I thought I could hear a wry smile in her voice.

I said, "Okay, well, let's both hit the hay before we talk so much that our tongues fall out of our heads." And she gave a little laugh, blew her nose, and said, "Right!"

I hated the idea of not being with her on her last Mother's Day, but it was what I had to do. After we said goodbye, I tried to distract myself from that unhappy prospect by watching obnoxious TV comedies, but that didn't work. At the end of the evening, I noticed I'd finished off an entire bottle of wine. That hadn't worked either.

WEDNESDAY, APRIL 21

Another phone call to Mom, but—surprise!—Mary answered the phone. She'd somehow managed to convince her husband to drive them down from Northern California to visit K.

I mentioned to Mary that K enjoyed looking at our family photo albums, and suggested she add that to their evening agenda. Mary loved the idea; she hadn't looked at them in ages herself. I hoped she would follow through, because it might be her last chance to share those special memories with Mom.

Mom sounded energetic and happy when she got on the phone, but when I told her I'd suggested the photo albums to Mary, she said, "But there's no identification in them, or dates or . . . ah, well . . . "

"Don't worry, Mom. Mary can help you identify people."

She sighed and said, "Thank you, Johnny, for your patience and for getting all these things together."

"Well, Mom, I love you. And that means I'll do anything and everything I can for you. And since patience is something I learned from you, it's only fitting that you're getting the benefit of it now. I'm sure I nearly exhausted your supply when I was a teenager."

She laughed and said, "Just about!"

After we rang off, I called Norma and learned that she was going to L.A. the following weekend. She said that when she'd called K about her visit, K seemed to be more "cloudy." Sadly, I had to agree.

I hoped Norma and K could have a few more good times together before the end. Coming soon. Very hard to think about.

I plunked myself down in front of the TV with a plate of cheese and crackers and a glass of red wine. Phooey—the wine was swill. I'd grabbed something off the rack at the store without thinking and had come up with a real stinker. So I poured it out, rinsed the glass with a vengeance, and returned to my good ol' reliable Jameson's. With a vengeance. Plenty of rocket fuel for my attempt at escapist flight. And I did fly high.

And a little later, I fell down the stairs.

As I'm falling, in seeming slow motion, I placidly think, *Swell, a broken back. Not a good thing. Not good for The Plan.* But when I land and look around, the only thing broken is the small plate I was carrying. No matter. The loss of a few crackers and chunks of cheese is acceptable collateral damage. The loss of some skin off my right shin is more personal, but that, too, is acceptable.

So, do I have a big epiphany now? Do I stop and think?

Nah. Maybe later. Right now there's a movie I wanna watch on HBO: *City of Angels*. How appropriate, on so many levels.

Before finally going to bed at a ridiculously late hour, I actually did stop and think for a minute: Why was I drinking so damn much? Pretty obvious, really: I had to keep so much knowledge to myself, hold everything in, make plans and arrangements without seeming to, do secret and important things with my right hand (and brain) while doing seemingly innocuous things with my left. Even in a steel trap of a mind, feelings can seep out the edges—like the blood of the animal caught in that same steel trap. Some things cannot be contained.

Thursday, April 29

Today would have been K and Jolly's fifty-fifth wedding anniversary. They married in 1944, when he was nineteen and she was twenty. It's impossible to imagine them so young.

I realized how constantly depressed I felt about all the stuff I'd bottled up inside: the knowledge, the planning . . . not to mention the plain old-fashioned *worrying* about my ailing mom. I knew that sitting on serious feelings could lead to depression, but there wasn't anyone I could talk to about it. I couldn't put The Plan in jeopardy by revealing it to anyone. Still, it was the main thing occupying my mind, and that made it hard to interact with others in any kind of normal way, because socializing is all about sharing thoughts and feelings. My nerves were on continuous high alert, which made it impossible for me to ever truly relax and have a good time with my friends. Faking smiles and making small talk simply had no value. So I found myself avoiding social occasions, even simple dinners at friends' homes. One of them, a baron of the barbecue, even accused me of having turned vegetarian! Of course, then I had to show up and prove myself still carnivorous, but I didn't stay long. Mostly I just stayed away. And that, of course, made me feel even more isolated and depressed.

Luckily, work was slow—partly because I'd stopped taking new cases. It was hard enough to concentrate on the work I already had on my desk. I couldn't focus all that well on other people's problems when I had this big-ass problem of my own (and K's) right in front of me all the time.

I felt anxious, distracted, and sad, but was I getting depressed, clinically? Hard to tell. Maybe it was only depression with a lowercase *d*, not a capital *D*. Getting more sleep and exercise was probably all I needed, not therapy or pharmaceuticals. Besides, I couldn't go to a shrink now—before K's departure—because the doctor-patient privilege isn't absolute, but The Plan was the one thing I needed to talk about. I also worried about what it might look like to Joe Friday if I went into therapy just before K's death. Maybe it wouldn't look as bad as I feared. After all, this was naturally a very difficult time for me, even without any huge hidden agenda. But I simply couldn't take any chances. I had to keep my own counsel for a while yet.

Although I'd known it intellectually for months, I finally felt—viscerally—that this was precisely why assisted suicide should *not* be attempted by amateurs, and why it should be a legally accepted part of the doctor-patient relationship. Family consultation might somehow be a part of the equation, but not direct involvement—let the doctors and patients do their thing. I just wanted to have my old relationship with my mom again. We didn't have much time left, and we should have been thinking and talking about all sorts of family things, good things, loving things—while we still could. We shouldn't have had to worry about hiding our thoughts from other loved ones, calculating drug overdosages, and avoiding prison.

I absolutely believed in the propriety of what I'd done for Jolly and what I was about to do for K, but that didn't mean I didn't feel all the emotions that it kicked up. Emotions I had to hide. Emotions that kicked my ass.

Saturday, May 1

I woke up very slowly, slogging my way through the tail end of some heavy dreams, and realized that I'd slept eleven hours. Obviously I needed it, after a long and frustrating week at work. I hadn't been able to pay much attention to things down in L.A., despite the number of calls I'd made to K to check in, but I hadn't been too focused in the office, either.

Everything seems so disjointed those days. I know I'm drinking too much, and that's not good. I don't want to get mush-minded, make a mistake, mess up The Plan. I'm sure that Jolly and K didn't want me to turn into an alcoholic over all this. Having seen Mom do battle with the bottle over the years, I should be more on the defensive.

Planning ahead is the key, and I'm doing that for all I'm worth. Thinking hard: *How will this look? How would that seem? Natural? Logical? What might this person do? How might that person react? What if this or that happens? What if something goes wrong? How will I contain it? Can I contain it? And if not, then what?*

Hundreds, maybe thousands, of variables.

I don't know how I'm coping with it all, but I am. I have to. And it forces me to ask the obvious question: If this is so damn hard for *me*, given my legal training and other advantages (like a flexible schedule and financial wherewithal), then how the hell could most other people cope with it?

The real question, of course, is: Why is assisted suicide illegal? Why not let people have the dignity and peace they want and deserve? It would certainly end all the skulking around and remove a ton of stress and anxiety from everyone. Dignity, finally. What's so wrong with that? As long as typical medical-safety protocols exist, then Self de-Termination can be handled just like any other serious medical procedure: the choice of the patient; the work of the doctor.

Even more than sex or abortion, Self de-Termination is the ultimate personal and private act. There's only one body involved. And the government, the church, and everyone else—whose body it *isn't*—should stay the hell out of the way.

I TOOK AN AFTERNOON plane down to L.A. and did a lot of thinking and looking out the window: snowy clear-cuts in Oregon's Cascades, ugly and depressing. The white-peaked, un-logged Sierras, gorgeous and inspiring. Shiny Reno. Beautiful blue Lake Tahoe. The flat, wide fertility of the San Joaquin Valley. The rugged, scrub-covered Sierra Madre Mountains just north of the L.A. Basin full of smog. The Sierra Madre's stark crags intrigued me: peaceful yet forbidding. Diagonal ridges jutting into the sky—a geologist's dream. No roads or buildings. I yearned for the peace of that kind of place. A real retreat, with sunshine, a slight breeze, a rock to sit on, a canyon vista to contemplate—a place where the mind could float and wander and relax. I promised myself that once all this was over, I'd get back up into the mountains somewhere and let all the built-up tension drain out of me until I felt like a natural being again.

I wondered if that kind of feeling was anything like what the drowsy dying mind experienced. I hoped so, for K's sake (and Jolly's too, of course, retrospectively). And for my own sake, down the road. For all our sakes. When we all eventually "go to our rest" or "rest in peace," let's hope it is indeed restful and peaceful. Most of all, let's hope we're free to choose what we want when our time comes.

Would anyone actually prefer to suffer? No one who's ever seen the suffering and dying of a friend or a relative—even a pet—can honestly say they prefer suffering. And we have mercy on our dying pets. Why aren't we merciful toward people? What's wrong with mercy and dignity?

THE PLANE LANDED, I bought a box of See's chocolates for K, rented a car, and headed up the freeway. My now familiar routine. After dinner, which I'd arrived just in time for, Mom and I shifted into the living room to continue our conversation. Just as we settled in, Maria Luisa started crashing around in the kitchen, cleaning up the dinner dishes. The woman was fantastic with food, but she threw pots and pans around like a sport. Even Mom grimaced at all the clatter, and she was accustomed to it. When the mechanical noise of the dishwasher added to the cacophony migrating from the kitchen to the living room, Mom frowned and said, "I hate the Christmas . . . uh . . . *kitchen*." A typical verbal misstep for her, but it showed that despite her out-of-sync synapses, she still knew where she was trying to go, and could get there eventually.

We turned on the TV to drown out the kitchen clamor, and later, when things had quieted down, we chatted until bedtime. But first K said she had a surprise; she had something to show me in Jolly's bathroom. I'd noticed earlier, when I'd put my suitcase in his bedroom, that the whole area seemed a lot less cluttered than when I'd last stayed there, but I hadn't yet looked in the bathroom.

Into the bathroom we went, and—it was empty! Not a toothbrush or bandage or medicine bottle anywhere on the counter, which used to be elbow-deep with such things. K winked at me, opened a drawer, and pulled out a sturdy Ziploc bag crammed full of small metal implements. It turned out to contain twenty-eight pairs of scissors, nail clippers, and tweezers, from tiny to large, that K had gathered up from the drawers in Jolly's bathroom and dressing room.

This bag of paraphernalia was Mom's surprise, but the real surprise, to *my* eye, was the absence of all the medicine bottles. All the prescription bottles and all the other bottles, bags, cartons, and containers of medical supplies that had cluttered Jolly's bathroom counter for so long were gone. The drawers and cabinets were virtually empty, too. All I could think, as Mom smiled proudly at her organizational achievement, was *Thank goodness I already snagged and hid the stuff she's going to need!*

SUNDAY, MAY 2

I asked Mom if she'd prefer to go out to dinner for a change, instead of eating at home. She suddenly got very still and thoughtful. "No," she said in a small voice. This seemed odd, but I chalked it up to her general reluctance to leave the house. Then she told me the real reason: She'd become extremely fearful about losing control of her bladder and wetting her pants in public, which had happened recently at her dentist's office. She'd been mortified, of course, and was terrified it might happen again. One more humiliation she had to endure.

Then she said, perhaps because we were already on the subject of her decline, "The problem is, I'm losing my language. I can't find the words for anything anymore."

I did my best to reassure her, again, that I understood her quite well, and she seemed relieved. But I was keenly aware of her verbal deterioration rate, and of my need to keep my ears well tuned. A sharp turn for the worse in her verbal skills could signal an imminent decline in her other abilities and compel us to put The Plan into action sooner.

Her verbal troubles were a terrible irony, given her previous superb ability with—and love for—language. In addition to her success in a highly intellectual and verbal profession, she'd been a superb crossword-puzzle player, a fine and serious poet, and a voracious reader. And now, none of that.

At bedtime we talked again about the mechanics of her pill taking. How many pills could she take per swallow? Two? Three? More? We used her regular evening pills for another practice session. Vitamins C and E together. Ambien and calcium together. Iron supplement, multivitamin, and Aricept together. A bit of coughing after that last one. Maybe three pills were too many, or maybe it was too much water, or trying too hard, but she recovered quickly and said she was okay. It was better to get used to this now, to practice and plan so that things would go smoothly when they needed to.

K enjoyed these trial runs because they gave her a sense of accomplishment. She liked being able to prove she could still learn new things. And in this case, she knew she was working to attain her profoundly desired goals: freedom and peace.

MONDAY, MAY 3

Today's big adventure for K: a trip to the dentist for one in a series of tooth-reconstruction sessions—a couple of misbehaving molars slowly being restored to proper chompers.

When we got to the dentist's building, we found that the only parking space near the entrance was inaccessible. The usual thoughtless idiots had parked over the lines on either side, so our car wouldn't fit. The nearest space I could find was at the far end of the lot. As Mom and I hiked toward the entrance, she seemed particularly unsteady on her feet, wobbling along, wielding her cane awkwardly. She used to be very physically coordinated—played tennis, was a great driver—but now she couldn't figure out how to use a cane. She just couldn't grasp the right rhythm. I was constantly afraid that she'd trip over the damn thing and seriously hurt herself, and the world did *not* need another elderly lady with a broken hip.

Once we got up to the dentist's office, though, everything improved. They all knew K quite well, and she was pleased by their warm welcome. Before we settled into the waiting area, K thought to check on the length of her appointment. She wanted to make sure she'd be okay bladder-wise, since this was the site of her earlier accident and she was determined that it would never happen again.

As we walked down the hall for a preventive visit to the ladies' room, K said: "This is why I know it's time for me to leave." She'd gotten used to making these sorts of comments to me in passing, pointing out the indignities and embarrassments that made her so unhappy to be alive. Her comments helped me to better understand the depth and breadth of what she was enduring, and they also helped reassure me of her unflagging desire to go through with The Plan.

When we returned to the dentist's office, they were ready to start on K, so she went off to the big chair while I caught up on my magazine reading. A *Newsweek* and *Sports Illustrated* later, K emerged, and the secretary scheduled her for the follow-up appointments to complete her ongoing tooth-rebuilding project. On the drive home, we discussed how these dental visits weren't all that necessary now, given The Plan, but canceling them might have tipped our hand, and we didn't want that. So we joked about K's finally getting her teeth rebuilt—just in time to "bite the dust."

THURSDAY, MAY 6

I had returned to Seattle physically, but my mind and heart were still in L.A. When I called K in the afternoon, she wanted to talk about The Plan. "I'm prepared to do some playacting," she reminded me.

And I reminded her that it wouldn't be necessary. What a ham! She *wanted* to perform. I teased her lightly about getting a late start on her acting career, and she laughed.

As I rang off I said, "I love you," and she said, "I love you too, and I think we're gonna make this." My mind automatically filled in the missing word "work" at the end of her sentence, and I told her I agreed.

It always took me a few minutes to "come down" after talking on the phone with K, especially when I called her from my office. My mind had to work so differently when we talked—following different cues and taking different channels to make proper sense of what she said. I was determined to understand everything she told me and not get anything wrong. I wanted to do whatever I could for K in the time she had left, and the one thing I knew she wanted—more than anything else—was simply to be understood, to feel that she wasn't a mental invalid. So I worked extremely hard whenever we talked, but it was well worth it.

MOTHER'S DAY

I had to settle for a telephone chat with Mom on this, her last Mother's Day, because of the Anne situation. But I did send her a huge bouquet of flowers that she loved. And apparently Anne was behaving herself; K said all was well. I hoped it would stay that way.

I still wished I could be there, of course, but I consoled myself with the knowledge that Mother's Day happened, in a manner of speaking, every time I went to L.A. So I figured I could miss this one and survive.

I also consoled myself with the memory of K's all-time-favorite Mother's Day cartoon, from a *New Yorker* years ago. It was a great example of K's sense of humor: A single panel shows two elderly female alligators taking tea in the parlor, one of them dressed in pearls and a flowered hat, the other one wearing a shawl and sporting pince-nez, saying, "Whenever Mother's Day rolls around, I regret having eaten my young."

MONDAY, MAY 10

Mom reassured me over the phone that all was well between her and Anne. But then she said, "Over the last couple of weeks, I can tell I'm becoming a non-creature."

That's a tough thing to hear your mother say. I ferreted out that she'd continued having difficulty operating the TV's remote control. On the plus side, though, Anne had taped large-print instructions onto the remote, and they seemed to help.

I called Cousin Dave to talk about K's decline. We discussed having more visitors for K, and perhaps asking Carol to move into the house. Dave also suggested that Maria Luisa check on K every half hour. I said that sounded like a good idea—for times when no one was visiting.

But the problem was obvious: Round-the-clock attention? Spot-checks? I wanted K to have all the help and companionship she could possibly desire, but at the same time, these impositions on her privacy could get in the way of The Plan.

Ordinarily I would have told K about these potential complications, but not anymore. She'd already made her decision, and she needed me to protect her from the confusion she now felt whenever she had to face options and complexities. She trusted me to keep her posted on the important things and protect her from the rest. It was an immense responsibility, and it felt like a scratchy second skin. It never left me, and I never forgot it was there.

MY ANXIETY GREW EVERY DAY. The anticipation of what I was going to be doing with K was intense and incessant. I felt as if I was constantly scrambling and probing, trying to predetermine any potential problems or barriers to The Plan's successful implementation—and at the same time trying to appear relaxed and calm, as if nothing in particular was going on behind my eyes, where a hundred scouts were searching, tracking, planning. This high-level concentration required tremendous, almost physical effort. After a while it started to hurt—my shoulders, my neck. Of course, my head and my heart had been aching for months in ways I'd never imagined possible.

As Mark Sandman, of the aptly named musical group Morphine, once wrote and sang: "Someday, there'll be a cure for pain. That's the day I throw my drugs away." Well, I had a houseful of drugs, including the attractively bottled liquid kind that's sold publicly on almost every corner, but the truth is that *none* of it can keep the pain away. Pain is powerful, and it only grows stronger when you're weakened by drugs or booze—and then it kicks your ass twice as hard. The only way to get past pain is to go into it and then through it.

But waiting to go through it was excruciating, as I knew how painful it would be to say goodbye to Mom and watch her go. The event itself would probably be much the same as it had been with Jolly—I'd have a concentrated practical focus, with specific tasks occupying my mind, leaving little room for self-reflection. Doing the job would be its own distraction, but the waiting was a torment.

I knew that afterward, I'd feel intensely bereaved. But I also knew—as strange as it was to think it—that I would feel relieved, mostly because Mom's agony would have ended.

Until then, though, I lived in a painful fog, with that rough second skin constantly scratching me. I rode the exercycle to blow off my pent-up steam, because if I didn't work out, the stress might overtake me. And I couldn't let it; I had to stay on top of it. I had to stay on top of so many things. So much to do; so much to hide.

THURSDAY, MAY 13

I didn't like Mom's latest news: She said she couldn't follow the information Dave had given her about some financial matter, and she worried that she was losing her grip faster than expected. I reminded her that arithmetic had been her first cognitive function to disappear, so this wasn't something new to worry about. But she did worry, and I did too, although I didn't say so.

Other news: Mom said she now had good feelings toward Anne. They must have gotten something accomplished during Anne's Mother's Day visit. What a relief! Maybe now Mom could relax and enjoy herself a little, and could feel free to go forward with The Plan before her condition got too bad.

Which might be soon. She said she'd wanted to call me earlier but had run into trouble. "I can't work the telephone," she said.

I'd been dreading that statement. My stress level instantly shot way up.

And then, as if she were reading my mind, Mom asked, "When are we gonna do this business?"

Well. That's not putting too fine a point on it, is it?

"Soon," I said. "As soon as you want to."

"I'm so relieved," she sighed. "I'm ambivalent, like when things go well around here and I think what I might possibly do, but . . . I keep thinking about Mary and Annie, how much they need my help, but . . . "

I reassured her again that she had done everything a mother could reasonably be expected to do—and then some. Now was the time for her to think about her own needs, and for others to take care of themselves.

She said that sounded right.

SATURDAY, MAY 15

I arrived in a cool and gray L.A.—for a change. "Late-night and early-morning low clouds" is the standard L.A. weather report in late spring and early summer, particularly on the west side of the city. My favorite description came from a local radio DJ who once called it "cream of elephant soup" weather.

Perhaps because of the contrast, L.A.'s springtime floral display seemed particularly amazing, and I had to take Mom for a drive to look at all the overflowing gardens. She loved it—the stately magnolias with their fat, languid blossoms; the jacarandas with their delicate canopies and clusters of purple flowers; white roses so abundant in landscaped hedgerows that they looked like snow-drifts. Weather and greenery like Eden. Air quality and traffic like Hell. Good ol' L.A.

Despite the scenery, my stomach hurt. For the tenth day in a row. Hmm. At first I thought I had stomach flu, or perhaps a touch of food poisoning. I felt "off," but I pushed through it and ate a bunch of Tums and Pepto-Bismol. After about a week it seemed to subside, but then I started getting a different kind of pain—not the dull ache and queasiness of flu or food poisoning, but sharpish pangs, closer to my thorax.

Could I be getting an ulcer? Certainly, all the stress of planning and waiting and worrying about K was enough to knock over a rhi-noceros. And it was about to get even more intense.

As we drove past a particularly pretty garden, Mom said, out of nowhere, "Johnny, I've decided. I want to go. Let's do it soon."

Luckily, we were on a side street at the time. I pulled the car over to the curb and looked at her carefully. "Are you sure?" I asked. "Where did this come from?"

Calmly and steadily, she said, "I've been thinking about it more and more. My skills are going fast. Soon I won't be able to do any-thing. It's time."

We sat there in the car and talked, and I asked a lot of questions, but it all boiled down to this: She was ready. It was time. So we set a tentative date: the weekend of June 19.

Only a month away.

TUESDAY, MAY 18

I awoke with a jump as my plane touched down in Seattle. When I got outside, I could tell that it had obviously been a rare dry spring day; the air still felt warm, though the sun had just set. As I drove north from the airport, the downtown skyline looked black against the darkening gray-blue of the twilight sky. A long, thin splash of salmon sunset across the western horizon highlighted the other skyline, the dusky purple Olympic Mountain range, as it faded into the night. Seattle can be a beautiful place. But although I could see it, I couldn't feel it. When someone you love is in trouble, no place is beautiful.

I got home and parked my carcass in front of the TV with a glass of wine, trying to distract myself a little from everything that lay heavily on my mind. On a cop show I liked, a middle-aged detective displayed an intense yet quiet grief over his son's serious illness. A good actor; his focus on the simple things felt wrenchingly real. Then the late news reported a terrible car accident and showed the distraught father bawling over his dead family members and being restrained by the cops.

Okay, that's enough. I turned off the tube and walked away, but I didn't get far before I started sobbing so hard, I had to sit down on the floor.

In public, I have to play the role of the quiet man—calm and under control—when all I want to do is cry and howl and berate the world for its unfairness. If I knew where the list was, I'd sign up to fistfight with God.

SATURDAY, MAY 29

Another Alaska Airlines afternoon commute to L.A. By this point I should have known the flight crews by name. I did know the flight *numbers* by heart, which was pretty weird. All this traveling was getting tiresome, but arriving and seeing Mom was always wonderful.

After dinner and TV, I dug out photo albums from the early 1960s to look through with Mom, and she loved them. She always lit up when she saw images from the past: Christmases when her kids were small, beloved pets we hadn't thought of in ages, visits from her parents, candid shots of her pounding away at her old manual typewriter (whipping her PhD thesis into shape), our first VW Beetle, trips she and Jolly had taken to Europe. She could re-live the best parts of her life this way. Even though she had difficulty remembering some people's names, she recalled interesting stories about them as we flipped through the pages of the past. And I got tremendous joy from seeing her face brighten. I savored every moment. I wish I could have videotaped these sessions with her, but all the lights and hardware would have changed the feeling. I'll just have to remember really well.

SUNDAY, MAY 30

In the middle of the quiet afternoon, Mom and I sat together on the living room sofa, gabbing about whatever came to mind and enjoying each other's company. After a lull in the conversation, as we let our thoughts wander and just held hands, she looked up at me and said simply, "I'm getting worse."

"How can you tell?" I asked.

"I can just tell. It takes longer to find words. I lose the thread faster."

"I've noticed that," I said, "but I can still understand you."

She nodded thoughtfully and then said very calmly, "I'm ready. We need to talk about ska . . . juh . . . " She heaved a deep sigh and frowned, her shoulders tensed and hunched up. She was clearly trying extremely hard to push this thought from her brain to her mouth. I didn't jump in to help her this time, because I really didn't know where she was going. She kept pushing at it, her mouth twisting around the effort: " . . . ska . . . jelly . . . "

It hit me, and I blurted out, "Scheduling?"

"Yes!" she yelped. Her shoulders dropped and she sighed deeply again, and then she started to cry. I put my arms around her and held her while she recovered from the effort.

"You see?" she asked between sobs. Sadly, I did.

"I'm almost totally helpless! It's so frustrating!" she cried into my shoulder. "I'm just on the fringe of not being able to run the TV."

That wasn't good. "What about the phone?" I asked. "Do you think you can still use the phone, at least most of the time?"

"No," she snuffled, "I avoid it."

That *really* wasn't good. It was the second time she'd said she couldn't use the phone.

She sighed. "I wake up every day and I cry because I'm still alive."

That settled it. I knew she was truly ready.

We just sat there for a while, quiet, while she recuperated from her crying jag. Then she thanked me for my patience with her, which she did from time to time. I smiled and said, as I usually did, something like, "I'm just returning the favor, from when I was a kid. That's only fair, right?" She smiled and nodded her agreement. She seemed to have regained her composure now, so I felt I could try cheering her up by teasing her a little, which she usually loved. I leaned away from her dramatically, gave her an exaggerated scowl, and announced, "Actually, I've just changed my mind! This very second I've run completely out of patience with you, and if you don't shape up I'm going to throw you to the crocodiles!"

She laughed loud and long, and I started laughing too, just from seeing her so happy.

MONDAY, MAY 31

After breakfast I lingered at the kitchen table, engrossed in the newspaper. Mom toddled around, dealing with dishes and such. When I got up for another cup of coffee, I noticed that she was wearing only her sweatshirt, underpants, and moccasins again.

Hmm. I thought for a second, then said gently, "Mom, why don't you go put on a pair of pants or something? Don't want to catch a cold on your kneecaps, right?" She looked down and said, "Of course, of course," puzzled, as if her pants had somehow walked away on their own. She shuffled off to her room, and I wondered if she felt embarrassed—and if she was declining faster than we thought.

When she hadn't returned after ten minutes, I went to see what she was up to. I found her fully dressed, hunched over her desk, looking through a pile of papers.

"Hey there, whatcha doing?" I asked, and put my hand on her back and gave her a little pat—one of my reminder signals for her not to hunch over like a little old crab-lady, to straighten up and give her poor spine a sporting chance.

She straightened up, but looked at me with a quizzical expression and said she couldn't find a letter from Genevieve. I could tell that she was already getting anxious. She *had* to find that letter.

"Why? What was it about?" I asked.

She couldn't remember, nor could she remember when it had arrived or where in the world she might have put it. And her awareness of not knowing these details made her even *more* upset.

She began puffing and panting, almost hyperventilating, then started to cry. We sat down on the edge of her bed and I put my arm around her until she got it out of her system. A few nose-blows later, she looked at me and said, "I hate this."

"I know," I said. I kissed her cheek and hugged her, and we sat there listening to the breeze ramble through the ivy outside her bedroom windows. She decided to take a quick catnap to recover, and I said I'd check on her later, in time to get ready for our lunch date with Walter and Mickey Seltzer. She smiled at the reminder; she always looked forward to seeing them.

I took a long, hot shower, and when I returned to wake K, she was already up and dressed—very snazzy, too!—and ready to rumble. Her morning confusion and anxiety had passed. For now, at least. So off we went to join the Seltzers.

Despite the entertaining lunchtime surroundings (the restaurant had an Amazon rainforest theme) and the very best of companions, when the Seltzers and I detoured from general conversation to the inevitable reminiscing, the inescapable contrast between past and present stabbed at K and she started to cry. It was such a quiet whimper at first that it was hard to tell, but when I realized she was crying, I leaned over and put my arm around her shoulder, as did Mickey on her other side. K recovered after a few moments, called herself an idiot for "turning on the waterworks" in public, and apologized profusely. Of course, we all said it didn't matter, and it truly didn't. We all knew what the deal was. And K knew she was surrounded by loved ones. Loving ones.

After lunch, we said our goodbyes and made promises to get together and do it again soon. It hurt to lie—K and I knew this was the last time she'd see the Seltzers—but we had to keep up appearances, even though it felt rotten. I wish we could have told them the truth. If any close friends of mine wanted to have a "farewell lunch," I'd sure as hell want to know that that was what it was. Then I could be sure to talk about all the important things, and tell them what I wanted them to know before they died, like how much I loved them, how much I appreciated certain things they'd done for me, what a pleasure it was to have had certain adventures together. It would be so much better that way.

Of course, there are people who would rather not have a heavy or dramatic farewell. They'd prefer to have a fun time and let that be the final memory. Fine. Great! But to *want* to share the knowledge and not be able to—that just stinks.

On the drive home, as Mom and I talked about the pleasure of spending time with people we enjoyed and cared about, she got teary-eyed again. I suspected that she was thinking about never seeing the Seltzers again, but neither of us could bear to say it out loud.

When we got home, Mom said she thought she'd take another nap. I wasn't surprised. Whenever she left the house these days, it took a lot out of her. I felt like resting myself, after having been K's valet, chauffeur, bodyguard, therapist, and stage manager of her farewell-tour performance these past few hours. Not to mention the two martinis I'd had at lunch, in a vain attempt to keep up with Walter. I shouldn't have tried that—he was a charter member of the three-martini-lunch generation, and even though he was eighty-four years old, his liver could beat up my liver with one bile duct tied behind its back.

Instead of napping I sat on the patio, had a cup of coffee, and thought about how things were going. Mom was definitely losing physical and verbal skills, and her memory was eroding as well, but even so, she was still herself inside. That was the key. I wasn't too worried that she'd take a sudden turn for the worse and not know who I was or what was going on, but I did fear that she might get more fragile in general, more fearful, more indecisive. And that would worsen the quality of her life. It could also be problematic for The Plan, so I had to stay alert.

After a couple of hours, I looked in on K and found her awake and rummaging through that same pile of papers on her desk. She said she'd been thinking more about that letter from Genevieve she'd been so worried about earlier, and had decided that she'd only *dreamed* about getting it, hence her confusion at not finding it. This flash of insight reminded me that she was, after all, a scientist. And despite her increasing opacity, her core intellect remained strong.

That night after dinner, TV, and a friendly bowl of ice cream, we looked at more photo albums from the late '60s. I was determined to get through all the family albums with her, to relive good memories together and elicit a few smiles—which was easy with these pictures. Just the hair on some of those people! Groovy, man. Tendrils reaching into space. Don't never have to cut it, 'cause it stops by itself. Beards, beads, braids. Overalls, caftans, op-art miniskirts. We could almost smell the incense and patchouli oil.

The 1969 album contained photos from Jolly and K's twenty-fifth wedding anniversary party, which had also been a surprise party for K. People from all over the country had snuck into town— a long sneak for many of them, since we lived in Oklahoma City at the time. Everyone had come to the house in the afternoon, and when Mom got home from work . . . surprise! I was just a kid then, so I wasn't sure who many of the people in the pictures were. When I asked Mom, she searched the faces and chewed her lip. Then she sighed and said, "Maybe someday you and your sisters will find out who all these people are . . . I wasn't the perfect mother to organize all these the right way."

I knew what she was trying to say, but it was hogwash, so I teased her: "Well, I guess you blew it, didn't you? You really should have done better with these photo albums, because you certainly didn't have anything else to do with your time, did you? Like get your PhD and work full-time and raise three kids and run a household and act as the perfect hostess for a world-famous psychiatrist and university department chairman all at the same time. No, you just sat around, reading movie magazines and eating bonbons. Some mother *you* turned out to be! I want a refund!" I looked at her sideways, and she looked at me sideways, and then she curled her lip and snarled at me. So I snarled back. And then she bared her teeth and roared at me, and by this time we were both laughing so hard, we fell over on the sofa.

Tuesday, June 1

Mom and I were at the kitchen table, and she got up to go to the bathroom—and left the door open again.

When she returned, she fussed with the newspaper TV guide but couldn't find what she was looking for. She shook her head, looked at me sadly, and said, "There's not much left." Then she took the TV guide into the living room and set it next to the oversize remote control unit. Maybe she could figure it out later, when she tried again.

And sometimes she could, at least enough to find PBS or A&E. But sometimes she couldn't. And when no one was around to help, she'd just quit after a while and lie down to take a nap. And cry, and dream of when she could quit entirely.

Soon, Mom, soon.

WE HAD SCHEDULED THE PLAN for the weekend of June 19 and 20 because it fit in best with my semiregular visiting schedule. I didn't want it to look like I was making a special trip that weekend. And I'd learned that Norma planned to visit L.A. then, too, to see Mom and other friends. Mom had told me that Norma's presence in the house would make her feel more comfortable, and I was all for whatever helped K in this business—even if it did add to the logistical complexity. And once it was all over, I would definitely appreciate having someone comforting and supportive there for me. I wouldn't be able to tell Norma what I'd done, of course, but I would be able to cry on her shoulder and get a godmotherly hug.

And I would need it.

WEDNESDAY, JUNE 2

In the afternoon Mom shuffled into the kitchen, where I was having a snack, handed me some papers, and said, "I just found this in a pile of things and thought you might want to look at it." I glanced up and saw that it was a reprint of a magazine article, and then my heart and brain almost jumped out of my body as my eyes processed the title: "Suicide Made Easy: The Evil of 'Rational' Humaneness."

Yow! I certainly did want to read it. Or, more accurately, I wanted to *have* it so I could *hide* it! We didn't want that bold title lying around the house, announcing itself to people. It turned out to be a review of Derek Humphry's 1991 book *Final Exit*, and the first couple of paragraphs revealed the reviewer's bias: Humphry's book was "evil" and "should never have been written." *There's* an open mind and a compassionate heart.

From a handwritten note at the top of the first page, I could tell that Jolly had given the article to K. And I later discovered that Jolly had given her a copy of *Final Exit* as a Christmas present in 1991 (they *both* had a dark sense of humor), with the following inscription: "For K—At her request, From the Ghost of Christmas Future (Distant Future!)." I'm sure neither of them imagined the book would become so relevant in their *near* future.

SUNDAY, JUNE 6

The big news of the weekend, and another almost-a-coronary for me (which I got from K over the phone this time, since I was back in Seattle) was that Mary was leaving her husband. She planned to move in with K and expected to come to L.A. in about three weeks—around June 26. So now Mom said that she wanted to wait a while and hold off on The Plan.

I was already going bonkers from anticipatory anxiety, and now there was a classic eleventh-hour delay! And maybe worse: With Mary living at the house, carrying out The Plan might be impossible. At the very least it would be far more difficult, because there would be much less privacy. Where would Mary sleep? Would K ever be alone? What other new variables would I now have to take into account?

It seemed as though everything was starting to unravel, and I felt as helpless as I ever had since The Plan began. Give me a job, and I'll do it. Throw things in my way, and I'll go over, around, or through 'em somehow. But this was starting to drive me nuts!

K's rate of decline was increasing, along with my fear. Would she start slipping too fast? Would it become totally unrealistic for her to have "done it herself," should that question arise? Her half sentences were deteriorating into quarter sentences and word fragments, and she knew it. She also knew that that foreshadowed a likely drop in her other abilities.

Despite my hopes, I knew that her descent was like a paper airplane's: slowly and gently downward most of the time, sometimes with a sharp dip followed by a slight bump up, but always down, inescapably down.

THE WEEK OF JUNE 7

Things got awfully raggedy, as Norma liked to say. As I contemplated the seeming disintegration of The Plan, I felt as if all my work and worry had been for naught. But as the week wore on, I came to accept that there was no way to change the situation, so I just had to cope and find a more creative and productive way to deal with it.

Several times in the past few months, Mom had said that her decision to end her life was based in part on her desire to not be a burden on the family. Often people say that and mean a financial burden, but K knew she had sufficient money to live very well for however long—her desire was to avoid becoming an *emotional* burden. As a psychologist, she had studied families and group dynamics for decades, and she knew the real score—that the financial burden was what people talked about, but the emotional burden was the far more serious issue.

K was not being a martyr; she was looking after her own best interests. She was choosing to end her life because it had become horrible to her. There was no cure, no hope of improvement, for her synapses and bones and lungs. But her sense of self, her ego, remained healthy and strong, and she would not allow herself to devolve into a walking broccoli, a drooling, diapered, disoriented "non-creature"—to use her own new word.

I started having wildly vivid dreams. If dreams are indeed the subconscious mind's way of bringing up buried feelings to remind us to deal with them, it's surely no surprise that my dreams now were about fun and frolic, as if my mind knew it needed to free itself from its intense plan-and-work mode and go outside and play. Hear, hear!

I obeyed my subconscious and started taking walks and shooting hoops over at Green Lake, a nearby park. I also threw myself into yard work: whacking at the English ivy, blackberry brambles, and an overgrown tangle of laurel hedge in my backyard was good for working off frustration. And I found myself watering the garden a lot—much more than necessary. Why would that be? Then I realized it was a simple case of psychological displacement: While my conscious mind focused on planning K's death, my subconscious was yelling, *Keep things alive! Nurture, support, nourish, protect!* The frustrated part of my heart and mind that wanted a living and healthy K needed an outlet, and my garden was it.

As the week went on, I began to feel better about the Mary situation. I knew how much Mom would enjoy having Mary back in the fold, after the many years when she'd lived far away from the family. We were all relieved to know that Mary was finally safe from her abusive husband, but Mom probably felt like she was recovering lost treasure: The prodigal daughter was returning. When Mom and I looked through the photo albums, she'd say things like, "Look how pretty Mary is!" and, "Isn't this a great picture of her?" Mary would be a great treat for Mom, a sort of dessert, here at the end. And despite the stress and complication it added to my life, I looked forward to her return, too.

I had no doubt that K still wanted to go forward with The Plan. She brought it up and confirmed it almost every time we talked on the phone. A bit unnerving, since I never knew who might be in the room with her. I would caution her, and she would assure me that she had privacy. And she called me twice during the week, which meant that she had re-learned the phone system. For the moment.

So my sense that things in L.A. were spiraling out of control had eased somewhat. The Plan wasn't scuttled, just delayed and more complicated. Norma visited K and reported on K's verbal deterioration, as well as her increased respiratory distress—just going from one room to another now, K huffed and puffed from her emphysema. But Norma didn't feel that K was in critical trouble or in danger of hospitalization yet.

This reassurance helped The Plan strategically: If the outside world saw K as ill enough *physically*, her death wouldn't be a complete shock. But she also needed to be seen as well enough *mentally* to have done herself in, without assistance, if the question arose. And I'd seen her acting as if she could do a lot more than I knew she actually could.

Just think how much peace of mind both K and I would have had if she'd simply been able to tell her doctor what she wanted, and taken care of business that way. Then we could have been absolutely certain it would be done right. Failing to do it right was my biggest fear. Once, when we were talking about The Plan's details, Mom asked, "Do you think it will hurt?" The question jolted my heart. I reassured her that it was just like going to sleep—no pain at all. I hoped like hell I was right. I hoped what the experts said was true.

ONE EVENING, I MADE MYSELF get out of my house and bicycle around my woodsy Seattle neighborhood. It was a beautiful, balmy, postcard-perfect summer evening. As I pedaled past serene front yards—people gardening, kids playing, dogs and cats sniffing and scurrying around—I realized how disconnected I was from my own world. I was here, but I wasn't. I lived here, but I was dwelling elsewhere, dwelling on other actions, other times, other people.

The next morning, as I sat on my back porch with a hot mug of coffee and my two tabby cats and the unseasonably warm sunshine, I pondered how the day could be so delightful without my feeling any delight. Nothing at all light was going on inside my heart or my mind. I figured it would be months, or longer, before I could even begin recovering my ability to enjoy things. I certainly couldn't enjoy anything now. Anhedonia, the professionals call it: lack of enjoyment of life. How can you enjoy life when you know you're about to grapple with something incredibly painful and you don't know how it's going to turn out? It's always gnawing at your mind, and you feel each bite.

WEDNESDAY, JUNE 16
Norma had just returned from seeing K again, and called me to report that K had been very tearful during the visit and generally

miserable about her declining condition. Norma said she realized that K's decline was accelerating, and that she seemed more physically fragile, but that at least she was still managing her personal grooming and medications by herself. And although Norma had growing concerns about K's condition, she didn't sense any imminent drop-off into non compos mentis.

I knew that whenever Norma visited, Mom perked up. I'd seen it myself. And it made perfect sense—they'd been best friends for forty-five years. But if Mom felt so unhappy, even with Norma there, how bad must she have felt when Norma was gone? Or when I wasn't there?

Mom called me in the evening (Carol was helping her with the phone) and said that the Yamamotos—old family friends—wanted us to join them for dinner the following Sunday. I said that sounded good to me. Then she said that maybe dinner was supposed to be on Saturday night, not Sunday, she wasn't sure, and she started to get flustered. I suggested she check the big calendar in the other room, and Carol volunteered to go get it. Moments later, mystery solved: Dinner was Sunday, as K had thought. Thank goodness for Carol, who had bonded so quickly with K and become like a daughter to her—a local, calm, and supportive daughter.

That night I got an email from Mary. Her timetable for leaving her husband was speeding up; now she'd be traveling to L.A. that coming weekend. It occurred to me that her early arrival might actually be a good thing for The Plan. The sooner she got to L.A., the better the chances that K would be ready to follow through with The Plan on our revised target date: the Fourth of July. Independence Day.

SATURDAY, JUNE 19

SEA-TAC to LAX once again. When I arrived at the house, I was delighted to find Marsha Addis chatting with K and sunning by the pool. Marsha was like a little sister to K and had been a close friend of the family for more than thirty years.

I changed into my gym shorts and joined the ladies on the patio. Very relaxing. We sat around, basking and yakking, until we got hungry, then we got dressed and went to Guido's for dinner. Mom had liked their cannelloni when I'd taken her there before. These days, it was more than just her familiar favorite dish; it was easy for her to cut with a fork. That meant she wouldn't need someone to cut up her food for her—one of the many new humiliations and indignities she tried to avoid, especially in public.

After dinner, as we walked to the parking lot, K tripped and started to fall, but I was holding onto her arm, as usual, and was able to keep her upright. She recovered her balance and muttered, "Shit!" and then took a few deep breaths to get herself under control. Then she gave me one of her dark looks, angry and imploring; I knew what it meant. And I thought: *It won't be long now, Mom; don't worry.*

SUNDAY, JUNE 20

A gorgeous morning. I took my coffee onto the patio to enjoy the sunshine, and a little later Mom came out and joined me, which she usually didn't do. We watched a fat dragonfly making its rounds a few inches above the surface of the pool, and enjoyed the humming-birds' noisy competition at the feeder. Idyllic.

It was also a chance for us to talk openly. Maria Luisa had the day off, so we had no need to censor our conversation or worry about being overheard. Sadly, I knew that this would be our last portion of extended time alone together because Mary would be arriving later in the day. After that, the only time Mom and I would have to ourselves would be through luck or craft; nothing simple and natural, like now. But now was quiet and peaceful, and we enjoyed it while it lasted.

The day passed quickly. Mom stuck to her usual rigorous routine of puttering around at her desk, sorting the newspaper, and napping. And I stuck with my routine of rooting through the boxes in the garage, working out, and worrying about The Plan.

At one point in the late afternoon, I went to K's room to see if she was up from her nap and getting ready for our dinner with the Yamamotos. I found her sitting on the edge of her bed and, as I found her all too often recently, crying. I gave her a big hug and let her cry for a bit, then asked her what was wrong.

She said, "I've neglected so much . . . "

"What do you mean?" I asked.

"My feet . . . No! My *teeth* . . . The wastes I've made . . . It's overwhelming."

She started crying again, but then it passed and she gathered herself and blew her nose. "I don't know what I'm talking about."

"Oh, yes you do," I said. "You know *exactly* what you're talking about. You may not get every word just right, but I understand you. It's all coming to an end soon, and it's damn hard to think about it, and to reflect on your life and how things have gone."

She nodded and sniffled, and I tried to think of a way to lighten her mood. When in doubt, I knew I could appeal to her sense of practicality—and her macabre sense of humor. So I looked at her sideways and said, "This going bit by bit is rotten. Better to get hit by a damn bus, or just wake up dead one morning after a good night's sleep, right?"

She chuckled, then grinned at me and said, "We're gonna need some liquor."

I hooted at that, then checked the clock and said, "Well, it's time to get our fancy duds on and go have dinner."

She nodded and said, "Right!" She stood up shakily, shook a fist at the ceiling, and said, "Onward and upward." She shuffled, hunched over, past the closets toward her bathroom, stopped, got her balance, and stretched herself feebly into an almost upright posture. Then she bent right back into a hunchbacked position and shuffled into her bathroom.

Soon we were off to meet the Yamamotos at their favorite restaurant, and right in the middle of dinner, Mary appeared. She'd found the note I'd left at the house and had tracked us down in Santa Monica.

And so that weekend was a reunion with Mary, instead of a bon voyage for K. For much of the rest of my visit I helped Mary settle in, but Mom and I still managed to talk while Mary slept or ran errands. K said she thought that two weeks would be enough time for her to get Mary situated, so our new schedule held: the Fourth of July it would be.

MONDAY, JUNE 21

That evening, just before our friends Fionnula and Garrett were to arrive for dinner, I wandered back to Mom's room to see if she was dressed. She was just about ready, brushing her hair—but it wasn't going quite right. I offered to help, and tried brushing a few stray strands back from her forehead. She thanked me and eyed herself in the mirror for a moment. Then she shook her head and said, "I can't do it anymore. I go to brush my hair and I can't tell left from right." She rolled her eyes, threw up her hands, and said, "It's all shit."

I gave her a mock glare and growled, "Knock it off, you—company's coming."

She snorted at me, then grinned and carried on with her makeup.

Later that night, as K got ready for bed, she said, "I feel like I'm in a cage, like a bird." She'd used this image several times before to describe her situation to me. She often felt trapped in the house—she couldn't drive anymore, couldn't find her way around. For some Alzheimer's sufferers, life is like being in a cage, and for others it's like being in a box. If you're in the box, you can't see outside yourself—you don't know what's going on. That happens usually in the latter stages of the disease. The cage comes first and is much worse because you *can* see outside; you *do* know what's going on. You can see the rest of the world and the life you've had, but you can't get there. You can never go back there again. And you can see that everyone else is watching you as you disintegrate. A good description of a living hell.

Does that sound like something you'd want for yourself? Or your loved ones? Would you want your children to see you in that condition? Your grandchildren? Spouse? Siblings? Friends? Neighbors? Is that how you want to be remembered? Lots of people don't.

K sure as hell didn't. And she was going to do something about it.

TUESDAY, JUNE 22

Midmorning, Mom took Mary and me into her bedroom, where she had set out her jewelry box and a pile of papers on the bed. The papers were insurance appraisals of her nicer pieces of jewelry, and K took comfort in them because they gave her a solid record, in black-and-white, of what she possessed that was valuable. She couldn't remember for herself anymore. She didn't own anything too pricey—she had never been that kind of woman. A thrifty Scot, she; a practical lass. And Jolly had never been lavish that way.

"Look through here, you two," Mom said, pointing at her collection. "Think about what you might want. I did this with Annie recently, so now it's your turn."

"Gee, Mom," I said, "I don't think any of this stuff goes with my wardrobe."

Mary giggled and K scowled at me. "Knock it off," she said. "One of these days you'll find a special lady who deserves a special bauble, and here's your chance."

"Besides," Mary chimed in, "you can always just enjoy something as a memento of Mom."

"Okay, I guess that makes sense," I said.

So Mary and I rummaged politely through Mom's collection for a while, and it actually felt less strange than I thought it would.

In fact, it was fun to see things we could remember Mom wearing in the past: colorful beads and clunky steel designs from the 1960s and '70s; formal pearl ensembles she'd gotten in the '40s and '50s but still wore occasionally; holiday costume jewelry and other fun items; and older things that had been her mother's.

As we reminisced, Mom got a bit tearful and then cross with herself for losing control. She recovered and said, "Tears are so ugly. I hate an ugly face like that." Mary and I hugged her and said soothing things to distract her, but the connection was obvious: These were pieces of her past, each one a link to happy memories of good times, good friends, a good life. And she knew that she would never wear any of them out on the town again. Which reminded her that she had lost herself, lost the identity she had worked so hard to build. And she hated the crying because it represented a deeper loss of self—the loss of self-control—that was particularly painful for her.

Later, we sat outside on the patio, talking and warming K up in the sun. Mary said she believed Mom's doctors were mistaken—Mom couldn't have Alzheimer's because she was still too mentally agile and seemed to have trouble only with her speech. Mary felt informed about this topic because her soon-to-be-ex-husband also had aphasia. Then she said, "I'll demand an autopsy after you die because I just don't believe that Alzheimer's is what you have."

Well, both Mom and I spit out our soup, metaphorically speaking, and our eyes met across the table, almost literally—like in a cartoon.

"No! No!" Mom blurted. And I'm glad she said it, because it sure would have sounded strange coming from me. She practically shouted, "I don't want that! Nothing of the kind!"

Mary was startled. She'd been sailing along happily on a sea of fond filial feelings, and this broadside caught her completely by surprise. I weighed in with small talk, trying to soften the blow and make Mom's reaction seem not quite so extreme or . . . *memorable*.

"You know, Mary, some people don't like that sort of thing, and we have to respect their wishes in these matters." Mary rushed to assure Mom that she'd really only meant it as a figure of speech, that she certainly would respect Mom's wishes, that she hadn't meant to upset her, and on and on. Mary had always been a cooperative person; luckily, she stayed true to form.

This was a good example of the gauntlet I'd been running for months now—people making apparently innocuous comments that made my ventricles jump up and do the Watusi. And I had to control my emotions and keep a straight face whenever it happened—Mister Spock without the pointy ears. No wonder I'd become so well acquainted with the Jameson family's special poteen.

THAT EVENING, I HAD TO FLY back to Seattle. The plane took an unusually westerly route out of LAX, flying close to the Channel Islands before turning north over land again, giving me a rare view of the San Luis Obispo area and the Pacific Ocean beyond. Dark clouds in the middle distance framed the top of a deep red sunset burning on the horizon, as if a volcano were emerging from the sea out there—Hephaestus on a bender, not going gently into the good night. I signaled the flight attendant and requested a drink, in solidarity with that ancient craftsman. I felt awfully ancient myself.

I mulled over the situation in L.A. and felt my insides squirm. The Plan would be delayed only briefly, but . . . who knew what could happen? What if K decided that two weeks with Mary weren't enough? Then what? Another delay? How long? How many more trips to L.A. would I have to take, all the while planning this most intense of plans but keeping it on hold, smiling and strolling through another series of social interactions with friends and relatives? And what if the delay were extended? Would Mom change her mind, or, more accurately, would her mind change on its own—would she *lose* her mind, thanks to the Alzheimer's, and "forget" what The Plan was? Then she'd end up exactly as she dreaded, because at that point The Plan would be over. I couldn't assist someone who didn't want to be assisted, or who didn't understand what the assisting was for.

OVER THE NEXT FEW DAYS, Mom and I spoke on the phone frequently. She felt that Mary was settling in nicely, which gave Mom a pleasant sense of accomplishment. But it was getting even tougher for K to talk on the phone. She sometimes struggled so hard to express a thought that her speech completely bottlenecked. That frustrated her further and made it even more difficult for her to get her ideas across. I did my best to keep her moving smoothly toward whatever her main point seemed to be, but her ability to focus was deteriorating, too, and she knew it. Which was sad but simultaneously impressive: The scientist was still able to observe herself.

But K's focus problem exacerbated my main concern, which was whether her feelings about Mary would change the timetable again. So I asked her—several times, gingerly—if she was still okay with the existing schedule, and she always said, "Absolutely."

SUNDAY, JUNE 27

Jolly's official portrait was finally installed today in the foyer of the Louis Jolyon West Auditorium at UCLA's Neuropsychiatric Institute. Mary said that Mom wanted to wait until I came down the following weekend, so we could all go see it together. Mom probably anticipated logistical problems that I'd be able to help with, like finding a close enough parking space, wheeling her through the hospital (she couldn't walk long distances because of her emphysema), dealing with stairs, and who knows what else.

I looked forward to seeing the full-on institutional reverence package: a large wall with Jolly's name on it in big letters, and his portrait hanging there. I wondered if seeing all of that would make his death feel more real to me, because it still seemed like a dream.

Mom got on the phone, then asked Mary to go get something for her. After Mary left, Mom told me quietly that she wanted to talk to me alone the next morning, when Mary was out of the house. Uh-oh. That made me nervous again. Or rather, *more* nervous. I don't think I'd been *not* nervous for about eight months straight.

MONDAY, JUNE 28

Mom answered the phone on the first ring, and almost before I could finish asking how things were going with Mary, she said, "That's what I want to talk about."

My stomach flopped and my heart sank as I suspected the worst. Did she want to change the timetable again? What new ulcer-causing glitch had popped up for me?

"Mary and Carol have made everything sound so good," K said. "But I don't want to go on with this . . . I can go on a little longer, to help Mary, but . . . Johnny, I long, I *long*, to be gone."

I felt a strange twinge of relief. After all my sweat and worry, she *hadn't* been distracted from The Plan. But I thought I could sense something else in her voice, so I asked, "Mom, is there anything in particular that's going on to make you feel this way, or is it just more of the same?"

"The symptoms are getting worse," she said. "And I've got nothing to look forward to, no improvement. And I know you've been 'on call' and that's hard, and I don't want to go on, even another month."

Usually she wasn't anywhere near this focused or articulate, especially so early in the day. Ironically, she talked about her symptoms getting worse when she sounded better than she had in months. But the damn disease is like that. It lifts slightly from time to time, but for just a moment—like a malicious mist in a fairy tale, giving sporadic false hope even to those who know that this particular path is one way only.

K continued, "But I don't want to break Mary's . . . progress. She's doing such a wonderful job getting rid of . . . the husband and . . . what's going on in her life. I don't want to ruin that . . . "

Suddenly, I heard a commotion on K's end. Mary and Carol had returned early from the store. Damn! But K was cool as could be. She said hello to them and told them she was talking to me.

They shouted, "Hello, John!" across the kitchen and went about putting the groceries away.

Obviously, Mom couldn't do any more talking about the subject now, but there was still a lot to discuss, so I went ahead.

"Mom, I'll talk now and you can listen and chime in with yes or no or that sort of thing, so that you can have some privacy on that end of the phone, okay?"

"Right," she said.

"You're very clear. I understand what you're saying to me and what you want. Mary is going to be okay. She's sturdy and resilient. The main thing is that she's finally gotten out of her abusive marriage. And you're right, there has been a lot of stress on me, but I want you to know that I can handle it, I can handle anything in order to help you in the way we've talked about. So I appreciate that you know how this is affecting me, but my needs are pretty far down the list. At any rate, what we'll do is stay on our schedule, and in a little over a week I'll come back down for another visit, and that's when we'll take care of business, okay?"

"Okay."

"I know I've said this to you before, but I'll say it again because I want to make sure you hear it enough to really remember it and have it sink in. We will all be very sad and mourn for you when you die, but we *are* ready. Anne's husband will help her with her grief. You've done what you can for her, as we've discussed. And Mary will rely on her faith and probably say something like, 'God doesn't give you more than you can handle.' And I'll be there for both of them, of course, as much as they need me. And Norma and I will lean on each other."

I also told her what Mary had told me a few months before, about how she'd come to accept Mom's choice—clearly stated the previous Christmas Eve—to end her life not too long after Jolly died. And I reminded K that Mary was much stronger than Anne, in many ways.

"You're right about that," she said.

Then I told her how much I appreciated her awareness of the stress I'd been feeling from being "on call," especially recently, ever since we'd changed the schedule for The Plan. I explained that it was like what an athlete feels when he prepares for a race or a fight—and then the event gets postponed. All of the intense focus, the rhythm, the adrenaline, the momentum—it's all leading to a particular point in time. And then you're yanked out of that rhythm, out of your frame of reference, into a kind of limbo. It's extremely discombobulating.

"Oh, sure!" she said emphatically, to let me know how well she understood.

I said that when we'd changed the schedule of The Plan because of Mary's return, I had been worried at first, but I'd come to accept it because of the important chance it gave K and Mary to reconnect. I now thought the new schedule was a good balance between Mary's needs and K's needs. But the dwindling privacy in the house was becoming a serious problem, what with Mary now in residence and Maria Luisa's instructions from Cousin Dave to keep a closer watch on K. A surprise benefit of the new schedule, however, was that Maria Luisa would be away on vacation at the critical time. That meant we'd have a bit more privacy.

K said she understood.

It felt a little strange being on the phone with K and having a one-sided conversation about such an important topic. But at the same time, it seemed completely natural. And then I realized why: It was a perfect example of the one-way conversations common between two people in a close relationship—a son and his mom, good friends, a patient and a therapist. We were all of those.

I told her what I'd been thinking. "What do you make of all *that*?" I asked.

"I think you get a passing grade," she said slyly.

"Just passing, huh? Thanks a lot!" I said, laughing. "It must be strange for you, too, listening to all of these serious, deep, and meaningful things I'm talking about while Mary and Carol are rattling around you, clueless as to what's really going on."

I could almost see the smirk on her face when she replied, in a controlled, calm voice, giving nothing away, "Oh, yes, I think you're rather accurate on that issue."

I knew she had more to say to me, but she couldn't because of Mary and Carol, so I told her I'd call back later when she wasn't in the middle of Grand Central Station. She laughed and said that would be a great idea.

After we rang off, I sat and thought for a while about our conversation. How amazing to think that she'd been considering my stress about being "on call," given what loomed before her. Then it occurred to me that as hard as it was for me now, doing all the preparing and planning and waiting, and as hard as it would be for me to carry out The Plan in just a few days, the hardest part would be afterward. The Before challenged my emotional stamina, organizational skills, strategic thinking, and much more. But it all was happening in a world I knew. The After would challenge all of my skills and emotions. And it would happen in a completely different world, a world I'd never lived in before—a world without K. I wouldn't have her support, her understanding, her unconditional love—the ultimate foundation I'd always had.

I called back after dinner, and K sounded much less focused than she had in the morning. It was usually the other way around. What was going on? Further slipping? She was struggling hard to tell me something but couldn't seem to get her thoughts in order. She said, "What I need to get, I need to know what kind of pro . . . procession . . . how to do some things. I don't know how to . . . Maybe I can get the big . . . in the other room . . . "

"The calendar?" I asked.

"Yes! Let me go get it. Just a minute."

I have no idea how I figured out that one. I guess I'd really learned how to tune in to her jagged wavelength. On the other end of the phone, I could hear her moving around and fumbling with things as she left the kitchen table and shuffled into the dining room to get the big calendar. It generally lived on the dining room table, along with the infamous Rolodex and other such items— what remained of K's organizational world. As she shuffled back to the phone, struggling with the calendar's large pages, I could hear her muttering to herself about not having any privacy. She got back into her chair and picked up the phone.

She whispered, "I thought Maria Luisa was going somewhere, but she's going in and out and this and that! I don't know when she's coming and going . . . And there's other things I fret about . . . Mary . . . one thing to another . . . whammo! She may feel a bit like I did when Jolly died."

I did my best to sort through all that, and then I tried my luck. "Mom, that 'whammo' you just mentioned—is that how you think Mary's gonna feel when you die?"

"Yes!"

"Okay, but don't forget that a big part of the 'whammo' for you when Jolly died was due to your illness. Mary's awfully sturdy, you know. She'd have to be to put up with that husband of hers for all those years. She's not a weakling."

K seemed somewhat relieved. "I guess you're right," she said.

But before I could change the subject, she started up again, and I could hear the tension and frustration in her voice. "I'm fretting because I don't know who's gonna take care of things when I'm dead!"

I quickly reminded her that I would be there, taking care of just about everything, and that Mary and Norma would be around and Carol would help, as would Maria Luisa and Marsha Addis and all sorts of people. I promised her that everything—every single thing—would get taken care of. This seemed to reassure her.

"I guess there'll be some time in the evening when Maria Luisa isn't around," she said. "Have you thought about that?"

That was a good sign: She wasn't fretting anymore; she was scheming!

"Yes, I have thought about that," I said. "I have The Plan all figured out."

I could hear the sly grin in her voice when she asked, "Will you tell me? I won't give it away!"

"I know you won't give it away," I said. "You're still sharp."

"Thank you," she said, sounding oddly subdued. And I realized I was probably the only person who could say, "You're still sharp" to her and mean it, and she knew it. She knew I understood that underneath the layers of crud slowly damming up her mind, streams of clarity still flowed and could rise to the surface on occasion.

So I laid out The Plan for her: Norma was coming to L.A. on Saturday morning to take care of some family business, and afterward she'd come over to our house. I'd arrive that afternoon and get settled. Maybe we'd all go out to dinner if K felt up to it, or maybe we'd stay home instead and have an old-fashioned family evening, just a couple of moms and a couple of kids. She liked the sound of staying home. Me too.

Sunday morning, I continued, we'd have a leisurely breakfast, and sometime later on we'd go over to UCLA to look at Jolly's portrait. After that, we'd do whatever else K wanted to do—take a drive to Santa Monica to look at the ocean one last time, or maybe even go out to Genevieve's in Malibu.

She said, "Wait just a minute, Johnny. I'm trying to write this down and you're going too fast."

What? Oh, no! "Mom! Stop!" I yelped.

"What? What is it?" she asked, flustered.

"Stop writing! You can't write this stuff down! Someone might see it, and that could wreck The Plan!"

"Okay, okay," she said, and then I felt bad because I hadn't meant to scare her, but if someone saw this schedule she was making, it might seem awfully fishy. Especially if she'd titled it "My Last Day" or something.

"Mom, I'm sorry if I startled you. I promise I'll remind you about any part of The Plan, any detail that you want to know about, at any time, but there *can't* be anything on paper, okay? Will you trust me on this one?"

"Okay, I understand," she said, but she sounded disappointed.

K had always been the queen of organization, a list-maker supreme, and I had learned very well from her. But throughout the whole process of The Plan—all of the organizing and preparing, for both K and Jolly—I hadn't felt like I could make any lists or notes. Everything had to be kept locked away in my head. It was extremely difficult, but perhaps my affinity for Cold War–era spy novels, especially those written by John le Carré, had proven useful. They were, after all, helpful guides for mentally keeping track of minutely planned details. And it was K who'd first gotten me interested in those books. How appropriate.

I wondered how much she'd actually written down, and how I could get her to dispose of it securely. "Mom, what does it say, what you've written down?"

"It says, 'Saturday: Norma in AM, Johnny in PM. Sunday: UCLA and Jolly picture.'"

I felt like a complete jerk. "I'm sorry, Mom, that's okay; that's not a problem. I thought maybe you'd written down something that would give things away, but that's fine. I guess I'm just getting a little jumpy, worrying about last-minute problems and all that. I'm sure you understand."

"Yes indeed," she said. "I understand."

Whew! I *had* to get a better grip.

Returning to our discussion of the weekend schedule, I asked her, "On Sunday, do you want to go out to Gen's in the afternoon?"

"No," she said, "I just want to be at home. UCLA, Gen . . . I'm not sure. I just want to be at home. I want to be really sure about what's going on."

"I understand," I said. Trying to inspire confidence, I continued, "I'll review all of this with you again when I get there, and throughout the process. You'll know exactly what's going to happen at each step, and what's coming up, and we'll do whatever feels right to you at the time. Okay?"

She sighed with relief and said, "Okay. That's good. I'm glad to hear it."

"Okay!" I said. "Well then, what else have you been doing down there, besides giving me a heart attack?"

She chuckled and said, "Lots of things. We pulled a lot of junk out of my desk."

"Upstairs?" I asked.

"Yes," she said. "You know, I can't get it all done in time . . . You kids"—she gave a wry snort of a laugh—"you kids are gonna have to deal with all this crap."

I laughed too, because I knew exactly what she meant: all the boxes in the garage, all the papers in her studio and in Jolly's den, the thousands of books . . .

She said, "I wish I could be watching from behind . . . to see how things go afterward." She probably meant "watching from above" or "from behind the scenes." I could hear the longing in her voice, and could almost see her half smile and furrowed brow—her typical expression when she discussed bittersweet things.

"Everything will be fine, Mom. I promise."

"Talking is so hard," she said. "I'm so relieved it's gonna change. It's gonna be real easy . . . It's gonna be *different*, that's for sure! There's no question in my mind that this is best for the family. It's not because of the pain . . . I could stay in pain for years, and clean out the house . . . but, it'll be okay, my dear, it'll be like . . . a movie . . . the woman who died, her brother . . . who lived in England . . . "

"What movie was that?" I asked. "Can you remember the name of the movie?"

"No!" she insisted, "it was *real* . . . a daughter, Annie's age . . . " She was sputtering and puffing now, and I could tell that she remembered whatever it was but just couldn't get the information from her brain to her tongue. She kept pushing: "It was the . . . the father . . . the friend . . . *Maggie!*" she almost shouted. "I want to go out like Maggie!"

Of course! She was thinking of Maggie Field, her great friend. Maggie's daughter, Gwen, who was Anne's age, was a movie producer. Her son, Joe, was an attorney who lived in England. Hence the curlicued thought process that K had verbally stumbled through to find Maggie's name.

Maggie had died a few years earlier, after a long battle with emphysema that had left her dependent on a portable oxygen tank during the last months of her life. Even after aplastic anemia had joined the attack on her body, she always seemed to have an upbeat attitude and a smile on her face. But when she decided she was ready to quit fighting, she stopped taking all her medications.

Then she gathered her family around her and asked a few close friends to come and say goodbye, and they all toasted her with fine champagne. Then she went upstairs to her bedroom, got into bed, and turned off her oxygen tank. Soon after that, she slipped into a coma, and 36 hours later it was over. Mom admired Maggie's courage immensely.

"She was so gracious," Mom continued, "and I've been going around like a baby, going, 'Wah, wah!'"

"No, you haven't!" I objected.

"Well, that's how it started," she said. "Now it's 'Rowr! Rowr!'"

"That's right," I said. "That's the real you."

"Damn right!" she replied.

THE LAST WEEK

So there I was, sitting in my office in Seattle, trying to pretend that nothing particularly interesting or important was going on, but knowing that in a few days I'd be flying down to L.A., seeing my mother for the last time, and helping her end her life. Can you imagine what a lighthearted, carefree week it was?

This was really going to happen, and in just a few days. It occurred to me that with Jolly, I'd had only a handful of weeks of planning, but with Mom it had been more than six months. That's a long time to hold your breath and try to act natural.

By Wednesday, I already felt exhausted—emotionally and physically. Sleep was a mere theory, and what sleeplike states I did manage to achieve were hardly worth my time. But each day somehow turned into the next, and soon I was on another airplane heading south.

SATURDAY, JULY 3

Mary picked me up at the airport. This worried me slightly, since my regular pattern was to rent a car. I wondered if this change would look suspicious to Joe Friday. But then I figured that since Mary was newly returned to town and family-starved, so to speak, and since I was "only down for the holiday weekend," it shouldn't seem too suspicious. I guess I felt particularly nervous about everything on this trip.

Another difference: The See's candy shop at the airport, where I usually stopped and got Mom a box of chocolates, was closed. Damn! That felt wrong. Was this a bad omen? Why was everything so different? But then I realized that everything was as it should be, because this wasn't going to be a normal trip. It was going to be *very* different. So it was only natural—even appropriate—for things to be different at the airport, too. That's how I decided to look at it, anyway.

On the way back to the house, Mary and I stopped and picked up lasagna and salad at Maria's Italian Kitchen in Brentwood. Then we got back on Sunset, went over the freeway and up Glenroy Avenue, then up the infamous steep driveway, and I was home.

Mom and Norma were yakking at the kitchen table when Mary and I walked in the front door. I heard the familiar sound of those old kitchen chairs scooting back from the table across the linoleum, and then Mom and Norma were in the front hall, welling up to greet me, and my hands were full but that didn't matter, and then there was hugging and the mass movement of bodies and food bags into the kitchen, and then I was able to get my hands free and do some hugging of my own, and it was the warmest homecoming ever.

And then Mom whispered in my ear, "I am *so* ready."

DINNER GOT DISHED UP, and it was simply the warmest, most comfortable meal four people ever had—four people who'd known each other for forty-plus years, and who loved and cherished one another. And the rest of the evening was just us, sitting around and enjoying ourselves, talking and laughing and living well.

EIGHT

K's Last Day

ANOTHER BEAUTIFUL, SUNNY day in L.A., cloudless and warming up to about eighty degrees. Idyllic. Perfect Fourth of July picnic-and-fireworks weather. But a very different kind of Fourth of July celebration was scheduled for later, for just Mom and me.

Mom had her usual breakfast of Grape-Nuts and raisins, carefully putting just the right amount of each into her bowl with her special little measuring scoop. She carried her bowl slowly to the kitchen table, walking in her hunched-over way, looking like the High Priestess of Cereal cautiously transporting the Holy Relics of Grape-Nuts to the round white Formica Altar of Breakfast.

She ate her cereal, sorted the newspapers, and looked at the funnies while I drank my coffee and glanced at the headlines. We were alone in the kitchen. Mary was still sleeping and Norma was on the phone in the den. We looked at each other.

"Well," I said, "today's the day. Are you ready?"

"You bet," she said, sounding very serious.

It was Independence Day, and she was going to get free.

We put together a mental list of things to do, working backward from the private party that would end the evening. We decided to have dinner at home. Going out would be too stressful, given our preoccupation with what was to come. The only other thing K wanted to do was to visit UCLA and see Jolly's portrait at the NPI.

Norma emerged from the den and joined us at the kitchen table, and a little while later Mary wandered in for coffee. They both liked the idea of going to see Jolly's portrait, so we all got ready and set out on our pilgrimage at around noon.

Mom had gotten all dressed up. This was, after all, her last outing. She looked great.

I heaved the wheelchair into the trunk of the car and made sure we had all the other necessities, like Mom's Kleenex. Mary brought her camera to take pictures of Jolly's portrait, and I brought mine to take pictures of Mom on her last day. I felt sure there would be a good photo opportunity at some point.

Everything seemed to move a little more slowly than normal. Everything we did, even the drive from the house to UCLA, seemed surreal, slightly enhanced—as if we were somehow part of a 3-D film. Each detail resonated at an altered pitch. I'm sure these effects were produced largely by my tightly wound-up mind, but also because Westwood Village, next to UCLA, was almost deserted because of the holiday. Our little corner of crowded, busy L.A. was eerily quiet and still.

We got to the campus and parked. Mom climbed into the wheelchair, and off we rolled toward the hospital entrance nearest the auditorium, but it was locked. And there was nobody around.

What the hell? And then it hit me: Of course—the holiday. Only the main entrances would be open. That meant we'd have to go all the way back to the car, stow the wheelchair in the trunk, drive around to the far side of the hospital, park again, get the wheelchair out . . .

Unless . . . perhaps we could avoid reenacting the D-day landing on the other side of the hospital after all. I went around the corner to a staff entrance I vaguely remembered, hoping to flag someone down who'd let us in. Bingo! A couple of med techs walked by, and I asked them to open up. They seemed skeptical at first, but when they saw the rest of my gang they realized we weren't likely to vandalize the place.

We continued our expedition westward, toward the elevators. Down to floor C, around the corner to the right, then another right, then up a few stairs on the left, and there we were, at the entrance to the foyer of the Louis Jolyon West Auditorium. Which was locked. Damn! Now what? We had to get in to see this portrait, one way or another. There would be no return visit another day. K wanted to see this thing *now*, and I needed to make it happen. I could already sense her anxiety level rising, and it occurred to me that she might be anxious just about being here, in this place where she'd worked when she was healthy. Maybe she even feared that a former colleague might walk by and see her in her debilitated condition. Whatever the reason for her unease, I wanted to assuage it promptly.

Then I saw what I was looking for: a house phone. I picked it up, got the hospital operator, and told her we needed to get into the auditorium, and to please send a security guard over to unlock it for us.

A sturdy female guard with a seriously tough attitude arrived promptly. She demanded my ID, which I was happy to provide, especially since I had the same last name as the guy whose name and picture were on the wall of the foyer, which she could see as she opened the door and let us in. Then she seemed to soften a little, gave us the standard "Have a nice day," and swaggered off.

And there was Jolly, gazing out from his pictorial perch, his name festooning the wall in big, bold letters beside the portrait. Not too shabby. The four of us just stood there for a minute, taking it all in. Then Mary started snapping photos. Mom seemed satisfied but quiet. Maybe she was thinking, *Well, Jolly, you got a small measure of permanent fame here, to go along with your writings and such. And tonight, after all is said and done, I'll be seeing you again and I'll have my verbal skills back, so I can chew you out for dying first and making me go through all this crap! Grrrr!*

Mom relaxed once we got back outside, and the sunshine reminded me of my camera, so I asked the ladies to pose. They all looked great, dressed up and feeling good. I took lots of pictures of Mom to make sure I had plenty of good ones. Some scenes can't be re-shot.

We decided to take the scenic route home—a leisurely drive through the beautiful campus. It was a fine final promenade to honor K's career as a UCLA faculty member and dedicated academician.

Back home, we all got comfortable again—K headed to the nearest bathroom, I got into gym shorts and a T-shirt, Mary checked the answering machine for messages, and Norma made phone calls. I was about to hit the patio for a workout when I remembered the Women's World Cup soccer game on TV: USA versus Brazil!

My exuberant shouts in the living room eventually brought everyone in to see what was going on. Mom had actually become a fan in recent weeks, having watched other U.S. women's games on TV with me, and Norma and Mary were up for anything, so they all joined me in cheering for our national team on this most American of holidays.

The action fascinated K. She couldn't understand the strategy or the rules, of course, but she liked the pageantry and the fact that these were fantastic women athletes. And she understood the most important thing, the final score, which was USA 2, Brazil 0.

Then K took a nap while I worked out, and Mary told Norma the long version of her split from her husband. And then it was almost dinnertime. I got cleaned up and dressed and went to check on Mom. She was dressed and seated at her bedside desk, sifting through a pile of letters and papers. As I entered the room, she turned and smiled. When I sat down on the edge of her bed, she gestured at the desk and shrugged. "Well, Johnny, I guess I won't . . . don't . . . have to worry about this junk anymore."

"Nope, I guess you don't."

She sighed, glanced back at the desk and shook her head a little, then looked at me sideways, grinning slyly. "Are you ready?"

I had to laugh. "Hey, that's *my* line!"

Then she stood up, and so did I, and we had a good long hug.

"Oh, my Johnny," she said into my shoulder. I just held on, for dear life.

NOW IT'S TIME TO GET STARTED. I've figured out the timetable, working backward, and now is when K should take her first antinausea pill: Compazine, 10 milligrams. That plus dinner should settle her stomach and the rest of her G-I tract, so her system won't reject the serious stuff when it comes down the pike in a few hours.

She's intrigued by the baggie of pills I've taken out of a cabinet, and I hand it to her so she can see what's coming later. It's not so much in terms of actual volume—really just a handful. She fondles the baggie, feeling its weight, probably thinking how small it looks compared with the effect it will have. She looks at me and smiles.

"What's for dinner?" she asks.

"Leftovers from last night," I tell her. "We still have a ton of lasagna and salad, and I think I saw other goodies in the fridge. But don't forget, you shouldn't eat too much."

"I won't," she says, grinning and holding up the baggie. "Gotta save room for dessert."

That's the real K. She still has her best wits, unquestionably. We both chuckle as I put the baggie away, and we stroll out to the kitchen for K's last supper. I'm glad that I remembered to get a bottle of her favorite wine for tonight. She deserves nothing but the best. (And *this* time, I'll remember to open it.)

I'm not too worried that she'll overeat; she's usually a light eater. I just don't want the drugs to have too much competition or inter-ference. I'm stressed out enough as it is, hoping we have sufficient drugs to do the job. From what I've read, it looks like we do, but I'm not a doctor, so I don't know for sure. And I don't want K drinking too much wine at dinner, either. Can't have her nodding off before she can get all the pills down. No Jolly-type mistakes, please. Not this time, thank you very much.

DINNER IS DELIGHTFUL—the four of us sitting around the small round kitchen table that's been in the family since the Stone Age; classical music playing softly on the radio in the living room. Mary discovers a bag of red-white-and-blue paper napkins and dresses up the table, making things quite festive. Mom is having a wonderful time.

After dinner, we all repair to the living room and the comforts of sofas and soft lighting. Just like the night before, we talk and talk, reminiscing about the olden days and whatever comes to mind. It occurs to me to get out a photo album, and K and Norma hoot and howl over their fashions from the early 1960s. Just how did horn-rimmed glasses ever come to be considered stylish in the first place? Pictures of our old house and old friends stir up memories and inspire the retelling of stories from the Good Old Days.

All of a sudden, Mom says she wants to do something, so the rest of us stop talking and focus on her. She says she's thought about this for a while, and now is a good time, so . . . she slips the opal ring off her finger and hands it to Norma—who is shocked speechless.

"You'll get a lot more use out of this than I will now," says K. "I'm not going to many cocktail parties or operas anymore, so you take this along, and it'll be like I'm there too."

Norma is almost crying now, and she leans over and gives K a huge hug. Then she puts on the ring and K smiles her approval; Norma is just beside herself. Mom tries to tell Mary and me the story of how she got the ring, but she can't quite get the details, so Norma leaps in and regales us with the full story—how she and K were in Westwood Village one day for lunch and saw the ring in a jewelry store window, and K fell in love with it, so Norma schemed and worked on Jolly to buy it for her, and he eventually did.

And then I realize it's time. I give K the surreptitious raised eyebrow, and she yawns and stretches (getting in a little bit of acting at last!) and says she's had a big day and, on this good note, thinks it's time to hit the hay. We all get up and say our goodnights, Norma showering K with more hugs and kisses, and head off in various directions for our evening ablutions and bed.

Mom and I walk to her room together, as always, and then it occurs to me to make a bit of a show for Mary and Norma. I don't want their last memory of me that evening to be my walking off with K, in case Joe Friday ever asks, so I return to the kitchen and rattle around. Norma's brushing her teeth in the front-hall bathroom around the corner, so I drop in and chat with her awhile. I tell her how tired I am from all the working out and World Cup soccer in the afternoon, and how I'm going to crash as soon as I get upstairs, and we say our goodnights again. Mary happens to be in the kitchen, getting a glass of milk, when I come back through, so I give her the same story and then head upstairs. Except I go up only to turn off the lights, in case anyone looks, and then I sneak back downstairs, waiting carefully for Mary to go into her room first so she doesn't see me slip into Mom's room.

And there we are. Just Mom and me.

NINE

——

The Last Goodnight

WE GO INTO HER BATHROOM and I get the baggie of pills out of the cabinet. It's easy to set things up in here—it's well lit, and the countertop is long and relatively uncluttered. I open the baggie and start to separate the pills into different piles. Then it occurs to me that this might leave a discoverable residue on the counter. How can I avoid that? Maybe put the pills on separate pads of Kleenex, or . . . I've got it! I tell Mom I'll be right back, and I slip out to the kitchen and snag a small cereal bowl. That'll work.

I'm almost out of the kitchen when I realize I'll need more than one bowl, so I go back and grab another one and then stop. And think. Anything else? Can't be running out here too often—that'll add to my chances of being seen. Think. *She's used to taking her pills from one of those little condiment bowls, and it's right here in her pile of pill-taking things. Wait! Don't take this one; it might look odd if it's missing. But there are others, somewhere down here in these drawers . . . there! Got one. Okay. Now what else?* Can't think of anything, so I leave the kitchen and sneak undetected back down the hallway.

Mom is waiting patiently right where I left her, standing at her bathroom counter, looking at all the pills. Her dessert. I use the bowls to separate the pills into piles: Compazine here, morphine there, Seconal here, heptabarbital there, the last couple of Jolly's mystery pills over there, and the phenobarbital right here. I have an idea of what should be taken and how much and when, and this will help me keep track.

The first thing I do is give K another Compazine, to suppress nausea and reduce the possibility of her barfing up the other drugs she's about to ingest. Then I line up twenty of the phenobarb. She takes two at a time easily, and then she tries three at a time. No problem—she polishes off the pile by threes, like candy. Great! I add in one of the Seconal and one of the morphine, which she pops down with ease, then another small pile of the phenobarb and a couple of heptabarbital. She's gobbling these guys down like nothing, so I line her up with a series of little piles of pills and cross my fingers that she'll get enough of them down to do the job.

But after only a few minutes, she stops. What's happening?

"Are you okay, Mom?"

She nods and says, "I'm okay, but my back . . . " She gestures toward the shower. What's that about?

"Johnny, I need to sit down."

"Okay." I look around and wonder if the edge of the bathtub will work. Should I bring her desk chair in here?

K points behind me and says, "There's a . . . it's in the shower."

And then I remember: the portable waterproof chair. I quickly get it out of the shower and set it where she's been standing. She sits down and sighs with relief, then smiles at me and holds out her hand for the next batch of pills.

I'm so glad that it's only her back. I remember how Jolly slowed down so incredibly fast, and I was afraid that if Mom slowed down the same way, she'd never get enough of the drugs in her to be effective. But this semi-glitch is just situational fatigue—she simply isn't used to standing up for very long.

It's amazing. Here we are, sitting in her bathroom as she downs a bagful of pills with ease and style. She even calls my attention to how well she's doing—how she's taking several pills at once and not using too much water, just as we practiced. She's bragging!

She takes a few more pills and then stops again. She has a concerned look on her face, and I'm immediately worried. What could this be? Is she hitting the wall?

"I think I'd like some ice," she says.

Ice! Of course! She always puts an ice cube or two in her red plastic pill-taking cup. Once again I nip out to the kitchen, fill a large cup with ice—being careful not to make any noise (hard as hell to do when digging ice out of a plastic bucket in the freezer in the dark)—and then scurry back to K's room.

With her water properly chilled, she downs the pills with renewed enthusiasm, and it isn't long before I notice that she's almost halfway through the entire stash. I take a mental inventory and realize she hasn't had too much of the morphine yet, so I add a few more of those to the mix. I want to be careful with her morphine intake, though, because opiates can cause nausea and I don't want her to feel bad. And neither of us wants her to upchuck all her good work so far. Conversely, the barbiturates (Seconal, phenobarbital, and heptabarbital) are slightly nausea suppressing—which is why they've historically been people's drugs of choice for overdosing. What quaint and delightful knowledge to possess. I learned it from Jolly.

I've also done my homework on all these drugs since January, consulting the *Physician's Desk Reference* and occasionally talking to doctors I met on my plane trips. According to my research, the seven Seconal won't be nearly enough, and the phenobarbital and heptabarbital might be stale and less potent. But we have ninety-seven phenobarbs, and unless they've gone completely inert, I figure they'll still have an effect. I sure hope so.

K shows no signs of being affected by the drugs yet, and says she feels perfectly fine. Still, quite a few pharmaceuticals have gone down the hatch here, and I don't want to tempt fate, so I suggest that now would be a good time for her to get into bed. She strides into her bedroom, fluffs up her pillow, and climbs aboard, smiling contentedly.

It occurs to me that she might be more comfortable with the head of her bed tilted up a bit. She has an adjustable bed, after all, and she might as well take advantage of it. I hunt for the control mechanism and start to fiddle with it, but K insists she can do it herself, and so she does. She arranges it so that she's sitting almost straight up, and then she smirks at me and says, "So there!"

She's clearly quite pleased with herself, and all I can do is bow and say, "Brava!"

And now it's back to business.

To "set the scene" for our fall-back scenario, I pour her a glass of her favorite merlot. That way, it can look like the classic "booze and pills" situation—just in case.

I pour myself a glass of wine also, then lift it in her direction. "Here's to you."

"Here's to *you*," she says, returning the gesture.

"Okay, here's to *us*, and the success of The Plan."

"Absolutely!" she says, and clinks the rim of my glass with hers. We take a sip and smile at each other.

So here we are: K sitting propped up atop the covers of her bed, with me perched on the side of the bed to her right, keeping an eye on things. I almost feel like I can relax a little now, because we've made such smooth progress.

I notice that she's wearing one of her favorite outfits: a pink fleece sweatshirt, black nylon sport pants, and white tennis socks. Very comfortable around the house. And what all the fashionable angels are wearing this season.

"I guess this is it, then," she says.

"Yep," I say, "this is the last bit. How do you feel?"

"Fine. Not feeling anything yet. Let's keep going."

I'VE NEVER SEEN ANYONE SO BRAVE. She keeps taking pill after pill, sometimes stopping to catch her breath, and when she does, I suggest that she take a break from the pills and enjoy a sip of her wine. She smiles and we toast each other again, and occasionally we even giggle a little because, well, here we are, actually pulling it off. Finally! The Plan is really being accomplished. K is finally taking back control of her life by taking control of her death, living the way she wants to by dying the way she wants to, making her own choices once again—and for the last time.

WE'RE GETTING CLOSE TO the last of the pills, and just after one of her short pauses to catch her breath, she starts slowing down. It seems as if she's getting drunk—slurring her words a little, leaning forward to try to focus on my face, swaying back and forth slightly. Then she starts to speak more slowly and deliberately, and I can tell she's working hard to stay on track with her final task. I keep offering her pills and she keeps taking them, but more and more slowly, and then she stops and a look of wonder spreads across her face.

"How are you feeling?" I ask.

"Just . . . I'm fine . . . I'm . . . this is interesting . . . , " she says, peering around the room as if it were changing dimensions. I suspect she's starting to hallucinate from the morphine.

"What do you see?"

"It's all so . . . it's different," she says in a loopy voice. "I think I'm seeing double." And then, as if coming back into focus for a moment to reassure me, she says, "Not bad, actually . . . " Then she smiles the sweetest smile at me and says, "You're a good boy, Johnny."

"Oh, yeah!" I laugh. "I'm good. I'm great—as long as they don't throw me in the pokey for helping you with this!"

She laughs too and leans back against her pillows, smiles and sighs, and closes her eyes.

"This is good," she says. "This is good."

I give her a few moments to savor the trip she's clearly embarking upon, then ask, "How about having some more of this stuff?" I hold out my hand with another pair of pills.

She opens her eyes, leans forward, and looks at the pills. Then she looks up at me and back down at them and back up at me. "What are those for?"

"These are your pills," I say, very slowly and clearly. "These are the pills you're taking to go to sleep and not wake up, remember?"

"Oh, yes . . . , " she says distractedly. She takes the pills slowly from my hand and starts to put them in her mouth, but drops them on the bed instead. She starts to search for them, but she can't see well enough or think clearly enough to find them in the folds of the bedding.

"Don't bother," I say. "Here's some more." I quickly hand her another couple of pills that she slowly manages to get into her mouth. She reaches for her wine glass but has obviously lost most of her coordination, so I retrieve it for her and place it carefully in her right hand, making sure she has a good grip. She takes a sip of wine and swallows the pills, and then I hand her another pair and she takes them, too.

She stops and catches her breath again. Her eyes are starting to glaze and lock, and I know we're getting close to the last part. I reach over and take her left hand in my right hand and give it a gentle squeeze. "I love you."

"I love you, too," she says.

"How do you feel now?"

"Fuzzy!" she says brightly, smiling at me.

"I can imagine." I smile back at her. "Can you take any more of these?" I hold out my other hand, palm up, with two more pills in it.

"What are those?"

"They're your pills."

"Okay," she says, and reaches for them, but her hand goes way past mine; I have to intercept it and put the pills in it. She looks down at them, cocks her head, and asks, "What are these?"

"These are the pills you wanted. Can you take any more?"

"I don't know . . . what were we talking about?"

I look closely at her eyes and can see that she's far, far away. The pills are kicking in strong, and then some. This is it.

ALL IN ALL, SHE'D TAKEN seven Seconal, eighty phenobarbital, fifteen morphine, four of Jolly's mystery pills (probably methadone), ten heptabarbital, six Ambien, three Compazine, and a couple of glasses of good merlot. Surely she would get her wish. But still, deep down, I couldn't shake my fear that we might fail.

Mom looked around the room in a daze, and I remembered my grandma Harriet, K's mother, lying in bed in this very same room in 1976, taking morphine for her cancer pain. One day, she accidentally took a stronger dose than usual and started babbling about seeing purple camels caravanning along the top of the wall near the ceiling.

I wondered if Mom was seeing purple camels, too. I asked her, but all she could do was stare at me quizzically, as if I were a purple camel myself and had just asked her for directions to the Panama Canal. She was beyond talking now, so I decided to talk while she could still listen. I wanted her to slip into her final sleep with happy memories and pleasant thoughts at the forefront of her awareness.

"Mom, I love you. You are the most important person in my life. I'm honored that you wanted me to help you with this, and I'm glad I've been able to help. You are so brave. You are simply wonderful. You're such a great mom. You've been so great to me and to everyone. And you were a great psychologist and teacher and mentor to all those interns at the VA and the psychology students at UCLA and all the NPI people you worked with. Everyone loves you. You're the best."

She smiled and nodded as I kept saying every loving, positive thing I could think of. As I kept talking, her nodding slowed and her smile faded and her eyelids drooped and closed. Then her head leaned back gradually and rested on her pillow, and her right hand, which still held the wine glass, sank ever so slowly to her side without spilling a drop—and then she was asleep.

I sat there and just looked at her for a long time. Looking at the face of the woman who gave birth to me, taught me to walk and talk, raised me, encouraged my creative spirit, supported me when I felt low, praised me when I succeeded, treated me when I was sick, took me to hockey practice at 6:00 AM on Saturdays, scolded me when my grades slipped, beamed with pride when I graduated from high school and college and law school, consoled me when I cried about lost loves and kicked my butt when I complained about lost jobs (and then told me to get back out there and keep looking—in both areas), shared with me her love of gallows humor and spy novels and travel, and passed along her curiosity about the workings of the human heart and mind. She'd shared it all with me: her thoughts, her feelings, her life—and now she was sharing her death. I hope I gave her enough in return.

THEN THE WAITING BEGAN. She snored softly as I sat and watched. I thought to check the clock, which said 12:30 AM. I also thought to get some baseline information, so I took her pulse, which was about fifty beats per minute and surprisingly strong, and counted her respirations, which were about seven per minute. I'd learned somewhere that three or four respirations per minute signified a coma state (twelve is supposedly waking/normal), and I expected that the real slowdown would come soon. I thought about how fast she'd gone from okay to confused to asleep—only about ten minutes.

As I settled in to wait, I thought about what else I should do to make The Plan work. I had to set the scene for when she was discovered, even though the first person to "discover" her would be me. I had to think about what it should look like to others. I walked around the room and took it all in. She was sitting in bed with a wine glass in her right hand, a little wine still in it. I considered that. It seemed reasonable to remove it, as that would be a natural reaction upon "finding" her and doing the various things one would naturally do at such a time. Besides, I'd already noticed her arm twitching a little—she was probably just dreaming—and it occurred to me that if she happened to jerk her arm in just the wrong way, then I might get wine on my clothes, and that would *not* be good. So I took the glass from her hand and put it on her nightstand. But something still wasn't right, and I couldn't place it. What was it? What? Of course! She was sitting up! She never went to sleep like that. So I found the control switch and lowered the bed to the standard flat position. Okay. I took a step back and surveyed the scene. Much better.

Handling the pill bottles earlier, I'd thought about using latex gloves, but there weren't any around, so I'd improvised and used Kleenex when I held the bottles. Then, toward the end, I'd wiped the bottles clean and had K handle them so that her fingerprints would be the only ones on them if Joe Friday ever looked.

I stopped strategizing for a minute and sat down again next to Mom on the bed. She looked so peaceful, having her last nap. I held her hand and talked to her for a while, telling her what I was doing, how the scene looked, and how confident I was that everything would work out just as we'd planned. And I told her how much I'd miss having her around to plot and scheme with. She was getting off easy, I told her. She could just kick back and relax, but now I had to do everything. Thanks a lot! I knew she'd enjoy a little teasing, even now.

I looked at the clock and couldn't believe it was already 2:00 AM. I checked her pulse again, and it was still steady and strong at about fifty. Hmm. But her resps were down to about six per minute, so that was progress. Okay, what other work needed to be done?

I got up and looked around with an eye toward incriminating detail. A lot of used Kleenex had accumulated in the bathroom while I'd fiddled with the pills, so I decided to take out the trash. But then I realized that completely empty wastebaskets would look odd, so I left a few of the Kleenex and miscellaneous tidbits from the day's other, innocuous activities in the bathroom wastebasket and the one next to her nightstand, and took the rest out to the trash bins behind the garage.

A beautiful night. Clear and cool. I stood on the patio awhile, eyeing the stars and appreciating the stillness. So serene.

An owl hooting from across the canyon shook me out of my reverie. I returned to K's room, remembering to be careful with the sliding glass door—it had a hitch in it that squeaked loudly when forced, and I didn't want to wake Mary or Norma.

Mom was sleeping soundly and snoring softly, just as I'd left her, and I felt a sudden pang of disappointment. Odd. Why should I be feeling that? And then I understood: When I'd come back into the room and heard her breathing, it meant that she was still alive, and subconsciously I must have been hoping it would already be over and I wouldn't have to watch while it happened. No such luck. Back to work.

I put a little bottle containing a few of the remaining morphine pills on K's nightstand, so the scene would look like what it was: K choosing to end things for herself. That would be the easiest explanation, it seemed to me. But something didn't feel quite right. I thought about it for a few seconds until it hit me, and then I felt like a complete idiot: Any apparent overdose would automatically trigger a coroner's inquiry. (My legal research had found that nugget somewhere.) What the hell was I thinking? I must have been getting sleepy, and this was the wrong time for that! So I removed the bottle from her nightstand and set it aside. She had to look like she'd simply died in her sleep. If there were any questions later, I could tell of having found some pills next to her bed but having put them away so as not to upset the family, and then I could turn over that one bottle to Joe Friday. But I had to get rid of all the other leftover drugs.

I was about to flush them down the toilet when it occurred to me that if the police were serious about an investigation, they might test the waste system. Maybe I was giving Joe Friday more credit than he deserved, but why take chances? So I put all the leftovers in a baggie, went out the patio door again, and got in the car.

My plan was to throw the stuff into the brush on a hillside up the canyon, but then it occurred to me that driving *up* the hill in the middle of the night might seem odd, should there be any witnesses—an insomniac neighbor, perhaps—to my leaving the house. I had to look like I was doing something I could explain. So I drove *down* the hill and headed west on Sunset. Now where? I turned onto the freeway, and once I got up to speed I opened the passenger-side window and ejected the pills into the brush along the shoulder. Mission accomplished. If anyone ever asked about my excursion, I could say I'd had a late-night craving for doughnuts but my favorite place had turned out to not be open twenty-four hours, so I'd decided to forget it and come home. A bit lame, perhaps, but it was all I could think of at the time.

I got home after about twenty minutes and checked on Mom immediately. She didn't seem much different than when I'd left, but her resps were down to about five per minute. Her pulse was steady at about forty-five, but it seemed weaker than before. She was in a very deep sleep, still snoring softly, but she hadn't yet slipped into that recognizably deeper state. Obviously, she wasn't going to make like Jolly and zip out of town. This made me both more and less comfortable—more because I didn't feel I had to watch her constantly; less because I didn't know how long it would actually take for things to end. And that could become a problem.

I tried to ease my anxiety by talking to her. Which didn't seem that odd, really; it was like thinking out loud. I talked about the good times we'd had—many of them travel adventures, like the time we drove cross-country together when I was thirteen, and the time she came up to Seattle and we went to a classical music concert in a former dairy barn at the foot of the Olympic Mountains.

And now we were having our last adventure together. I told her about the strategic moves I'd just been making—the Kleenex in the trash and the "doughnut run"—and I filled her in on the stealth work I'd been doing in recent months, things I'd felt I couldn't tell her earlier because they were complicated and I hadn't wanted to over-load her synapses. I knew she'd understand everything just fine now.

I checked her vitals again. Her resps were down to about four, her pulse was down to about forty, and her snoring was a little deeper. But the clock was moving along—it was already after 3:00 AM, and I realized I wasn't going to get any sleep before I had to perform my morning theatrics for Mary and Norma. And Carol would probably come over right away. Swell. I'd have a houseful of wailing women. (*Hey, Mom, wait—I'll join you!*) No, it wouldn't be that way; it would be fine. But whatever happened, I knew I could handle it. Because I had to.

I knew that Norma would be strong, but K was her best friend— like a sister, really—and this would be extremely hard for her. On the other hand, Norma had been a surgical nurse in her early years, and I'd seen how composed she was after Jolly died. And her maternal instincts toward Mary and me would probably kick in and distract her. She'd want to be particularly helpful to Mary, I thought, but she'd comfort me too, of course. After all, she was my godmother. Carried me home from the hospital and all that. So I wasn't too worried about Norma. But Mary . . . I really didn't know.

It was getting close to 4:00 AM, and K looked about the same. But as I listened more closely, I could tell that she was starting to snore in that deeper, more meaningful way, making a rasping sound in the back of her throat as she inhaled, her mouth open and jaw slack. But the snoring was solid and regular, not weak or sporadic. She'd always been a tough bird, and now she was proving that she really hadn't been as frail as she'd seemed recently— a good example of why people who choose Self de-Termination are so concerned about "success": The human body is remarkably resilient.

Jolly, in contrast, had been a lot weaker than he'd seemed. It had taken him only a few minutes to die after he'd fallen asleep. But he'd been full of cancer and morphine, so he had a hefty head start.

I started thinking ahead and got worried again. What would happen if K had hit a plateau and couldn't get over the edge? What if she was still hanging on when morning came and Norma or Mary—whoever woke up first—walked in to say good morning? They wouldn't assume K was merely sleeping, because she would be in obvious respiratory distress. They'd call 911. Would the paramedics be able to revive her? Or the doctors at the hospital? And if so, what kind of state would she be in? Shit! This was *not* good.

Stay calm, John. Focus! Remember, she took enough drugs to knock off a water buffalo. This was only a slight glitch. Perhaps she'd had a bit too much to eat at dinner, and the drugs were just taking a little longer to act. And as they *did* act, they were slowing down her metabolism more and more, which was slowing down the absorption of the rest of the drugs. Slower and slower. Yeah, that's all it was—a self-slowing process. So there really wasn't a problem. *Just relax, it's okay. Everything's fine, slower and slower, everything's right on schedule, it's only a matter of time, slower and slower . . .*

223

I must have dozed off thinking about all that slowing and slowing, because all of a sudden I was wide awake and it was bright and sunny outside. It was morning! I started upright in my chair and looked over at Mom. No movement. Was I sure? Yes. Well. Finally, it was over. I took a deep breath and sat there contemplating how the next few hours would go. And then I heard something. Was that her snoring? Was I imagining it? I jumped up and went over to her, grabbed her hand, and felt her wrist for a pulse. I'd learned my lesson with Jolly. No more ear-to-chest listening for *this* puppy. I wasn't sure if I could feel her pulse, or if it was my own pounding heartbeat that I felt as I held her wrist. I waited. All was still. And then she snored again. It was true: She was still alive. Just barely, but she was. Very shallow breathing, very weak pulse, but they were there. Oh, man! Now what?

The first thing I needed to do was calm down. I forced myself to breathe deeply several times, to help me focus. *Okay. That's a little better. Now walk around the room. Okay. Breathe deep again. Okay. Now. Think. What are my options?*

Option one: Let it be. She's deeply into it. It can't be long now.

I don't think that's good enough. She's taken so long already, I have no good reason to believe that she won't keep going for quite a while. Which could open things up to outside scrutiny and possibly a ton of trouble for me. That's not what either of us wanted. What's option two?

Option two: Speed things up. Oh, no. Not that. What's option three?

Option three: . . . Shit! There isn't any option three.

There's no way to avoid it—I have to speed things up. Dammit! Well, if that's what I have to do, that's what I have to do. I'm in this thing because Mom needed me, and I said I'd make sure it worked. Okay. Now. How do I do it? I have to be careful not to do anything too obvious. Taking pills is one thing; someone can do that easily by herself. But external help—that can be obvious, and if they catch it . . . shit! Okay, I need to calm down. Think. How do I disguise my help? If there's a coroner's inquest, what will they look for, and what can I do that will be hard to detect? Ah, fuck it. The modern tools are all too good. Basically, I'm screwed if they look at this at all. The new technology can spot a dimple on a flea's ass. I just have to get past the level of what's obvious to the naked eye, and get K to the mortuary and cremated without anyone putting a magnifying glass to her.

So what do I do?

First thought: *Avoid anything that might leave bruising.*

Obvious first answer: *Use the pillow.*

Reality check: *Thinking time is over. It's time to do it.*

I take a deep breath and exhale, hard. Then I walk over to K's bed, get down on one knee next to her, and look into her face.

"Okay, Mom, I'm sorry things had to get to this point, and I know you are, too. I know you didn't want me to have to do this. And I sure as hell didn't want to have to do this. But you wanted The Plan to work, and I promised you that it would, and now I have to be true to my word. So . . . here goes."

I kiss her on the forehead and stroke the side of her face with my left hand. Then I remove her glasses, fold them, and set them on her nightstand. I'd forgotten and left them on her earlier. No one sleeps in glasses! I feel a small twinge of relief at catching another detail. Then I reach over and get the other pillow and place it gently over her face. Don't want to bruise anything, just need to restrict the already slow and shallow airflow until it stops providing enough oxygen for her to keep going. I fold the pillow slightly around the edges of her face and wait. She takes a breath. It's more labored, but clearly there. Then nothing. Then another breath. About fifteen seconds go by. Then another breath. I wonder how long this might take, but figure it can't be too much longer.

I'm wrong. The pillow seems to make no difference. Maybe the compression of time in a crisis makes it seem like it's taking forever, but the sun is now piercing through the bedroom blinds and morning is fully upon us. When will Norma and Mary wake up? What if they're already awake? What if they walk in?

How can I make this go faster? I pull up the pillow to have a look. Her mouth is open. Perhaps if I close it, that'll make a difference. So I curl the end of the pillow under her chin and press gently upward to close her mouth and keep it closed, and then I lay the pillow back down over her face and wait. I hear something, but I'm not sure what. There it is again. Is she still breathing? I look over and I can see her chest rise and fall. How can this be? Think! Of course—she must be breathing through her nose. I take the pillow away from her face and look at her again. She takes a raspy breath through her slightly re-opened mouth, and I notice that the pressure of the pillow has pushed her right eyelid open slightly; I can see some of the white of her eye exposed. Shit! I put my hand over her eye and coax the eyelid back down. It resists, but eventually it cooperates and stays closed.

Thanks a lot, Mom. I know you want to keep an eye on me to make sure I'm doing things right, but watching me work right now is just not helping! I can't resist a snort of laughter at the thought—a much needed tension release. Mom's macabre sense of humor is definitely haunting my chromosomes.

Still, this is far less than ideal. Dignity is a great goal, but getting there—as an amateur—is virtually impossible. If I do say so myself, if *I* can't do it, then I don't know who can. This is why the laws *have* to change. But philosophy has to wait for another time and place. I have to get this job done *now*.

So I do what I have to do.

I kiss her cheek and tell her I love her. And then I put the pillow back over her face and under her chin, push gently upward with my right hand to keep her mouth closed, and with my left hand, through the pillow, I gently pinch her nostrils together. I can't pinch hard because I know she bruises easily and I don't want to leave any telltale marks around her nose, but I have to finish this.

She gets in one or two more slight breaths before I exert just enough pressure to shut off her nasal airway. Her chest rises once or twice, reflexively trying to get air. Then a little shudder. Then stillness.

I wait. I do *not* want to have to start this over yet again, so I wait until I am certain that there is no movement of any kind, and that several minutes have gone by and it is all over. Then I slowly ease the pressure and take the pillow away from her face.

She looks up at me.

"Hi, Johnny!" she says.

AND THAT'S WHEN I really woke up.

I sat frozen for a second, my head still leaning against the high back of the chair I'd fallen asleep in, staring at the ceiling, wondering what the hell had just happened.

Holy shit! I jumped up and looked around to see where I was. Okay, Mom's room, that's right. *Mom!* I leaped over to the side of her bed. Was she . . . ? I looked and listened for breathing. Nothing. I felt for a pulse. Nothing. Her skin was cool, her fingernails bluish, cyanotic. Still no breathing or movement.

My own heart was pounding like crazy from the dream, the nightmare, the worst nightmare I could possibly have had under these circumstances. I wasn't sure I could trust my own senses anymore. I went into the bathroom, turned on the light, splashed water on my face, hit myself on the leg a couple of times, did ten quick push-ups. Okay. Now I felt pretty sure I was awake. I took several deep breaths, clearing my head and calming myself down. *All right. Now go double-check.*

I went back into K's bedroom and just looked. No movement, no breathing, no snoring. All quiet. I reached out and checked again for a pulse. None. Just cool skin. It was over. For real this time.

I sat down on the edge of her bed and looked at her. There were no surprises. No unexpected paroxysms. Just peace.

"Well, Mom," I said, "you did it. The Plan worked. Happy Independence Day. You're free."

I looked at her some more, and felt sad that I hadn't been awake and sitting with her when she died.

But I also felt glad. Glad that it was finally over for her. And for me, too—at least this part. I knew I still had a lot of hard work to do, but that would be later. For now I just wanted to sit quietly with her. She looked as if she were only napping and about to wake up, exactly as I had seen her so many times in recent months. But this time she wasn't going to wake up.

So there we were. Just Mom and me on a sunny morning in July, saying good morning and saying goodbye.

TEN

—·—

The Morning After, Again

THE EARLY MORNING LIGHT filtered through the vertical blinds of K's bedroom, casting a faint golden glow on the scene. I sat on the edge of the bed, looking at her and reflecting on how far we'd come, how much we'd done, what a wild ride it had been. Her joy and relief last night had been so obvious, so palpable, as she eagerly embraced her Self de-Termination. Clearly, she felt it was the right thing for her—her last adventure, her last psychology experiment. And finally she had peace. No more of the emotional pain she'd called "torture."

My own pain began to intensify, even though I knew K was better off now and I would get past my grief eventually. She'd still be alive in my memory and in others' memories, and in that way she'd still be part of our lives, as vibrant and verbal as ever.

But now I had to face the day and do another dog-and-pony show. One more time.

I started to leave the room, but something didn't feel quite right, so I stopped, looked around, looked at Mom, and thought for a second. Her glasses were still on! I'd taken them off only in my dream. So I went over and gently removed them, placing them on her nightstand.

It felt awkward to leave her without saying something—she always appreciated being kept informed—so I said, "I'll be back in a little while. I'm gonna go make coffee and get started on my chores. I'll probably even make a list, just like you taught me. And I'll bring Norma and Mary in to see you when they wake up. You can catch a few more winks." Mentioning winks reminded me of the glasses, so I added, "And don't you put those things back on, you hear me?" She didn't argue, which was a good sign.

I closed her bedroom door gently behind me and moved slowly down the long carpeted hallway, past the spiral staircase leading up to her studio, past the hall closets where she stored her mother's good china that we never used, past Jolly's bedroom where Mary now slept, past the large living room where so much had happened over the last twenty-nine years, past the dining room table covered with all of K's various papers and calendars and the infamous Rolodex, past the kitchen counters holding her basket for Doritos and her pillboxes and her special cup, until finally I arrived at the coffeemaker next to the sink.

I looked out the window at the fresh, clean morning, the early sun spreading long fingers of warmth across the foliage at the top of the canyon. It was all so peaceful and still.

The first hummingbird of the day swooped down to the feeder that hung just outside the glass, eyed me warily, then tucked into the red nectar with gusto. *Life goes on*, I thought. *The cycle of life is unchanged. But my life is changed. Forever changed. No more Mom.*

And that's when I lost it. Tears spilled down my cheeks into the sink and I started to sob, my movement scaring off the hummer. I didn't want to wake everybody up, so I lurched into the laundry room and closed the door behind me, grabbed a towel, and buried my face in it to muffle my howls. I leaned face-down on the washing machine, my head wrapped in the towel, letting it all out—the pain, the loneliness, the anxiety, the fear, the unknown future—all kicking me in the gut one after another until I had nothing left.

When the beating finally stopped, my head seemed to continue vibrating, like a thick metal bell that had been struck and had finished ringing but was still quivering. I slowly unwrapped myself from the towel and slumped to a seated position on the stepstool next to the laundry hamper. I huddled there, elbows on my knees, head down, just trying to breathe for a while and imagining Mom's reassuring voice saying, *It'll be okay, Johnny—you'll get through this*. And I realized that if I ever felt overwhelmed, I'd only have to think of her strength, her courage, her incredible grace in the face of all her challenges, and I'd have my role model. I'd be fine.

But first I had to put myself back together—find the couple hundred pieces I'd just broken into and get them reattached in something like the right configuration. Coffee would be a good place to start, so I dragged myself back into the kitchen and went through all the ingrained motions. While it brewed, I stood looking out the window again.

Another hummingbird flew up to the feeder and tanked up on the nectar, then just sat there looking around, pleased with himself, swaying a little on the tiny plastic perch. That gave me an idea. I got a couple of ice cubes, a glass, and the bottle of Jameson's and poured myself a long slug. I wasn't going to get drunk; I doubted that I even could. My adrenaline level was way too high. But maybe this would help start the insulation. Or at least take the edge off my jagged emotions. Whatever.

Emotion was for later . . . Much later. I'd had my emergency valve blow wide open a minute ago, but now it was over—for the moment. All that emotion, all those hard-to-control waves of it, had to be kept in check. Control was all-important again. I had a lot more work to do to make sure that everything went according to The Plan.

When the coffee was ready, I filled a mug (guess which one?) and drank it, sipping at the Jameson's, too, and thought about my next moves. *Norma first*, I thought, *then Mary*. Norma would be okay; she wouldn't fall apart. Then she could help me with Mary, who just might.

My main concern, of course, was Dr. Davis. What would he do? I wasn't ready to face that question yet. I needed more time to regain my composure. Everything could wait just a little longer.

I took my coffee and whiskey outside and sat in the still of the morning, watching the sunshine stroll slowly down the canyon, and rested my mind, letting it float for a minute. I wondered if any meandering mule deer were breakfasting on the bushes up the hill, but I had no real urge to get up and look. I wanted only to be still and gather myself for all that was about to happen. The amazing athletics of two competing hummingbirds caught my eye and made me smile. A diligent dragonfly patrolled the pool. I closed my eyes and leaned my head back on the deck chair. This was good. The Jameson's had begun to steer me toward a lighter frame of mind.

When I opened my eyes, sunshine had reached the top of the plumbago hedge at the far edge of the roof, so I decided I'd better get going and break the news to Norma. I drained the glass and then the mug, took a deep breath, looked around at the last bit of early-morning peacefulness, and went inside.

I knocked softly on the den door and pushed it open. Norma rolled over, yawned, and said brightly, "Hi, honey!" Even at the crack of dawn, Norma was always upbeat. I don't know how she did it, but it was a true gift. And I was grateful; I knew I'd need all the positive energy I could get today.

"Good morning, Norma," I said, and although I thought my tone was neutral, I guess it wasn't, because she immediately asked, "Is everything okay?"

She sat up in bed, suddenly alert, as I walked over and sat down next to her, sighed, and said, "K passed away in the night."

"What!" she gasped, grabbing my shoulder and searching my face, as if she were trying to decide if I was a dream or real.

I continued, "I woke up a little while ago and couldn't get back to sleep, so I came downstairs and made coffee. For some reason, I decided to check on her, and she wasn't breathing; then I double-checked and she was cold." I shook my head. "She's gone."

Norma hugged me fiercely and moaned, "Oh, Johnny . . . oh, Johnny," and we held each other for a minute. Then she got up, grabbed her robe, and threw it on. "I want to see her," she said, suddenly all business, marshaling her old nurse's experience and getting her self-defense mechanisms up and running. We walked to Mom's room together, but just before going inside we stopped and I gave Norma a hug, knowing she'd need one.

Everything was just as I had left it, only a little brighter because the sun had risen higher. I hung back while Norma strode over to

K's bed, sat down, and took Mom's hand and held it. She leaned down close and said a few soft words that I didn't hear, and then she just looked at K and cried. I waited a minute, then went over and sat down on the other side of the bed. Norma looked at me with moist red eyes and said, "She's better off."

"I know."

We sat in silence awhile.

"I just can't believe it," Norma said. "She's really gone."

"Yeah."

"It's really better for her," Norma said. "She was *so* unhappy, *so* miserable with the way she'd gotten. But oh! I'll miss her *so* much!" And she started to cry again.

"Me too." I reached over and put my arm around Norma's shoulders. After a minute, she sighed and straightened up.

"Have you told Mary yet?" she asked.

"No," I said, "I wanted to tell you first and let you get your breath. Then I thought we'd tell her together."

Norma leaned over, hugged K, and said, "Everything's going to be fine now, dearheart—you wait and see."

I stood up, and Norma got up, too, and we left the room, holding on to each other to keep our balance. We went to the kitchen, had coffee, and let the situation sink in.

"Should we wait until Mary wakes up," I asked, "or should we wake her up now?"

"I think we should let her sleep awhile. It's going to be a rough day, and she'll need her energy."

"You're right, that sounds good," I said. Then it hit me: "I'm sorry I didn't let you sleep in, too."

She shook her head and said, "No, no. You did the right thing. I get up about this time anyway." She reached over and squeezed my hand. "K wouldn't have wanted you awake and all by yourself right now, so it's a good thing you woke me up, or she would have been really aggravated." We both tried to smile.

Norma said, "Okay, I'm going to get out of this robe and into my clothes, put my face on, and then we'll start doing what we need to do." She stood up and went back to the den.

I fetched the Rolodex from the dining room table, and when Norma reappeared we started making a list of people to call.

Then we heard Mary emerge from her bedroom, and I realized that Norma and I hadn't talked about how to break the news to her. I took a deep breath and stood up. Norma swiveled her chair around to face the doorway. Mary came in, still groggy with sleep. She smiled, murmured, "Good morning," and made a beeline for the coffeepot. I shot a questioning look at Norma and she shrugged, so I decided to jump right in. I walked over to Mary and hugged her, interrupting her search for a coffee mug and gently leading her over to the kitchen table.

I said, "Mary, we have some bad news."

"What is it?" she asked, suddenly wide awake. "Is it Mom? Is she all right?"

Norma sighed and reached out to Mary. I held on to Mary too, and told her what I'd told Norma, about how I'd found Mom that morning.

Mary stood still and listened. I hadn't known what her reaction would be, but the one reaction I didn't expect was what happened: She slowly disengaged herself from Norma and me, sat down and stared at the tabletop for a few long seconds, then looked up at us with a wan smile and said, "She's at peace now."

Then it all started to sink in and she began to cry, but soon she stopped and said she wanted to go see Mom.

"Do you want me or Norma to come with you?" I asked. She shook her head and left the kitchen.

"Well!" I said to Norma. "That was a lot better than I thought it would be."

"I'll say," she agreed.

After a few minutes Mary returned, poured herself a large mug of coffee, and headed back toward K's room. I called out to her and she said, "I just need a little more time alone with Mom," and kept going.

Norma and I made another run at the phone list, adding names and making notes about who would call whom. We knew that Mary would pitch in when she was ready, and when she rejoined us in the kitchen about half an hour later, she was indeed quite helpful.

Since the people we'd be calling would want to know about memorial service plans, I suggested that we aim for the following Sunday, July 11. Mary agreed, and Norma said it sounded sensible.

Norma went to the den and made her calls from there—her family first, and then the other people on her list. Mary went to her room to call Anne and the others on her list. And I stayed in the kitchen and prepared to make the most important call in this whole business: Dr. Davis. I paced and thought about how the conversation might go—what he might ask and how I should respond in order to get the result I wanted, needed, dreamed of. Finally, I took a few deep breaths and dialed his home number. His wife answered and went to get him, so I had another few seconds in which to try to breathe deeply and focus. Then he picked up the phone and I started my pitch.

He sounded surprised, but not overly so. And he was very sympathetic and solicitous, asking how Mary and I were holding up. He also asked how K had been feeling recently, and whether I had noticed her having any trouble. I told him that she'd been a little more huffy and puffy than usual, and a lot less energetic, but she got that way regularly, didn't she? Yes she did, he said. (I thought that playing up the emphysema angle would be the best strategy.) He asked a few more questions, but I never felt as if he was interrogating me, or that he had any heightened concern about the circumstances of K's death. When he asked if we'd made arrangements with a mortuary, I said I thought we'd use Hillside Mortuary again. Then, after what seemed like the longest pause, he said, "Well, have Hillside send me the papers when they're ready, and I'll take care of them."

That was it!

"Thank you, Dr. Davis," I said, as calmly as I could, suppressing my urge to shout with gratitude. "I appreciate your help. The whole family appreciates everything you've done for us." Then we said our goodbyes and rang off.

I could hardly believe it. What a relief! A warm sensation cascaded down the back of my neck, and I slumped into the nearest chair.

Dr. Davis wasn't concerned, which meant—once again—that there would be no coroner, no inquest, no investigation, and no Joe Friday!

I should have leapt for joy, but suddenly I felt too tired to even stand, too drained, almost numb. I could hardly move. I put my head down on the table and gathered my wits for a minute. That had been the last main hurdle, and I'd cleared it. The finish line was right in front of me, and unless something bizarre happened, I was finally done. There were still important matters to attend to, but they were only details and I knew I could manage them.

I found it hard to focus on making notification calls at this point, but there wasn't much else for me to do. I got up and poured myself another splash of Jameson's—to toast my clearing the Dr. Davis hurdle. (Toast for breakfast!) Then I sat back down and called Hillside to get that piece of business started. I also called Carol. She and K had become quite close in the short but intense time they'd spent together, and she was extremely upset and tearful at the news. I told her the mortuary people were coming to get K around noon, and asked if she wanted to come over and say goodbye to K "in person" beforehand. She said yes, very much. I asked her to bring her dog Daisy with her too, because we could use all the extra friendly faces we could get. She sniffed back her tears and managed a little laugh at that, and said they'd be right over.

I decided to take one last look around K's bedroom for any stray pills or anything else that might seem out of place or attract unwanted attention. Her room was lit brightly now by the mid-morning sunlight streaming through the patio windows.

"Nice day, huh?" I asked Mom as I entered the room and walked over to her bed. "I'll bet it's even nicer where you are now." I looked around again for anything that seemed off, but nothing did. Just in case, I bent down to check under the bed.

Ack! A pill! How the hell did that get there? I thought I'd looked everywhere and given the room the all-clear hours ago. This was not good. Where else might stray pills be lurking? I looked at Mom and said, "Sorry, old girl, but I've got to do one last bed check." I started rummaging through the sheets and blanket and bedspread, and around K's edges.

I kept up a running commentary as I went, letting her know where I was looking and how strange this felt, and telling her that I was sure she understood. Then I found another pill, in the bedding, tucked in by her right side.

"Hey! What do we have here?" I scolded. "Holding out on me, huh? Thanks a lot! You're still trying to give me a heart attack, aren't you?"

I'm sure it isn't all that odd for a dead person to have a pill or two floating around in the bed when the mortuary personnel arrive to collect the body, but I sure as hell didn't want that to happen here. Maybe an esoteric health code or mortuary-industry regulation would require them to catalog or retain whatever medications they found with the body, the same way they catalog personal effects, like jewelry and clothing. I'd promised K there would be no foul-ups, and I wasn't about to let any stray pills ruin The Plan.

I finished searching the bed, then went through the wastebaskets next to it and in the bathroom again. I found nothing else that could have registered on anyone's radar, and I pocketed the last two telltale pills. I'd throw them out later, somewhere safe.

Before leaving the room, I stood there for a moment—one last quiet moment alone with Mom. I thought about all that had happened here, all our plotting and scheming—and what we'd ultimately accomplished. It was finally over, our mission a success. I felt like a spy whose deep-cover assignment had just ended— nine months in the cold finally over, about to begin readjusting to life without tradecraft. *Thanks, Mom, for all those spy novels. And thank you, John le Carré. I do believe that Smiley himself smiled on this operation.*

I gave Mom a kiss on the cheek and headed back to the kitchen, but I just didn't have it in me to make any phone calls. As I headed toward the den to check on Norma, the front door opened and a yellow Lab came trotting into the front hall. I knelt down and gave Daisy a big hug and then stood up and gave Carol one, too. She was crying, but she recovered her equilibrium quickly. Then she and Daisy went off to find Mary.

I found and refilled my Jameson's glass and returned to phone duty. Cousin Dave almost jumped out of his socks when I told him the news. Then I called the Seltzers, Marsha Addis, the Yamamotos, and a few others.

The doorbell rang and I almost inhaled an ice cube. Who the hell could that be? It was two men from Hillside Mortuary. Already? It felt like I'd called them only a few minutes earlier, but in fact it had been a couple of hours.

As with Jolly, the removal procedure with K went smoothly and efficiently. When the Hillside men had secured the gurney inside their van, shut the doors, and gotten into the front seat, I stepped forward, thanked them for their help, and complimented them on doing such a professional job. They looked surprised. I guess they weren't used to people thinking about them or their work in positive terms at times like this.

As they drove off, I stood there at the top of the steep driveway—alone, contemplating, trying to compute the gravity of the past twenty-four hours. Very heavy. The July midday sun beat down on me like a broiler. No breeze. Everything quiet. But then I heard the next-door neighbors' young children squealing and laughing, playing in their backyard. It was summertime. Life goes on. What a strange dream it all seemed. K would have been able to write a beautiful poem about it, I'm sure.

The strafing run of a nectar-crazed hummingbird right past my head brought me out of my reverie, and I blinked my way back to awareness.

Mom was gone. That was it. It was done.

Now I had to face the people who remained: my sisters, relatives, family friends, K's colleagues. And I had to handle the work that remained: K's memorial service, the house, all the things *in* the house. And I had to learn how to live in this strange, empty new world.

MORE CALLS WERE MADE, people came, food happened, people left. I didn't feel very involved, although I was in the middle of it all. I was exhausted. Eventually it was bedtime, but before I crashed, I looked in on Mom's room. How weird it felt not having her there to say goodnight to.

I stepped outside for some fresh air. It was still warm from the day but cooling down quickly, the way it does along the West Coast. I looked up into the clear night sky. A few stars twinkled there. I smiled and said goodnight to the sky, and to K, who was surely looking down and smiling back.

ELEVEN

———

The Aftermath

I STAYED IN L.A. FOR QUITE A WHILE, dealing with estate matters and decelerating from the wild ride I'd been on for the past nine months. A few days after hosting K's memorial service, I finally had some pure peace and quiet, a completely empty house for a few hours. No sisters, no friends of the family, no out-of-town relatives. And that was when I finally let my guard down entirely and had a good, long, uninhibited cry. By the end of it, though, I found myself laughing. This ordeal hadn't been a tragedy, but a success story. Both Jolly and K had gotten exactly what they wanted. So I had to feel good.

But I still wrestled mentally with an assortment of loose ends that I feared might pose a threat to The Plan's official, final, and complete success. A good night's sleep eluded me. I had so much on my mind, so much that I felt I still had to do, so much to worry about. And I continued to find too much solace in the sauce. Not good.

Not much dignity for *me*, apparently. But this wasn't about me. It was about Jolly and K. It was about their personal autonomy, their wishes, their choice. They deserved to end their lives the way they saw fit. I just honored their wishes and did my part.

But what a *hard* part.

EVENTUALLY, THE ESTATE GOT SETTLED, and I returned to Seattle. For months I fooled myself into thinking that I had handled the stress of it all. I took time off work and told myself it was a vacation, a sabbatical, a well-earned break from the intensity of practicing law (and knocking off my parents). Then I started to write this book. And as I did, I found myself drinking an awful lot, and I finally realized why: Each time I sat down to write, I was thrown back in time—to holding K as she cried, to pushing on Jolly's leg . . . all of it. I didn't live through those events just once; I lived through them hundreds of times, in excruciatingly slow motion. But I had to do it—I had to write it all down so that people could see it, and perhaps feel it and know it, and maybe even be empowered by it, which had been K's fervent wish. I had to answer The Call.

I didn't feel that my obligation to K was finished yet. She and I had talked about my writing this book; it meant a lot to her. And the more I reflected on everything that had happened, the more I wanted to write it. Jolly and K were intelligent, creative, thoughtful, independent, self-determined people who took charge of their lives and made their own destinies—as much as anyone can. In this way, the story of their deaths reflects their character and their life goals, and is a much more fitting eulogy for them than what I was able to give at their respective memorial services.

As I continued to write, I realized I was depressed as hell. With a capital *D* this time, no question about it. All that hiding, all that repressing of emotion, had affected me far more deeply than I'd wanted to admit. But eventually I found my way into counseling, started a tough workout regimen, and finally got my snout back above the surface.

My psychologist helped me unearth and address the deep feelings of grief that I had put away when I'd needed to harden my heart and focus on the job at hand: assisting Jolly and K with their suicides. He also helped me navigate the peculiar tides and currents of those deeper, stranger, weirder thoughts and feelings that I had guessed might eventually emerge, back when K asked me about my mental state (after Jolly's death). I'd said I was fine, but had secretly wondered about time-delayed fallout. He also helped me deal with the lingering, mammoth loads of stress I still felt just from the logistics of it all, as well as the ongoing trauma of reliving my parents' deaths over and over and over during the writing process. Two deaths became hundreds, maybe thousands. Not so easy to process. Makes perfect sense when you can see it from a distance, which is one of the reasons why counseling is so valuable in these situations.

And time has helped, as it naturally does. Jolly often said that the "tincture of time" has great healing properties.

Eventually I regained a social life, did that hiking and decompressing in the mountains I'd promised myself, reduced my Jameson's intake to a proper level, and never heard a peep from Joe Friday. (Not yet, anyway.) And I'm confident that whatever legal jeopardy I may face by writing and publishing this book pales in comparison with the book's value for society.

George Bernard Shaw wrote, "All great truths begin as blasphemies." So I guess it's up to us blasphemers to keep pushing forward, revealing the truths that are currently shrouded by ancient mores and doctrines that have outlived whatever usefulness they may once have had.

This book may upset a small number of Jolly's and K's friends, colleagues, and relatives. I'm sorry for that, and I'm sure Jolly and K would be, too. But the close few with whom I've already shared this story not only have *not* been upset, they've been deeply supportive and encouraging. They were glad to know that both Jolly and K got what they wanted and needed. They were grateful that I helped. They were proud that I was telling the story, too, because they knew that the one thing Jolly and K believed in, above all else, was helping others. And they're convinced, as I am, that this story will indeed help others, and perhaps help change the current laws—a change that ultimately will help countless more.

As painful as writing this book was at times, it helped me through the grieving process—maybe because it *was* so painful. And now that I've gone through it and am on the other side of it all, I realize how much I've learned and grown, how much valuable perspective I've gained about what's truly important in life: living it, not just enduring it. And while I can't exactly recommend the path I took, I do recommend traveling whatever road you need to in order to find this wonderful clear view. The old words are true: Life is short. Life is precious. Live it and savor it—while you still can.

afterword

THE EXISTING LAWS AGAINST assisted suicide are well meaning, certainly. They keep things simple for the general public, and they help protect people from enemies disguised as family members or friends. But they also prevent people like Jolly and K from getting the peace they want and deserve, unless family or friends are willing to risk becoming "criminals." And that's an unconscionable alternative.

Surely we can do better. Surely we're smart enough to find a way to protect people without forcing them to die slowly, in a cage. Switzerland is smart enough. So are The Netherlands and Belgium. And so are the states of Oregon and Washington—at least, they've made a good start. What's holding the rest of us back?

Well?

Ask yourself the following questions, and answer them honestly: How do I want to be treated when I'm dying? Do I want to be forced to suffer? What about my loved ones? Do I want my dying father to be *required by law* to spend his remaining days or weeks in agony? Do I want my mother to be *required by law* to spend her remaining months of awareness knowing that she's turning into a vegetable?

Jolly once darkly joked that dying was hard work, and there ought to be a union. Well, actually, there *is* one. And we're all in it, every one of us who's alive and can vote. And we all must vote to improve our "working conditions"—our dying conditions.

K called her condition "torture." Do you want to be tortured to death? Is that what you want for yourself and for your loved ones? Or do you want a choice?

I certainly do. I bet you do, too.

To that end, let's make sure that we change the laws so that our end-of-life choices are protected by the doctor-patient relationship. If you choose to fight tooth-and-nail at the end, you are free to do so. If you prefer to avoid the pain of that fight, then you should be just as free to do so. It's really nobody's business but yours.

Let's all have more compassion for one another. Let's all behave with more dignity. And let's extend our compassion to—and provide dignity for—those who want it and need it. Because we all will want it and need it eventually.

So let's start now.

The Wind of Fate

How like the wind of fate to blow so fair,
To tender such remarkable caress
As bears the heart beyond the realm of care
And thaws the frigid marrow of distress.

Yield to the embrace of that fair breeze,
Drink deep of its intoxicating breath,
Avail yourself as it is wont to please,
For, in the hour, it brings the chill of death.

Its mischief knows no measure by my pen.
What frail barometer could hope to know
The passions set against the heart of man
That rend the fabric of affection so!

No consolation that it dries the tear
I shed for you who are no longer here.

—KATHRYN WEST, 1969

acknowledgements

THERE IS A VERY SMALL group of people who helped me bring this book from plan to reality: Anne Melley is the book's godmother, without whose friendship, integrity, and initial editorial efforts I doubt the book would ever have made it out of my house. The book's godfather is John O'Leary, my friend indeed—a man of uncommon spirit and supportive zeal. Walter Seltzer provided great wisdom and much-needed avuncular affection. Sue Aran, Colby Chester, Lou Oma Durand, and Ken Patten gave me the great gift of their collective friendship, which kept me going during some of my darkest times while I was writing this book. Lance Rosen and Amber Pearce provided invaluable friendship, as well as savvy legal counsel. I will be forever grateful for the very special refuge and solace given to me by Karen and Darold Gress. Don Lamm guided me through the publishing jungle, and his sagacity was invaluable. David Groff provided excellent editorial acumen. Marilyn and Scott Blair are quite simply the best neighbors and supporters that anyone could ever have. Mona Golabek's deep empathy and timely encouragement were a tremendous gift. George Bird and Tony Glassman supplied extremely helpful legal advice. The perennial kindness and support of Patsy and Chet Pierce are unforgettable. And Chuck Nelson has been such a truly great friend over the years that I cannot even begin to put into words my gratitude to him.

Norma Richland, my real-life godmother, sadly did not live to see the publication of this book. She knew I was writing it, though, and she supported me and my quest to get it published with the ferocity of a tigress. There's a good reason that she and K were best friends: sisters under the skin. I also wish to acknowledge, *in memoriam*, for their influence on my life, especially with regard to this book: Hal Williams, Lucy Schilling, Hume Hopkirk, Harriet Hopkirk, Enid Sepkowitz, Jano Burroughs, Lunda Hoyle Gill, Phil and Genevieve May, and Johnny Flinn.

And I want to particularly acknowledge Jack Shoemaker—who saw what my story had to offer, believed in it, and put his publishing company behind it. To Jack, and to everyone at Counterpoint Press who helped make this a real book, my sincerest thanks.

Printed in the United States
by Baker & Taylor Publisher Services